DEFIANCE

THE SHORTEN CHRONICLES BOOK 4

ROSALIND TATE

You might have a missed a book in this series!

Defiance is Book 4 of the *Shorten Chronicles*. If you've not read Book 3.5, *Intermezzo,* you'll be reading out of order.

Intermezzo is a little different from the main fantasy books. A fun, rom-com novella, it's set in modern London — just before the gang cross universes in *Defiance*.

If you haven't read *Intermezzo,* don't continue reading *Defiance*. Spoilers ahead!

Only available from my online Fantasy Bookshop, grab *Intermezzo* now: *https://bookshop.rosalindtate.com.* Click on 'Exclusive To This Bookshop' to choose your preferred format.

Defiance
The Shorten Chronicles Book 4

When Sophie time-travelled into the past, it took a while to adapt to living in Shorten Manor, a grand country house. After that, she landed in a terrifying medieval kingdom and nearly died before returning to modern London.

Over the next eighteen months, she married and had a baby. Life was good.

But the baby's father, Freddy Lacey, is determined that his parents should know his daughter, so Sophie must return to Shorten...

Shorten Manor
Estate Chapel
Families' Rooms
Armoury
Stables
New Graveyard
Servants' Hall
New Greenhouse
Office
Allotments
Manor
Bower
Tennis Court
Greenhouses
Lucy's Cottage
Mrs Evans' Cottage
not to scale

"I need ammunition, not a ride."
Volodymyr Zelensky, President of Ukraine
February 26, 2022

CHAPTER 1

12th November 1927. England.

The grass verge in the country lane had an icy, grey-silver sheen and the tall hedges flanking the road were swathed in ghostly morning mist. Everything was hushed, cowed by winter.

Sophie stretched, breathed in fresh air, and felt an intense rush of relief. Safe, and in the correct universe.

Hugo and Freddy looked equally relieved. Freddy adjusted the sling his daughter was sitting in, closer to his chest. Behind them Sophie's labradoodle, Charlotte, sniffed the air, not sensing any danger.

Hugo glanced both ways along the lane. 'Seems to be the right place.'

Sophie pulled her holdall onto her shoulders and let out a groan. Almost as heavy as her. 'This crossing was drama-free. We're getting the hang of it.'

'Perhaps.' Hugo's holdall was even heavier than hers,

weighed down with water flasks and self-heating army rations. Enough to survive in most places — and times.

Sophie looked back at the lift that had brought them here. Sparkling gold, it resembled a swanky elevator in a pricy hotel, but its appearance was an illusion. Its angular lines were already softening, the gilt façade fading, camouflaging itself. Soon the doors would close, and it would disappear, beginning another journey, shuttling between universes.

'Thank you, Janus, for a safe crossing.' Sophie meant it, which was fortunate, as he could read her thoughts.

'You are welcome.' Janus' deep baritone boomed from the lift's software.

Despite wearing ski clothes good to minus thirty, Sophie shivered. She'd been careful to give Janus this world's exact designation: 422. Ambiguity would have given him a deadly discretion to land somewhere of his choosing. And he was clever, could twist the clearest intention.

Sophie tightened the scarf around her neck, pulled a hat from her jacket pocket and jammed it on. Charlotte, dressed for the weather in a navy dog-coat, bounced over the verge and marked her territory by a skeletal elm tree.

'Thank goodness we've landed safely.' Freddy stroked his daughter's silky hair. Bella was well-wrapped up in her fleece-lined babygro, sucking on her dummy. He gazed up the lane. 'I'd rather not be the one carrying Bella as we approach the Manor. I feel … undignified.'

Sophie rolled her eyes. In 21st century London, Freddy had been a very hands-on father. She'd worried that once he returned to the Manor, he might step away from childcare, in line with this society's expectations. Hadn't expected him to go all Victorian Dad straight out of the lift.

'When we get near the house,' said Sophie, 'I'll carry her.' The Manor was a twenty-mile trek, but the buggy wouldn't have been practical if they'd landed on a mountain or in the sea.

They set off, the thud of their hiking boots on the tarmac clipped and loud. The trees and looming hedges seemed to watch them. Silent and brooding.

'I was correct about the time of year,' said Freddy. Ninety-two years and two months behind Sophie and Hugo's home. An easy calculation for maths-obsessed Freddy. He yanked his ski hat further over his ears. 'It's inconvenient that the lift opens so far from the Manor.'

'But there's no militia around,' said Sophie. 'So safer.'

'We should still be vigilant.' Hugo bit his lip.

'The revolution may be over,' said Freddy. 'The militias disbanded.'

Hugo frowned. 'Or they've taken the Manor, and your parents have emigrated.'

History was unfolding differently here. In this 1920s, riots had led to revolution — and civil war. But Freddy had been adamant that Bella belonged with his family, so they'd returned as soon as they could. It had been two years…

Charlotte snuffled at the verge, her awesome canine nose picking up scents unique to this world. Then she raced to and fro, a spring in her step. Not long before she'd be reunited with Jack, the Manor's black retriever.

Before a bend, Charlotte slowed, checking the road ahead was clear. If she'd heard or sensed trouble, she'd have barked, but she was being thorough.

'No harm in being cautious, Mrs Harrington,' Hugo said to Sophie.

Since having Bella, caution had been her mantra. She gave him a droll look and responded to the familiar teasing. 'Mrs *Arundel*-Harrington is always cautious.' Most people would find her relationship with these two men confusing. She was married to Hugo, but Freddy was her daughter's father. Tricky, but somehow they were making it work.

'My turn to carry her,' said Hugo.

Freddy lifted Bella up and Sophie unclipped the sling and fastened it onto Hugo. Freddy lowered his daughter back in.

Hugo wiggled his shoulders as he walked. 'She gets heavier every day.'

'Bah,' said Bella, pointing at Sophie. She'd only learned one word, used it for everything.

Hugo kissed the top of Bella's head. 'When I imagined life as a grown-up, it didn't include hiking in a parallel universe with someone else's baby.'

Freddy guffawed. 'You look like a Red Indian squaw.'

'You shouldn't say squaw,' said Sophie. Freddy had been born here in Shorten in 1904 and personified political *in*correctness.

'All right,' said Freddy, 'Red Indian lady.'

'It's not okay to say Red Indian either,' said Sophie.

'Why ever not?'

'It's based on a mistake,' said Hugo. 'Christopher Columbus called the native population Indians because he thought he'd arrived in India, not America.'

'You could say Native American woman,' said Sophie.

'Has their skin changed colour?' said Freddy. 'I don't understand.'

'That's not the point,' said Sophie. 'Saying "Native American" shows respect.'

'But there aren't any … Native Americans in the lane,' said Freddy, 'so they won't know.'

Sophie sighed. Change the subject. 'Have you decided what to tell your parents about Bella?'

'I'm more worried they won't be there,' said Freddy. 'And there'll be no one to tell.'

CHAPTER 2

Four hours later and about sixteen miles further along the lane, Charlotte barked a warning. From up ahead and out of sight beyond a bend, came the roar of car engines.

Militia.

Sophie was carrying Bella and she cast around for somewhere to hide. There was nowhere. No ditch, no trees—

Hugo and Freddy stepped in front of her.

An open car, pitted with dents and holes, raced towards them, another vehicle close behind. Beside the driver in the first car was a man in a black coat and a cap, aiming at them with a rifle.

The vehicle screeched to a halt and the guy jumped out. 'What the hell are you doing?'

Sophie froze, her insides churning. Bella wriggled and wailed.

The man lowered his gun and took off his cap, and Sophie did a double take. His face was smeared with grime and his fair hair had been cut short, but those startling blue eyes were unmistakable.

'Rupert?' Sophie sagged in relief. Standing before her wasn't a member of the militia, but an aristocrat. Two years ago, he'd courted her, offering an 'open marriage.'

Rupert glared at them. 'You're out here — with a *baby*?'

Freddy offered his hand. 'Good to see you, old chap.'

'Get in.' Rupert gestured with his rifle at the cars. 'Now.'

They all hastily obeyed. Sophie squeezed with Bella into Rupert's car with Hugo, and Freddy and Charlotte clambered into the second. The brown leather of the seats was split and scratched, and the doors were grey except for a sliver of green paint. No, it couldn't be. 'Is this the Laceys' car?' Sophie asked the driver, her voice tentative.

'It is, Miss.'

Sophie swallowed. What state was the Manor in?

The vehicles turned around and sped off.

With the holdall on her back and Bella on her chest, Sophie sat straight and upright, holding on to the half-height door. There were no seat belts in this world.

Sophie shuffled forward, closer towards Rupert in the front passenger seat. The collar of his coat was frayed and grubby. Very different from his regular clothes. She yelled over the wind whistling around the car. 'Rupert, what are you doing here?'

'A militia has taken Radden Hall.' He kept his eyes on the road.

Rupert's home was the other side of the county. Grand, rambling, but with no moat. Impossible to defend.

'I thought you were emigrating?' shouted Sophie, as they rounded a bend.

'I am. The Laceys are too.'

A sharp crack like a breaking branch joined the sound of the wind.

'Down,' yelled Rupert.

Sophie and Hugo huddled as low as they could. Bella, squashed under Sophie in the seat well, screamed.

Bang … *bang*.

Oh god. Sophie pressed her face into the seat. Thud, *crack*, bang. Bella screaming…

Sophie pushed her face harder into the seat. If a bullet hit her, would it also kill Bella? Would the holdall protect them? She unclipped the sling and shoved Bella further into the seat well. Please, please make it stop.

But the bangs grew louder. The car swerved as Rupert returned fire. Metallic thumps punctuated Bella's cries.

Finally, the shooting stopped.

Bella was still full-on screaming and Sophie desperately felt her baby's body for blood. No blood. Dazed and thankful, she grabbed Hugo's arm.

'I'm okay … somehow.'

She glanced back at Freddy and Charlotte in the other car. The driver gave a thumbs-up sign.

'Waiting by the field gates, nearer the Manor,' shouted Rupert to his driver. 'They're getting bolder.'

Sophie was shaking. She pulled Bella from the seat well and cuddled her. 'Shush. It's over now. Over.'

The cars drew up in front of a gate covered in hammered sheets of metal. At the top of the gate was a roll of barbed wire, and the same wire crowned the flanking walls.

The gate was hauled open, and Sophie held her breath.

But the moated house looked the same: crenellated wings, handsome tall windows, and the Virginia Creeper, winter-brown, starting its conquest of a new gable.

They slowed to a crunching halt on the drive, and Sophie climbed out, cradling Bella. Freddy and Charlotte had left the rear car and were running towards them.

Freddy helped Sophie secure the baby back in the sling.

'You were lucky you met us,' said Rupert from the passenger seat. 'We only check the lane once a week.'

Sophie shuddered. They'd have walked straight into the militia's ambush. Stood no chance.

'I need to patrol again.' Rupert gave them a mock salute.

The cars turned and headed to the road.

The moment the convoy left the drive, two gamekeepers Sophie vaguely recognised closed the gate and thumped down a long horizontal bolt.

A grinding noise came from the Manor. The drawbridge was winching down, providing a bridge across the filthy water in the moat.

Sophie's legs trembled as she stumbled over the bridge, the sound of bullets still echoing inside her brain. She clutched at Hugo, and he steadied her. His expression was drawn and tense. Likely, his legs were trembling too.

CHAPTER 3

$\mathcal{I}$n the Manor's grand hall, two scruffy-looking boys wound up the drawbridge, laboriously turning the large handle.

Sophie slipped the holdall from her back, dropping it with a thump on the oak floor, then took off the sling and gently put Bella down next to the bag.

Bella promptly crawled at speed towards a large wooden box, so Sophie picked her up. Other boxes, some big enough to hold furniture, filled half the hall, and stacked in a corner were travelling trunks.

Across the room, the Manor's housekeeper stared at Bella, managing an expression of polite surprise. The baby returned the stare, her clear blue eyes wide with curiosity.

The housekeeper came towards them. 'Master Freddy.'

Freddy smiled and shook her hand.

'I hardly recognised you, what with that beard.' Mrs Rawlings' thin lips trembled. Her black gown with its white frilly collar was unflattering, washing out her pale, elderly face. She glanced at Hugo and Sophie.

They nodded politely and Sophie breathed in the musty

air, furniture polish, and the cleaning mixture the scullery maids used: faint, tangy lemon.

The grandfather clock was ticking as loudly as ever. That used to upset her, a reminder of when she'd learned her parents were dead, but now the sound was entangled with happier, more recent memories. This house, and her life here.

The housekeeper clasped her hands. 'I'll fetch Lady Lacey.'

'We'll meet her in the small drawing room,' said Freddy. 'Could we have tea?'

'Of course.' Mrs Rawlings hurried away.

They left their bags and coats and trooped down the corridor. The royal blue runner carpet was grey with dust. Two years ago, an army of servants had kept the house spotless. Where had they all gone?

In the small drawing room, the green, damask-covered couch wasn't dusty. Sophie sat down, put Bella on her lap, and peeled off the outdoors babygro. Bella yawned, looking cute in a blue woollen dress and thick tights.

Sophie's shoulders relaxed. She loved this room. Despite its name, the small drawing room was not small at all, would have filled the whole ground floor of a 21st century suburban house. Sofas were arranged around a coffee table near the elegant fireplace, where a healthy fire was burning. The rest of the room was cluttered with armchairs, lamps, a sideboard, and occasional tables.

A new walnut cabinet had been squeezed between the sideboard and a floor lamp. A little taller than an armchair, the cabinet was polished and embellished with an arch, nestled within Greek-style columns. Above that was a stylised acorn, and at the top were protruding buttons and a dial.

'A wireless!' Hugo bent down to examine it.

Freddy joined him and fiddled with the buttons, creating a loud static noise. 'Interesting.' He switched it off and looked towards the door.

Anne Lacey hesitated on the threshold, leaning on the door jamb. Her hair, pulled into a bun, was streaked grey, and she was thinner. A navy silk gown matched the shadows under her eyes and emphasised her dull, pallid skin. She swayed.

Freddy rushed forward and caught her. Limp in his embrace, Freddy led her to the couch opposite Sophie and sat her down. He sat beside his mother and took her hand in his. Bear hugs and extravagant displays of emotion weren't the Shorten way. Sophie had dubbed it the 'Shorten Code.'

Anne sat up straighter, struggling not to cry.

'I'm so sorry we couldn't get back before now,' said Freddy.

They'd agonised about when they should return, waiting until after Bella's first birthday. Crossing universes with a new-born would have been beyond crazy.

Charlotte cautiously approached Anne and leaned against her legs, her canine way of showing empathy, offering comfort. Anne gave Charlotte a tremulous smile and stroked her.

'Where's Richard?' asked Hugo.

'On patrol,' said Anne, her voice unsteady. 'He should be back soon.' She drew a deep breath.

Decades ago, Anne had come through the lift from the 1980s, the first 'visitor' as the locals here called them. She'd done good. Married the heir to Shorten Manor.

Bella squirmed on Sophie's lap, and Sophie moved the baby onto the sofa. Anne gave them a tearful smile, and another wave of contentment enveloped Sophie. She returned the smile.

Sir Richard Lacey marched in. 'It's true. You're here.' Like

Anne, Richard must have feared his only child had gone forever.

Freddy stood up and shook his father's hand. 'We're very glad to be here.'

'And it's wonderful you're back.' Richard's hair was grey, and his patrol clothes were as grimy as Rupert's.

Hugo got to his feet and shook Richard's hand.

Cradling Bella again, Sophie stood and kissed Richard on the cheek. He grinned at her before turning his attention to the baby. 'And who is this?' He closed his fingers round her chubby fist.

'Bella,' said Sophie, hoping she'd settle, lulled by the conversation and the warmth of the fire. 'Short for Arabella.'

Charlotte trotted up to Richard and he ruffled her head, before sitting on the couch next to Anne.

Miss Parry came in, laid out crockery and poured tea. She'd briefly been Sophie's lady's maid and they exchanged smiles.

After Miss Parry left, Richard said, 'Much has happened since you disappeared, and not for the good.' He sipped his tea.

'We also have much to tell you,' said Freddy.

'You go first,' said Richard, his astute brown eyes on Bella.

'May I present Arabella Deborah Anne Lacey.' Freddy pointed at Bella with a flourish. 'Your granddaughter.'

Bella gurgled.

'Oh.' Anne took a handkerchief from her sleeve. 'Everything worked out how it should.'

Freddy hesitated, then blurted, 'Bella's my daughter and Sophie is Bella's mother.'

'Obviously,' said Anne.

Hugo cleared his throat. 'But Sophie married me.'

Anne gaped.

'Sophie and I found ourselves in some difficulty.' Freddy folded his arms.

'In a medieval, parallel world,' said Sophie.

Richard's jaw dropped.

'In particular,' said Freddy, 'we fell into a bear pit.'

'With a bear?' said Anne, her voice high with alarm.

'No,' said Freddy, 'but we were trapped there, and we were sure we were going to die.' Freddy turned his back and studied the fireplace. 'One thing led to another.'

Sophie briefly closed her eyes. *Embarrassed in a bear pit* would be carved on her gravestone.

Anne turned to Hugo. 'But you are Sophie's husband?'

'We married, um, a while after the bear pit.' Hugo put down his teacup.

Sophie shot Hugo a sheepish glance. Anne had been sort of right. Things *had* worked out. But only because Hugo had forgiven her.

'I can't take this in.' Anne shook her head at her son. 'You were madly in love with Sophie. You don't seem upset that she's married to Hugo.'

'Much has occurred since we left.' Freddy unfolded his arms. 'I intend to turn my attentions elsewhere.'

Bella was casting around for her dummy, attached to her dress with a safety pin. Sophie returned the dummy to Bella's mouth. 'We've come up with a cover story to protect Freddy's reputation here, and mine.'

'As far as the household and society are concerned,' said Freddy, 'I married a lady called Jane Smith.' They'd chosen a name they could easily remember.

'She died in childbirth but the baby, um Bella, survived,' Sophie added.

'This woman is fiction?' said Richard.

Freddy nodded. 'Entirely.'

'We'll propagate the story,' said Richard.

Bang. The mullioned windows rattled, and Sophie jumped. Bella cried out, and Charlotte barked.

Bang.

'One of our chaps on the roof is returning fire across the moat,' said Richard. 'Nothing to worry about.'

Really? Did people shoot across the moat every day?

Anne had regained her composure. 'Bella's a Lacey and she's home. That's the important thing.'

'We wanted her to know her family,' said Sophie, 'but it's too dangerous here—'

'We'll be in New York soon,' said Richard.

Hugo caught Sophie's eye. He wouldn't emigrate to 1920s America. He intended to return to modern London, with her.

Sophie busied herself with straightening Bella's dress, the problem whirring in her head. Freddy belonged here, would never agree to be separated from their daughter, and Bella needed her mother, living in the same universe.

Charlotte barked.

A knock and the door opened, revealing Miss Blackmore in her gamekeeper clothes. Her curvy figure had expanded, reinforcing her hearty air and confirming her penchant for game pies. Beside her was Jack, a sleek black retriever. Jack had cataracts, had been nearly blind when they'd left. Miss Blackmore unclipped his lead.

'Miss Blackmore keeps Jack in her room while she's out patrolling,' said Anne.

Jack and Charlotte met in a bundle of joyful barking. But the next instant, Jack retreated and cowered by Richard's legs.

'I'll help with minding Jack,' said Sophie, taking his lead from Miss Blackmore, 'so he can get to know Charlotte again.' Jack had sensed Charlotte was different, was understandably confused.

Miss Blackmore left, and Sophie said to Charlotte, 'Jack needs to adjust to the new you.'

Charlotte did her unnerving, human-like nod.

Anne gasped and Richard stared.

'Charlotte understands us,' said Freddy. 'Every word we say.'

'How?' asked Richard.

'Her DNA's been altered.' Sophie had adapted to the new Charlotte so entirely that she'd almost forgotten what she was like before. 'But she's still Charlotte.'

'She was changed by a lady whose ancestors built the lift.' Freddy glanced fondly at Charlotte.

'You mentioned DNA when you were here before,' said Richard to Hugo. 'But this is more advanced science?'

'Yes.'

'We don't want scientists prodding and poking her,' said Sophie. 'We'd be grateful if you could keep Charlotte's new nature a secret.'

'Of course.' Anne's eyes lit up. 'What a lovely day this is.'

Sophie's biological mother was gone, and no one could replace her, but Anne came close.

Freddy pointed to the old-fashioned radio. 'When did you acquire that?'

'About a year ago,' said Richard. 'The local militia broadcasts, as does the British Broadcasting Company.'

'And this is new as well,' said Freddy, gesturing at an oxblood-leather fender club seat in front of the fireplace. 'A fine addition.'

'We needed more seats,' said Anne, 'with the Armstrong girls staying, and Clarissa.'

Hugo paled. 'Clarissa's here?'

CHAPTER 4

Two years ago, convinced that returning home was impossible and equally sure Sophie would marry Freddy, Hugo had been days away from proposing to Clarissa Maine. They'd met at a ball in Shorten and a few weeks later, he'd visited her in London, staying at her family's town house.

The only child of a wealthy politician, Clarissa was direct, perceptive, and her caustic wit reflected a sharp brain. So, of course Hugo liked her. And she'd really fallen for him.

But against crazy odds, he and Sophie *had* returned home, leaving behind this universe — and Clarissa.

Hugo shifted in his chair in the small drawing room, guilt turning his stomach.

Sophie was settling Bella on the floor beside Charlotte, Freddy was sitting on the fender club seat, staring at his feet, and Richard had steepled his fingers, deep in thought.

The only sound came from the fire, crackling in the grate.

'There were mobs targeting politicians' families,' said Anne. 'Clarissa couldn't remain in London.'

'And the Maines' house in the country was undefendable,' said Richard.

'I have no idea what to say to her,' said Hugo. 'No apology can make this right.'

Sophie frowned. 'You don't want her hearing a garbled version from the gossip mill.'

'She'll be in the large drawing room,' said Anne. 'You should take her somewhere more private to explain.'

Hugo nodded, forced himself to stand up. News of their arrival would spread fast. He couldn't put this off.

He left the room and made his way to the oldest part of the house, following a winding corridor. Oil paintings, cracked with age, lined the walls. Kings and queens and other worthies. In the pit of his stomach, dread joined guilt. He paused before the door.

The summer ball had been held in the large drawing room. Over a hundred guests, the men in black tie, the women in formal gowns and white, elbow-length gloves. Dancing with Clarissa had been such fun, first one waltz, then more. New to waltzing, he'd stepped on her foot, but she'd only smiled, made him feel at ease. Then she'd flirted... Seemed like another life.

Just do this.

The door was ajar. He pushed it and gasped.

The Jacobean stone-framed windows and the medieval fireplace were the same. So was the double-height ceiling, coffered into rectangles with the Lacey coat of arms in the centre: brown, prancing stags around a royal blue 'L' outlined in gilt.

But everything else was shockingly different.

The huge space was filled with hospital beds, arranged in regimented rows. Except for a few wooden chairs, there was no furniture, and no carpet. Only oak boards.

Every bed had a patient. Some were sitting up reading,

but most were lying, still and silent. A man in the nearest bed was moaning in his sleep.

All the windows were open, and the chilly air was imbued with a strong tang of disinfectant. A textbook implementation of Florence Nightingale's belief in ventilation and cleanliness. Must be a version of her here.

This parallel universe had the same people as at home. Some eerily similar — others not.

Nurses in black dresses and long pale aprons flitted between the beds, their hair gathered up under starched white hats. Hugo recognised many of them. They'd previously worked as maids.

Ethel Armstrong was making notes on a clipboard, her delicate face so set in concentration she hadn't noticed Hugo come in. Ethel's younger sister, Alice, was with Harry Richards, talking quietly, their heads close together. Harry was hatless, his red hair neat and short. A stethoscope hung from his neck over a doctor's coat. Two years ago, he'd been a medical student.

Clarissa was sitting beside a bed at the end of the room, her head bowed, reading to a patient. Like the Armstrong sisters and the former maids, she was dressed like a World War One nurse. But her brown hair had been cut into a classic bob with a straight fringe. She seemed older.

Hugo squared his shoulders and walked towards her. His hiking boots snicked on the hardwood floor, and the Armstrong sisters and Harry looked up.

Clarissa saw him and froze, but a moment later she jumped up and ran into his arms. She sobbed into his chest and, inwardly cringing, Hugo hugged her until she'd cried herself out.

Finally, she stepped back. 'Apologies. Bit of a shock.' She found a handkerchief hidden in her sleeve and dabbed at her face.

Harry hurried over to them. 'Goodness. We assumed you were gone forever. What on earth happened?'

'A long story,' said Hugo.

'I look forward to hearing it,' said Harry. 'Perhaps over dinner?'

'Absolutely.' Hugo smiled at the Armstrong sisters who were staring at him. He turned to Clarissa. 'Can we speak in private?'

He held her arm, guided her out into the corridor, and they walked to the library. Hugo could feel her trembling and he felt physically sick. At least they'd never been formally engaged. Broken engagements here ruined reputations — and lives.

He shut the heavy library door and Clarissa settled herself in the red, wingback chair, her eyes bright with tears. 'I thought you were dead.'

'I nearly was. I only survived by going through the lift.' Hugo strode over to the cold fireplace and faced her.

Clarissa held her hands together in her lap.

'Sophie travelled in the lift as well to escape.'

'The police said Sophie tried to kill someone in the lane.'

'No,' said Hugo. 'Alan Parkes, who ran the pub in the village, nearly killed *us*.'

Clarissa frowned, bewildered.

'Freddy also went into the lift. After many months, he married, but sadly his wife died in childbirth. The baby survived.'

Clarissa's mouth dropped open. She shut it. 'Freddy was engaged to Sophie. I can't imagine him marrying anyone else.'

'While we were … away, his feelings, and Sophie's, changed.'

'How strange.' Clarissa looked directly at him. 'I don't

understand why you were by the lift in the first place. Academic curiosity?'

He could lie. Grab 'academic curiosity' and run with it. Claim he only got into the lift because of Alan trying to murder them all. No. He owed Clarissa the truth. 'I wanted to return home, and I wanted Sophie to go with me.'

Clarissa shook her head. 'But she was marrying Freddy.'

'She wasn't in love with him.'

'I still don't understand. You were happy here. With me.'

Hugo dearly wished to retain Clarissa's friendship, but no friendship could survive this, and sugar-coating it would just prolong the agony. 'In our London, Sophie and I talked through our feelings for each other. And we got married.'

For a moment, he thought she hadn't heard him, but then shock and dawning comprehension showed in her face. '*No.*'

'Hear me out, please.'

Clarissa clutched the arms of the chair. 'You were in love with Sophie the entire time. At the ball, in the cocktail bar at the Ritz...'

'I'm really sorry. I was in love with her, but she didn't realise, so was intent on marrying Freddy—'

'You're a cad and a liar.' Clarissa stood up abruptly. She slapped him on the cheek, the force of the blow jerking his head sideways, and before he could say anything, she ran from the room.

Hugo swore. He should have locked the door and pocketed the key, given himself time to explain better... No, she wouldn't have listened. Too shocked. Too hurt.

What a mess. He could avoid meeting her around the Manor but that wouldn't be possible at mealtimes. Anyway, hiding away from the dining room would be cowardly. For him, this was difficult. For her, it was devastating. Humiliating.

He closed the library door and leaned back against it, trying to calm down.

There was kindling in the grate. A box of matches was beside the wood basket and he lit the fire. When it caught, he added more wood and settled in the red chair, watching the flames.

He'd always liked this room, though in winter it was chilly, even with a fire. The arched leaded window was wide, took up half a wall, the top almost reaching the vaulted ceiling. Elizabethan bookcases held large tomes at the bottom, the smallest books at the top. Hugo drew a slow breath, inhaling the traces of dusty vellum and old ink.

But as he calmed, another worry nagged at him. Sophie might not go home with him if that meant being separated from Bella. And missing the gene, he couldn't cross universes by himself. Not that he'd want to, without Sophie.

He gazed up at the bookcases. Stop thinking about it. Find something to read.

He ignored the hefty books on the lower shelves and clambered up one of the bookcase ladders. As he reached across the shelf, he brushed against a book not set squarely, and it fell off, landing on the floor with a thud. He climbed down, retrieved the book, and climbed up again to return it.

The space was blocked by a book which had been tucked in behind. Hugo bent forward, pulled it out and slid the original book back into place. He wiped a thick layer of dust from the hidden book. The cloth cover was an unattractive yellow-brown and plain except for the title in an italicised dark font. *Classical Myths and Legends: A Convenient Guide* by George Herbert. Hugo had spent months searching for clues about Janus and the lift in here, thought he'd seen every relevant book. But he hadn't checked for books behind others.

He stepped down the ladder and opened *Classical Myths*

and Legends. The binding was new and stiff and groaned in protest. Had this been lost before it could be read?

Fitzroy Publishing 1889. He turned the page. *Education is the kindling of a flame, not the filling of a vessel.* Socrates.

Hugo sighed at the weak joke. Yes, the contents of this short book wouldn't fill a vessel, but on the upside, it wouldn't take long to read.

No, Sophie would be worried about him and about Clarissa. He should read this later.

CHAPTER 5

After Hugo left the small drawing room to speak with Clarissa, there was an awkward silence.

'Can we listen to the wireless?' said Freddy.

'The militia do their broadcast around now.' Anne walked over to the walnut cabinet and turned a knob at the top.

Static, and a click. '*This is the British People's Alliance.*' The man's accent was as clipped as Richard's. '*Militia recruitment continues apace. Join us now for a steady wage.*'

Jack was staying close to Richard and, evidently used to the static and the voice, he lay down and closed his eyes. Charlotte, though, pricked up her ears.

'*Local news. Today, the post office van was prevented from delivering letters to Shorten Manor. In the encounter, one game-keeper was killed.*' Static.

Sophie looked at Richard and Anne in horror.

'Tell me this isn't true,' said Freddy.

'It's not,' said Richard. 'He was shot in the arm, only a flesh wound.'

'They exaggerate our losses and play down their own,' said Anne, turning the wireless off. 'As do we.'

Twenty minutes later, Hugo returned, a deep frown between his dark eyebrows.

Sophie frowned too, feeling for Clarissa.

'I can't face seeing her in the dining room.' Hugo checked his watch. 'I'd rather miss lunch.'

'Clarissa won't be there,' said Anne, getting to her feet. 'She'll have tea and sandwiches in the hospital bay with the others.'

'I know this is unlikely, but do you have a highchair?' Sophie picked up Bella and the sling.

'We do. It's stored away near the kitchens.' Anne smiled at Freddy. 'Last used two decades ago.' She rang the bellpull and despatched a maid to find the highchair.

Richard clipped on Jack's lead, Freddy took the holdall with Bella's stuff, and they all walked down the dusty corridors. The new Charlotte didn't rush down the passage. Instead, she walked at a sedate pace like the humans.

In the dining room, the Lacey ancestors peered down from their oil-paintings. The long table was set for five, but the butler wasn't there, nor were the footmen.

On the sideboard were hot lidded dishes and the smell from them made Sophie's stomach rumble.

A maid came in, carrying a wooden highchair. There were no straps, so Sophie used Bella's sling to secure her.

Charlotte sat beside the highchair in guard mode, also looking forward to food. Jack was keeping his distance, whimpering if she came too close, but Charlotte wasn't pushing. She knew to bide her time.

Anne and Richard helped themselves to lunch and Hugo stood in line behind Richard by the sideboard. 'Where are the footmen?' Hugo asked him.

'On patrol.'

Sophie sat at the table to feed Bella from one of the jars

they'd brought. Freddy poured water from a jug into Bella's tippy mug and helped her eat the puréed carrot.

Bella taken care of, Sophie stood up, went over to the sideboard, and selected a boiled egg, potato mash, meat pie, and cabbage. She fed Charlotte meat pie and ate the mash.

Richard poured himself a glass of water and fed Jack a piece of pie. 'We grow potatoes, but we're far from self-sufficient. Most of the food deliveries and medicine get through from the town, but at a terrible price. Every week, men are killed and wounded.'

'I'm glad the broadcast was wrong,' said Freddy, 'and the gamekeeper's all right.'

'In war, truth is the first casualty,' said Hugo, his voice sombre.

'Who said that?' said Sophie. 'I mean, I know you just did—'

'Aeschylus,' said Freddy, wiping Bella's lips with a napkin. 'He wrote tragic plays in ancient Greece and died when an eagle dropped a tortoise on his bald head. The eagle mistook his head for a rock that he could use to shatter the tortoise's shell.' Freddy had enjoyed a classical education, as befitting an Edwardian gentleman. 'It's such a ridiculous story. I love it.'

Sophie smiled at him. 'So ridiculous, it might be true.'

'Hugo, could you join me in the estate office this afternoon?' said Richard. 'I'd appreciate a fresh eye on our security arrangements.' Richard winked at Sophie, and she gave him a 'message understood' nod back. He hadn't asked her because she needed to keep a low profile.

But it was two years since she'd killed Barty Inkpin to escape the militia. Dealing with her would be way down the militia's to-do list.

'What's happening with the army, the local regiments that returned from India?' said Hugo.

'They're in London,' said Anne. 'The fighting's particularly unpleasant there.'

Freddy looked up. 'Is the government still in power?'

'Hanging on by their fingernails,' said Richard. 'Parliament can't sit so they're ruling by royal prerogative. That can't go on forever.'

Those packing boxes in the hall … they really were emigrating. 'The militias can't be defeated?' Sophie asked Richard.

'We can't turn the tide by force. Every day they recruit more men.' Richard glanced across at Hugo. 'When you stayed at the Maines' house, you mentioned to Clarissa's father that the government in your world make payments to the unemployed.'

Hugo nodded.

'Lord Maine has persuaded the cabinet to bring in a similar scheme,' said Richard, 'and raise the old age pension.'

'How does any of that help us?' Freddy vigorously cut into his pie. 'And the Manor?'

'If these payments enable a man to feed his family,' said Richard, 'receiving a militia wage, risking serious injury or death, becomes less attractive. The hope is that men will leave the militias and support for their cause will dwindle.'

'How much do the militias pay?' said Sophie.

'Eight shillings a week,' said Anne. 'The unemployment benefit will match that.'

Eight shillings wasn't much. When they'd first arrived in Shorten, two beers in The Crooked Gate, the village pub, had cost half a shilling.

'Unfortunately, the Poorhouse Payment Scheme's proving difficult to set up through the post office,' said Richard.

Bella wailed, the sound echoing around the dining room.

How could she still be hungry? Sophie rooted about in the holdall for another food jar underneath a jumble of nappies, a thermometer, wipes, and 'just-in-case' amox-icillin.

Bang. The windows rattled, sending shards of panic into Sophie's heart. That settled it. It wasn't safe here. 'We should take Bella back to the lift,' Sophie said to Richard. 'Could you spare some cars to escort us?'

'We've only just got here.' Freddy's face hardened.

'Leaving the Manor could be more dangerous than stay-ing,' said Richard. 'You were lucky in the lane.' His words echoed Rupert's comment before he left to patrol again.

Sophie swallowed.

'The militia are everywhere.' Anne tightened her lips.

'Where's the local militia based?' said Hugo.

'Little Shorten,' said Richard. 'Miss Small's requisitioned The Crooked Gate.'

'*Irish* Joan Small?' said Sophie.

Richard nodded.

Sophie pictured Joan from when she'd briefly seen her in the bakery in Shorten town: a 'hard-life' expression and wearing men's clothes.

'By all accounts,' said Anne, 'Miss Small deals with Mrs Hill about pub matters, merely tolerates Mr Parkes.'

'Why isn't Parkes in prison?' said Hugo. 'Reynolds must have gone to the police.' The Laceys' chauffeur had witnessed Parkes trying to kill them.

'No charges were ever brought. It was Reynolds' word against Mr Parkes's.' Anne stared into her glass of water. 'And you were ... gone.'

'How is Reynolds?' said Sophie. Without the chauffeur's help, she'd have died in the lane.

'He's well,' said Richard. 'He replaced the head game-keeper as patrol lead.'

'What happened to the head gamekeeper?' said Hugo.

'He lost his life patrolling.'

The man's face appeared in Sophie's mind. 'I'm so sorry.' She steeled herself. 'Has anyone else been lost?'

'Albert Garnier,' said Anne. 'He died in the summer, defending Fissington Hall.'

Sophie had danced with him. She pushed away her plate, her appetite gone. 'Do the militia ever take days off?' The question was flippant.

'Actually, they do,' said Richard. 'Sundays tend to be quieter.'

'What day is it today?' said Sophie. Freddy had calculated it was a Saturday, but he'd called that 'an educated guess,' could have been wrong.

'Saturday,' said Anne.

Sophie drank the last of her water. 'I'll take Bella to the lift tomorrow.'

'Perhaps that would be prudent,' said Richard, glancing at his granddaughter. 'We're travelling to Liverpool next week, taking anyone who wishes to sail, but it's a hundred miles, there's three militias to negotiate, with numerous checkpoints.'

'I can protect Bella on the road to Liverpool,' said Freddy, his determined face on.

'I'd love her to stay with us,' said Anne, 'but Sophie's right. Bella will be safer in the 21st century.'

Freddy stood up and dropped his napkin on the table. 'This isn't decided.' He strode from the dining room.

CHAPTER 6

Freddy and Anne were happy to mind Bella, so after lunch, Sophie put on her red ski jacket and hat and ventured outside, wanting to look up an old friend. She kept Jack on a lead and Charlotte stayed close, snug in her expedition dog coat. Note to self: find Jack's dog coat.

Even within the moat, the Manor gardens were large enough to get lost in, but mindful of the recent exchange of fire from the house, Sophie avoided open lawn, choosing paths through evergreen trees. On the far side of the moat, the grand octagonal greenhouses were still there. Looked deserted. Next to the servants' hall was a new, much smaller greenhouse, basic and square. Adjacent to it were rows of vegetable plots.

Inside the greenhouse, Lucy Hemmings was watering plants with an iron can. Over her black trousers and top, she wore a short cardigan, and her brown bobbed hair was hidden under a grey beanie. Lucy had come through the lift years ago, was the Manor's head gardener.

Sophie ran over and hugged her, and Lucy dropped the can.

'When you and Freddy didn't come back,' Lucy said in a rush, 'everybody thought you were dead.'

Sophie winced. 'We couldn't risk returning earlier. Not with the baby.'

'A baby?'

'She's called Bella, but, um, it's complicated.'

'I'd never have guessed.' Lucy shot her a wry smile.

'Can we chat in private?'

Lucy gestured at the empty greenhouse. 'Trust me, this is entirely private.' She sat on a rickety wooden chair. 'I've missed you.'

'And I've missed you.' Sophie brushed green cuttings off another chair and sat down. The air was hushed, and there was a faint earthy smell. 'Where are all the gardeners?'

Lucy pressed her lips together. 'Some are on patrol, some are between shifts, staying in the town. Three are dead and one's in the hospital bay.'

Sophie was lost for words. Jack lay down as near as possible to Sophie, but Charlotte was exploring, sniffing at a plant pot and a raised bed of tomatoes. It was warm, and Sophie took off her jacket and Charlotte's.

'The electric heating's working. Not sure how long that'll last.'

'It breaks down a lot?'

'And always when the only gamekeeper who can fix it is out on patrol.' Lucy exhaled. 'Every day, life here gets harder.'

'You're emigrating?'

Lucy nodded. 'Where Anne goes, I go, but getting to Liverpool won't be a walk in the park.'

'We know how to call the lift,' said Sophie. 'You just say "Janus" out loud.'

'Really?' Lucy looked shocked.

'You could go home.'

'Back to the future.' Lucy smiled nostalgically. 'I enjoyed those movies.'

'If travelling to Liverpool proves too dangerous, we could evacuate lots of people through the lift.' It should be possible, in theory.

Lucy raised an eyebrow. 'There'd only be room for three or four at a time.'

'The lift expanded when we needed to sleep, so it might get bigger according to what's needed.'

'Mindboggling,' said Lucy. 'Like the Tardis in *Dr Who*, but flexible.'

'Maybe. I'm speculating.'

Lucy chuckled. 'I can't see many families rushing to get into an alien spaceship. They're worried enough about America. Many of them have never ventured further than Shorten town.'

'It'll be stressful,' said Sophie. 'Anne looks so much older than when we left.'

Lucy lowered her head. 'When Freddy disappeared, it nearly broke her. Reynolds said one moment he was in the lane, then he was gone.' She glanced up. 'Do you know what happened to him?'

'He was with us and he's here,' said Sophie. 'Safe and well in the Manor.'

'That's fantastic!'

'And Hugo's here too.'

Lucy blinked. 'He was obsessed with getting home. Why on earth has he come back?'

'Turns out, he was obsessed with getting home — with me.' Sophie summarised the weird 'Freddy's baby but married to Hugo' situation.

Lucy grinned. 'The servants will be over the moon.'

'Why?'

'The gossip mill is starved of feel-good drama, and we could do with cheering up.'

Hell no. 'The truth is for your ears only.' Sophie laid out the cover story.

'Not as juicy, but better than nothing.' Phew. Of course, Lucy was joking. She hated gossip.

Lucy frowned. 'We're reduced to boiling moat water. It's a miracle nobody's gone down with dysentery.'

'You're looking fine.' And she was, if a bit skinny.

Charlotte sat on the floor opposite them, her golden eyes on Jack, but she was following their chat.

Lucy stroked Charlotte. 'I've missed you too.'

Charlotte nodded and Lucy nearly fell off her chair. 'What was that?'

Sophie explained how Charlotte's DNA had been altered by Naga in a different universe. 'Naga's a descendant of the people who built the lift.'

The head gardener leaned forward and hugged Charlotte who responded with a contented sigh. Lucy straightened and grinned. 'I'm glad you married Hugo. Found your happy ever after.'

Their love triangle was complicated, and the future uncertain, but she was certainly happy to be married to Hugo. 'You could still find that special … someone.'

'Nah. You know my happy ever after is being single.' Lucy folded her arms. 'All this trouble has been hard on the estate families.'

The families' cottages were beyond the moat. Richard had worried the militia could take them hostage, force him to surrender the Manor. 'What's happened to them?'

'They all moved out. I had to, as well.' Lucy stood up. 'I'll show you.'

Sophie followed her outside with the dogs. They walked past the servants' hall and the stables to a fenced yard with chickens strutting around a coop. Further on, between the armoury and the moat, was a sprawling, one-storey building.

'Forty rooms, built from repurposing part of the stables,' said Lucy. 'Not ideal, but safe.'

They went inside. Lucy's room was sparsely furnished with a tatty armchair and an old wooden bookcase, but it was as neat as Lucy's cottage had been.

'I have two rooms, this and a bedroom,' said Lucy, '*appropriate for the head gardener*, to quote Mr Crawford.'

Sounded like the butler.

'And as Reynolds is patrol lead,' said Lucy, 'he has the two rooms across the corridor.'

Even in the middle of a war that had changed so much, Shorten was strong on hierarchy—

Boom!

What the hell was that? Everything shaking. The whole room. Piercing pain in Sophie's ears. Dust in her mouth and eyes. She put her hands over her face.

When she looked through her fingers, the wall in front of her was gone. Just. Not. There. An angular gaping hole. No, no. This couldn't be happening.

Lucy's bookcase was twisted and in pieces. Tapping. A ragged curtain was flapping, boat-sail loud. From the nearby moat came a faint slushing sound.

A movement in the room made Sophie turn around. Lucy was covered in red dust. The dogs were shaking themselves to remove the powder from their fur. Sophie stared down at herself. All over her was the same stuff.

The sound of screaming from outside galvanised her. Sophie pulled Lucy through the gap in the wall and the dogs followed.

The red dust was from shattered bricks, and the particles were dancing in the air. Part of the families' rooms had been reduced to rubble. Men, women, and children were standing about in a daze, others were shouting.

People were running towards them from the servants' hall. Richard and Rupert pushed through the throng. 'Quiet,' Richard yelled, his voice clear above the shouting. 'Listen.'

In the silence, a faltering woman's voice could be heard from under the debris.

'Direct our efforts there,' said Richard.

'What did this?' whispered Sophie to Rupert as they hauled up a wooden truss.

'Must have been a field gun.'

Artillery? From where?

Freddy and Hugo ran up and they hugged Sophie in turn.

'Where's Bella?' said Sophie.

'Safe in the house,' said Freddy.

A gamekeeper and a gardener joined the effort to move bricks and beams and Sophie went with Lucy to the ruined sitting room. Carefully, and as quickly as possible, they retrieved jackets and gloves.

Outside, Charlotte was pawing the ground. 'If anyone's alive under this,' said Sophie to Freddy, putting Charlotte's jacket on her, 'she'll find them.'

'Yes. Everybody move back, please. Mrs Harrington's dog can find the exact spots to clear.'

The gamekeeper frowned at Charlotte and the gardener shook his head, but they stepped off the debris.

'Go,' said Sophie to Charlotte.

Charlotte sniffed, then sprang onto the rubble and followed her nose. A few minutes later, she stopped snuffling and barked.

'I can't hear anything,' said the gardener.

'Clear that location,' said Richard.

Sophie dropped brick after brick into a wheelbarrow, her body screaming at her to stop, to rest, but she kept going.

Fifteen minutes of concerted effort later, a leg could be seen, then the rest of a woman.

'Unconscious, but alive,' said the gardener. He stared at Charlotte in awe. 'I'd never have believed it.'

Charlotte advanced, sniffing again, then stopped and barked.

Freddy moved bricks at the spot and froze. He picked up a child, a few years older than Bella, and cradled him, tears streaming into his beard.

Charlotte worked until nightfall. She sat on the rubble, her head lowered.

'We'll begin again at dawn,' said Richard.

Charlotte, Sophie, and Hugo shambled to the house, numb with exhaustion.

Freddy caught up with them. 'I was wrong about Bella. You must take her to the lift tomorrow and, Hugo, you must go too.'

Sophie nodded, too tired to talk.

At the house, Sophie quickly washed and changed, and fell into bed with Hugo. They'd washed Charlotte in the bath, and she was dozing, wrapped in a towel. Bella was asleep in the cot, but Sophie was wide awake, and so was Hugo.

'That shell could have been fired from miles away,' he said.

'Whoever did this has no soul.'

'Richard said the militia don't target civilians,' said Hugo. 'It may have been a mistake.'

Sophie frowned, trying to forget what she'd seen.

'The Derby militia has a 19th century artillery piece. It could have misfired.'

'That child dead,' said Sophie. 'And for what? Pointless, *pointless* war.'

'The militia believe they're fighting for a fairer society, to help future generations. Richard's fighting for the Manor.'

'Nothing is worth this.' Sophie gave in to tears.

'At home, we owe our comfortable lives to those who fought the Nazis.' Hugo stroked her hair. 'Kept going when all seemed lost.'

Sophie looked over at Charlotte. 'Hitler was supposedly kind to dogs. I never got that.'

'Not a redemptive feature,' said Hugo. 'A quirk.'

'My parents believed no human could be completely bad.'

'I think that's a fiction we tell ourselves, to make us feel better.'

'But no single evil person started this, stirred up hate,' said Sophie. 'It's just … a mess.' She pulled the blanket further up, covering their shoulders. 'Lucky evil people are rare.'

'I'm not sure they are.' Hugo sighed. 'We only notice the ones who have power. Who kill with impunity because they can.'

She wiped her eyes. 'Not helping.'

'It feels wrong, leaving Freddy to defend the Manor.'

'I know.' She didn't want to leave Freddy, but she could lose Hugo and Bella to this war if she stayed.

'In any event,' said Hugo, 'once we're well down the lane, there'll be no militia, and missing a hand, Parkes won't be waiting by the lift to finish us off.'

Alan chasing them … the lift doors shutting, slicing off his hand. Two years on, the memory still made her shudder.

CHAPTER 7

*B*etty Hill was serving behind The Crooked Gate's bar. The last militia patrol of the day had returned. Thirsty, exhausted men who'd soon be drunk and fighting over her.

Which was just fine.

She'd grown used to the table-banging and the banter, and she hardly noticed the smell of the beer. The sweet scent was part of the pub, part of home. She'd given up trying to get the smell out of her figure-hugging work dress. The endless cigarette smoke was tedious though. Irritated her eyes.

Alan Parkes did his best to help, despite his missing hand. Two years before, when he'd staggered into the pub, bleeding like water from a tap, she'd cauterised the wound with a hot poker, and he'd been grateful. But afterwards he'd gone surly, taken her for granted.

Now, with the militia in residence, he had competition, needed to keep on her good side.

Betty smiled at a young man with a mop of sandy-fair hair and gave him a drink. He smiled back. Roy Ducker reminded her of Freddy Lacey. Not just his hair. Roy was easy going — like the heir to Shorten Manor. Years ago, in Cambridge, she'd had a dalliance with Master Freddy, initiated him. He'd been sweet. Perhaps Roy would be too?

She caught his eye. 'Thank you for watching Frank.' Her young son was preoccupied in the brown armchair by the fire, doodling on scrap paper with a crayon stub. She'd taught Frank his letters, but he was happiest drawing.

Roy wiggled his eyebrows. 'You can rely on Roy.'

He was only minding Frank to seduce her into bed, but survival involved making friends — and keeping them.

Away from the bar at a corner table, Mary James was nursing her beer, talking with two burly men. Mary was slight with pale skin and had the sort of red hair that artists liked to paint in posh pictures. Joan Small was at the same table, writing in a notebook. She'd fought in Ireland and run guns to London. A man who'd questioned Joan's right to be in charge was in the ground. She made the fiercest suffragette look shy.

'Everyone quiet for the broadcast,' ordered Joan, turning on the small wireless. Due to it being thrown in a fight, the wooden casing was cracked and bent.

Betty sat in the armchair opposite her son, grateful for a break.

Static. *'Local news. There's been a surprising development at the Manor. Mr Lacey, previously presumed dead, is alive and well, as are the visitors, Mr Harrington and his wife, formerly Miss Arundel.'* Static.

Alan stopped drying glasses and briskly wiped down the bar. He was a visitor, had come to Shorten through the magic lift. Scientists had found no evidence of a portal or whatever it was, but visitors coming and going still set tongues wagging.

Static. *'A misfired shell has damaged a building on the Lacey estate. Casualty numbers remain unclear. The Laceys are leaving for Liverpool soon and we look forward to requisitioning the Manor. Mr and Mrs Harrington go back to the mysterious lift tomorrow with the Laceys' baby granddaughter.'* Static.

The Manor's gamekeepers kept their patrol cars in the town, visited cafés and pubs, and gossiped. Juicy titbits for the broadcasts.

Mary turned off the wireless and winked at Roy who pretended not to notice.

'Do you believe in the lift, Miss Small?' Taffy Morgan was short, with black hair and a Welsh accent that matched his nickname.

'No.'

'Mr Harrington thinks it's a machine,' said Roy.

When Roy had worked as a footman at the Manor, Alan had paid him to spy on the visitors. What he'd overheard had been fascinating, if far-fetched. A way of crossing universes...

Joan made a gesture for more beer.

Betty brought them over and picked up dead glasses. Mary ignored her, as per usual. Mary had been a maid in the Manor and could barely hold a rifle. Joan thought her a useful distraction for the men, though, so they were stuck with her.

'Mrs Hill, let me take that.' Roy stood up and relieved her of the tray.

Alan was shuffling around, tidying up. Only Mr Morley acknowledged him as he cleared his table. Mr Morley was teetotal and educated and so useless on patrol, Joan had crossed him off the rota.

Roy took the dead glasses through to the kitchen and Betty changed the cloth she'd left on the counter to soak up spills.

'Mrs Harrington leaves tomorrow.' Joan got to her feet. 'If we're laying the mine, it needs to be done at first light.'

'We shouldn't do it,' said Roy. 'She's a defenceless lady.'

'She's not defenceless.' Jim Hayden ran his fingers through his greasy hair. 'She murdered Barty, robbed us of a great leader. Why should she escape justice?'

Betty frowned. Barty Inkpin, the son of the man who started the militias… Difficult to believe Mrs Harrington had killed him.

Pitter-patter. Alan was behind the bar, agitated, drumming his fingers on the counter.

'What Mrs Harrington did is common knowledge in London,' said Jim. 'If we don't act, it'll make us look weak.'

Mr Morley put down his teacup with a clink. 'The crux of this discussion is whether we should distinguish between combatants and civilians. In Britain, at least in recent times, we have categorised individuals as one or the other and treated them differently.'

Taffy nodded.

'The distinction is not straightforward, however.' With Mr Morley's prominent blue eyes and receding hairline, he could have been a vicar giving a sermon. 'We should continue to respect the difference, as civilised men, but the status of an individual can be dynamic.'

'What?' said Jim, confused.

'The difficulty here is that, with due respect to Miss Small…' Mr Morley gave Joan a polite nod. 'Mrs Harrington's conduct is not typical of her sex or that of a civilian.'

'So, what are you saying?' said Taffy.

'I'm saying,' said Mr Morley, slowly, 'that we need to decide whether Mrs Harrington, through her own choices, is no longer afforded civilian status. If that is the case, then the mine should be set.'

'She's going down the lane with a baby,' said Roy. 'Surely,

Mr Morley, an infant is a civilian and shouldn't be punished for the actions of others.'

'If it's reasonably foreseeable that an action will harm non-combatants, the general must be convinced that the action could be pivotal, change the outcome of the war.'

'On that basis, you could justify anything,' said Roy. He cast around for support but only Taffy acknowledged him.

'Would Mrs Harrington's death, the death of Lady Lacey's grandchild, so materially affect our ability to seize the Manor, that it can be morally justified? Hasten our victory and the fortunes of other militias?'

'No,' said Roy. 'The Laceys are leaving anyway.' He narrowed his lips. 'I'm having no part in it.'

'Nor me,' said Taffy.

'It would hurt the Laceys hard, all of them up there,' said Jim. 'They'll flee with their tails between their legs. And once word spreads that we've avenged Barty, we'll have much more clout in London. I reckon the militia there will soon be running the country.'

'There is seldom a clear-cut answer,' said Mr Morley.

'Right,' said Joan. 'All those in favour, raise your hands.'

Much later, when Alan, and Betty's son were asleep upstairs, and the militiamen were unconscious from drink, Joan wrote in her notebook and Betty sat beside her, cleaning captured shotguns. Thanks to Joan's patient tutelage, Betty was now a decent shot.

As they worked, they listened to the wireless.

'This is the British People's Alliance. First, the weather forecast.'

Joan recorded how many inches of rain were expected, how many hours of predicted sunshine or cloud. The numbers were code for militia successes and failures.

When the broadcast finished, Betty said, 'Did Mrs Harrington really kill Barty Inkpin?'

'Yes.'

'Why hasn't anyone mentioned this before?'

'The militia's not proud Barty was bested by a girl,' said Joan. 'She stabbed him through the heart.'

Dear heaven. 'That's awful.'

Joan hesitated. 'Barty was a nightmare. A psychopath.' She moved her tongue against the inside of her cheek, considering something. 'But dealing with Mrs Harrington would boost morale.'

'Alan said she made the lift cut off his hand.'

Joan rolled her eyes. 'Do you honestly believe that?'

Betty put aside the shotgun. She had believed it, accepted everything Alan had told her. If the visitors opened the lift, the pub would be destroyed, and they'd all die.

Trying to stop the visitors opening the lift had cost Betty's brother his life, but the visitors were back, and nothing had happened to the pub, or Alan, or her. Had anything Alan told her been true?

CHAPTER 8

The next morning, Sophie woke up beside Hugo in her Shorten bedroom and relived what had happened to the families' rooms. Trying not to think about it, she stroked his hair as he sleepily snuggled into her, and she breathed him in. The room was chilly, but underneath the heavy blankets in the four-poster, they were cosy-warm. Hugo was wearing silk pyjamas and the material caressed her skin. She stretched in her prim nightdress. Brazenly sleeping with Hugo in the Manor felt ... odd.

Jack was asleep by Bella's cot and Charlotte was snuffling around, reacquainting herself with the room's freshly scrubbed scent. The antique French windows, the dressing table by the smaller window, and the tall, free-standing mirror were the same, though the side table was covered with Hugo's correspondence, along with his fountain pen and a box of Clarissa's letters. All brought over from his previous Shorten room.

Bella gurgled, her highly tuned baby-instinct sensing her mother was awake, and someone knocked, opening the door a crack. The caller couldn't see the bed, but Sophie jumped, startled. She might be married, but Shorten habits — fear of gossip, the need for propriety – were as ingrained and stubborn as a tattoo. She pulled the silky blue counterpane up to her shoulders. 'Come in.'

Maud Watkins came in with a tray of tea and toast.

Stuff propriety. Sophie slid out of bed, careful not to disturb Hugo, and hugged her.

Maud set down the tray and hugged her back. 'I'm so glad you're all right, Miss.' She hesitated. 'Er, Madam.'

'Let's keep with Miss,' said Sophie. 'Madam makes me feel way too old.'

'I would have helped you retire last night, but when the rooms got shelled, I was needed in the hospital bay.' Maud hurried to the fireplace to light the fire. Jack woke up and Charlotte sat to attention, waiting to be offered toast. Jack stayed a foot away, still wary. 'I've another nursing shift.' She hurried out, closing the door softly.

'Has she gone?' whispered Hugo.

'Yes,' whispered Sophie. 'I can't believe you're embarrassed. You've never been shy about … bedroom stuff.'

'I don't know Maud as well you do.' Hugo sat up and arranged pillows behind him. 'It's like waking up in a hotel room with the chambermaid making notes.'

They wouldn't be here long enough for Hugo to get used to Maud. Soon, they'd be in modern London.

Sophie bit her lip. Saying goodbye to Anne and Richard would be difficult enough. Much harder for Freddy, saying goodbye to Bella. Who knew when he'd see her again?

After breakfast, on the drive, Anne and the Armstrong sisters made a fuss of Bella. When Anne embraced her, Sophie blinked hard. Hugo shook hands with Rupert, Harry, and Richard.

'Take care,' said Richard, kissing Sophie on the cheek. Rupert kissed Sophie on the cheek too.

Freddy's eyes were red-rimmed but he was somehow keeping it together. 'I'll drive you down, say properly goodbye to Bella there.' He gave his daughter a long hug before handing her to Sophie.

Three cars were escorting theirs. Freddy drove the second. Hugo sat in the front passenger seat and Sophie was with Bella in the back, squished in with Charlotte and Jack. Jack would adapt to the new Charlotte. Just needed time.

Gamekeepers drove the other cars, their passengers armed.

Jack was snug in the tartan jacket that Sophie had found in a bedroom drawer. Everyone else wore their ski gear, wrapped up against a bitter wind that whistled around the windscreen and half-height doors.

Freddy maintained a steady speed, keeping the same distance from the vehicle in front. 'The moment it becomes safe here, I'll cross to the students' union,' he shouted over the wind. 'Collect my phone from Elliot and call you.'

'Absolutely,' yelled Hugo.

Shorten might not be safe for years… Sophie kissed Bella, who was restless, squirming in her sling.

Two miles out, Freddy slowed, negotiating a bend. 'You're right to leave,' he shouted to Hugo. 'This isn't your fight—'

His words were cut off as the car up ahead exploded with an ear-splitting roar.

~

Why was it dark?

Trapped in a tiny space. So cold. Freezing, hard tarmac,

hemmed in by steel and leather and fur. The fur was moving, pushing, licking Sophie's chin. Charlotte?

Bella! She was still in her sling. Sophie was on top of her. Move. No, can't move. Bitter, tangy air, hurt to breathe, her chest too tight, her brain pounding, ears ringing. Too many cymbals, deafening, stinging—

'Now.'

A screech. Complaining metal. A tremendous thump.

Blinding light.

Next moment, Sophie was hauled up by her shoulders. Set down.

She stayed where she was, collapsed in a heap. Something gritty filled her nostrils and throat, and she coughed.

She was in the lane. Grey smoke was drifting into the trees. A car had blown up...

Bella was coughing. Why wasn't she screaming her head off? Her little face was red with agitation and confusion, and Sophie frantically inspected her. Part of the sling was torn, but she seemed okay. How was she okay?

Charlotte was beside them. Quiet. Stunned.

Their car... Battered but intact. It must have been upside down. She and Bella and Charlotte had been pinned under it. The gamekeepers had managed to right it, get them out.

Hugo, Freddy, and Jack were sitting on the tarmac a few yards away. Hugo had a gash on his nose. He wiped his eyes, spreading blood from the gash over his cheeks. Freddy was staring into space.

But they were safe. All safe.

Sophie stood up on shaky legs, her chest hurting with every breath. The car that had been in front of theirs was now *behind* their car. A burning, twisted mess.

Freddy must have swerved past it.

Near the wrecked car, someone was sprawled on the tarmac.

A gamekeeper was talking to her, but she couldn't hear him with the noise in her ears. He took her arm and guided her to an undamaged vehicle.

Sophie half fell into the rear seat, and with the sudden movement, Bella's mouth opened. But the baby made no sound Sophie could hear. After stroking her daughter's fragile downy head, Sophie covered her own ears. *Please* stop the ringing.

Freddy and Charlotte got into the back with her, Hugo and Jack in the front, and the gamekeeper turned the car around and sped off. But the ringing drowned out the sound of the engine, and the trees by the edge of the road were passing by too fast. Maybe this wasn't real?

The Manor loomed up, mixing in with the numb, trance feeling.

The car stopped with a jerk on the drive, but Sophie's whole body hurt. Climbing out, moving at all, wasn't happening.

The gamekeeper opened the door, was pulling at her, saying something.

Must try. Sophie swung her feet out and shakily stood up.

Freddy took Bella out of her sling. He mumbled and prodded her, then held her close.

The gamekeepers were carrying the man who'd been lying in the road, taking him into the house.

Sophie staggered across the drawbridge into the hall. The cymbals repeating in her ears were still clanging but they were fainter.

The gamekeeper addressed Richard. 'They've mined the lane.'

Richard embraced Sophie and Bella. An ache in Sophie's hip was spreading, and a stabbing pain in her neck made her gasp.

But with the pain came clarity. She met Richard's eyes. 'I guess we're staying.'

CHAPTER 9

The following morning, Sophie had breakfast in bed. A quaint perk of being married. The tradition only applied to women, but as Hugo had been badly shaken up by the mine, this time he was included too.

The ringing in Sophie's ears had mercifully stopped and her chest didn't hurt with every breath. But her neck was still agony, the paracetamol she'd brought from the 21st century not touching it. She swallowed a teaspoon of laudanum and screwed up her face. The alcohol mixed with opium tasted yucky-bitter but it would sort the pain. She swirled tea around her mouth to wash away the taste.

Hugo took himself off to the bathroom and Maud added wood to the fire.

'The lane's bad luck for you, Miss. Better to stay here.' Maud peered into the cot. 'It's a miracle the baby wasn't hurt.'

'After the car turned over, she was underneath me,' said Sophie. 'My body must have shielded her. Mr Lacey and Mr Harrington were thrown clear.'

'I would never have guessed about you and Mr Harrington. Not in a hundred years.' Maud straightened Bella's bedclothes. 'And Master Freddy courting another lady so soon after a broken engagement…'

The gossip mill was alarmingly efficient. Maud could keep secrets when prevailed upon, but she was also the Shorten Gossip Queen. Sophie embellished the cover story, adding spurious details about Jane Smith.

Maud frowned. 'So sad.'

Bella's piercing wail cut the conversation short, and Sophie forced herself to climb out of bed. She opened the holdall and dug out a nappy and Bella's changing stuff.

'What's that?' asked Maud.

'Disposable nappy.'

Maud watched her change Bella, fascinated.

'Will you emigrate with Mr Watkins?' asked Sophie.

'We don't want to.' Maud sighed. 'America's very far.'

Sophie lined up the clean nappy on Bella and fastened it. Just two left.

'After you disappeared, and with so many maids working in the hospital bay, I've been doing all sorts, Miss. Helping in the kitchen, laying fires in the public rooms.' Maud pursed her lips. 'It's not right.'

Maud left, and Sophie climbed into bed, trying to get comfortable. The laudanum would kick in soon.

Hugo returned from the bathroom. He touched the ugly scrape on his nose. 'When the car hit the mine … to sitting on the road, it's all a blank.'

'Same. I wonder if Freddy remembers swerving.' That had saved them.

'Why mine a quiet country lane?' said Hugo, getting into bed. 'Makes no military sense. The gardeners don't collect wild garlic anymore. The only person who might be down there is the farmer.'

Sophie nodded. 'Who has fields by the lift.' The pain in her back and hip was fading, but a dawning realisation was

so horrible, she didn't notice. 'The militia radio broadcasts…
They knew we were going.'

'It wasn't a secret,' said Hugo. 'Targeting Freddy?'

'They couldn't have been. He decided to drive us at the
last minute.' Sophie gasped as it sunk in. 'Hugo, they were
after me, because of Inkpin.'

Jack was snoozing by the fire, but Charlotte was listening,
her furry head tipped to one side.

'I'd forgotten about Inkpin,' said Hugo.

Sophie addressed Charlotte. 'You were in the Manor
when it happened.' She explained how she'd been taken
hostage in the town and had killed Barty Inkpin to get away.
Charlotte didn't look shocked, just listened. 'Later on, when
Inkpin's father was assassinated, I presumed his plan to
avenge his son had died with him.'

A Charlotte-nod.

'Joan Small was disgusted when Inkpin shot an innocent
bystander in the bakery,' said Sophie. 'I can't believe she'd
have ordered that mine.'

'She must have done,' said Hugo. 'According to Richard,
nothing happens without her say-so.'

'I need more of this.' Sophie reached for the laudanum
bottle, but Hugo snatched it off her.

Sophie sighed and finished her tea. Laudanum was definitely moreish.

'The gamekeepers on patrol pick up info from the town.
They'll soon learn why the militia mined the lane, and when
they do, what you did to Inkpin will get back to Freddy. Tell
him first.'

Sophie clunked down her cup onto the saucer on the tray,
her heart sinking. 'I can't. How I finished off Inkpin was too
horrible.'

'Compared to killing a whole army,' said Hugo, drily, 'one
man is small beer.'

In the parallel medieval universe, protecting Hugo, Freddy, and Charlotte, Sophie had used a goddess-like power. Then, it had seemed sort of okay. Now, not so much.

She lay flat, her head on the pillow. Directly above her, on the underside of the bed's wooden canopy, was the Lacey coat of arms: the cream background, the stylised blue 'L,' and the noble stags faded with age. 'How I killed him is too gruesome. I can't tell Freddy.'

'You must,' said Hugo. 'Or he'll hear a more gruesome account from someone else.'

Later that morning, the laudanum properly kicked in, and Sophie sat on the sofa in the small drawing room, imbued with a warm, hazy glow. Freddy sat opposite her, dressed in male Shorten Casual: suit and tie, but he could take the jacket off. He smiled at nothing, laudanum-happy.

The dogs were half-dozing, Bella was preoccupied with her plastic rattle, and Hugo was in the library. A good a moment as any to share about Inkpin.

Sophie blurted out what she'd done, glad that neither Jack nor Bella could understand her words.

Freddy swallowed. 'You pushed a *hatpin* into his heart?'

'I didn't tell you then because I thought you'd be … disgusted. That *I* would disgust you.'

Freddy guffawed. 'I became accustomed to you wreaking havoc in a horrible medieval place. Why would I be disgusted that you're a lady assassin?'

Relief coursed through her. 'Not a lady assassin, Freddy. An assassin.' Lady assassin sounded pervy. 'Please keep this to yourself.'

'I'm hardly going to discuss it over lunch.' He stared at

her. 'It would make a good tawdry newspaper headline, though. Inkpin ended by hatpin.'

'The point is…' Sophie stood up to retrieve Bella's dropped rattle and returned it to her. 'The militia wanted revenge. They set the mine to kill me.'

'Goodness.' Freddy leaned forward on the couch. 'My father must be told. Additional measures should be put in place to ensure your safety.'

Sophie sat down. This was awkward. 'Your father knows. I told him straight away.'

'You confided in him but not me?' Freddy glared at her. 'Why?'

'How would you have reacted back then? Honestly?'

Freddy studied the coffee table between them. 'I wouldn't have believed you, or if I had…' He looked up. 'Everything would have been different. I wouldn't have proposed. I wouldn't have followed you and Hugo through the lift. We wouldn't have ended up in that bear pit.' He glanced over at Bella. 'Our daughter wouldn't exist.'

Sophie flinched. She hadn't thought of that.

'In a parallel universe, would another version of you have told me?'

Sophie tried to think through the laudanum fog. Cause and effect in one universe were complicated enough. 'It wasn't a finely balanced decision.' Imagining Freddy's revulsion had given her nightmares. 'The versions of me in other universes, unless they're very different, wouldn't have shared.'

'Hmm,' said Freddy.

Anne came in and sat beside her son. 'You're both looking serious.'

'I have to tell you something,' said Sophie.

'You don't,' said Anne. 'Richard's explained how you escaped from Inkpin. That's why I'm here.'

'Oh.' She'd spent months worrying about Freddy finding out, hadn't considered how Anne would react. Sophie held her breath.

'I was surprised,' said Anne, carefully, 'but I was more shocked that Richard hadn't trusted me enough to tell me at the time.'

Sophie winced, hating that she'd affected their relationship. 'It was a military secret. Otherwise, he would have.'

'Perhaps,' said Anne, her shrewd eyes on Sophie. 'But we talked it through, and as a result he shared other information, and I'm thankful for that.' Anne glanced at her son, then at Sophie. 'And I'm also thankful you escaped the mine unscathed.'

'I can't imagine how horrible it was for you when Freddy disappeared,' said Sophie.

'You're both here now.' Anne smiled. 'Miss Hemmings is back at work, seems to have recovered herself after the shelling.'

'I should tell her about Inkpin,' said Sophie.

'You can leave Bella with us.' Anne gazed fondly at her granddaughter.

Lucy was in the lean-to greenhouse, talking to a gamekeeper about the heating. He opened a tool bag.

'Are you up for a mini-archery session?' Sophie asked her.

'Definitely,' said Lucy. Most of Shorten believed she and Lucy practised mini-archery, a 'ladylike' sport, but the assigned room in the Manor had no archery board. Only a punchbag on a stand.

The gamekeeper was setting out tools on the floor. 'The heating should be up and running in about an hour.'

Lucy and Sophie went outside.

'My heart stopped when I heard about the mine,' said Lucy. 'Are you really up for a workout?'

'No, just a chat.'

They walked into the house and down the corridor to the gym. Sophie unlocked the door, and they stepped inside. She re-secured the door, leaving the key in the lock. Empty keyholes could be looked through.

Lucy strode over to the diamond-paned window. Outside, a dense line of elm trees formed a natural privacy screen. She drew the heavy curtains further apart to let in light and spluttered in the resulting cloud of dust. 'We don't need to keep our kickboxing under wraps anymore, and I'd enjoy telling Mr Crawford. He might lose the butler poker face.'

'I like his poker face,' said Sophie. 'And, anyway, I'd like this to stay secret. Precious downtime.'

Lucy nodded. 'Mr Crawford wouldn't be that surprised. With maids doing roof-duty, this isn't a big deal.'

Sophie lifted an upright chair from a stack, sat on it and rubbed her neck. 'What's roof duty?'

'Watching for anyone trying to swim the moat. Shooting them if they try.' Lucy placed her hands flat against the wall and did her pre-workout stretching. 'But now I'm sleeping in the attic, the girls on roof duty thump up and down the stairs and wake me up.' She yawned. 'I'm not complaining. The bombed-out families have it worse, camping in the servants' hall.'

'Do you do roof duty?'

'I've got my hands full with the one-woman greenhouse.'

'What's happening with the old ones beyond the moat?'

'I've no idea what state they're in.' Lucy finished stretching. 'But everything outside the moat has been looted, including my cottage.'

'I'm sorry, that sucks.'

'And the few knickknacks I had in my rooms are gone as well.' Lucy shot her a resigned smile and did a flurry of punches. 'The gossip-mill is loving Freddy's beard, and everybody's agog you're married to Hugo.'

Gossip had been the bane of Sophie's life here. It was fortunate that the head gardener passed on gossip just to Sophie. She exhaled, and summarised about Inkpin, not glossing over the hatpin. 'That's how I escaped.'

To her dismay, Lucy looked horrified. 'I … can't believe you did that.'

'We hoped the militia wouldn't find out it was me.'

Lucy steadied the punch bag.

'I told Hugo, but only once we were home, a universe away.' Freddy and Anne's reaction to how she'd dealt with Inkpin had made her complacent about Lucy's. 'Are we still friends?'

'I've seen a load of bad stuff here, but this is something else.' Lucy executed an impressive kick at the punchbag. 'Why is a pin more shocking than shooting someone?'

'Up close and personal.' Sophie chewed her lip. 'Freddy wasn't as shocked as you.'

'Really?' Lucy stopped the bag swinging.

'He's been through a lot since we disappeared.' Sophie shifted in her chair. 'The mine in the lane was payback for Inkpin.'

Lucy gave a low whistle. 'I wondered why they'd set it there.' She executed another targeted kick.

Sophie moved her neck from side to side and gave in to the need for more laudanum. She measured out a teaspoon and swallowed it fast.

Lucy watched her. 'You'd be better off drinking brandy. One of the gardeners who was shot on patrol … he's completely recovered but still on laudanum. The opium starts slow, but it draws you in, doesn't let go.'

'Noted,' said Sophie, a weary edge to her voice. 'I'm glad you don't patrol.'

'When they're very short-handed, I patrol.'

'And how is it, the patrolling?'

'Hours of boredom, seconds of terror,' said Lucy. 'But the terror's growing on me.'

'What do you mean?'

'Adrenaline rushes are as addictive as laudanum.' Lucy did a balanced turnaround kick. 'Might get me killed.'

Was she serious? 'Do you have to patrol?'

'Yes.' Lucy stepped away from the punchbag. 'I'd never ask my gardeners to do a job I wouldn't do. Patrolling's no different.'

CHAPTER 10

The shell that hit the families' building had demolished two rooms and damaged four others. One woman had died of her injuries and so had her young child. Another resident had lost a leg and three others had serious shrapnel injuries.

Hugo was still too sore from being thrown from the car to help with the clear-up. So, when Sophie left to confess to Freddy about Inkpin, he slipped off to the library to read *Classical Myths and Legends*. He took with him his old 'lift puzzle' Shorten notebook and a pencil. The notebook's plain cardboard cover was getting shabby, fraying at the edges.

He lit the fire, sat in the red chair, and scanned an unremarkable list of Greek and Roman gods, including Janus. The next page was entitled *Mythical Symbols Reimagined*, with sketches. And Hugo caught his breath.

The first drawing was of a long, grey key, with a heart-shaped handle, and in the hollowed-out centre was a figure T.

Janus' key symbolises the Roman god's protection of doors, gates, paths, and thresholds, he read.

Below it was a sketch of a walking staff, drawn in the same tidy style and shaded with tiny strokes, but it wasn't flat like the key. The walking stick had depth, the shape and proportions so cleverly done, it seemed to be jutting out from the page. Though the stick was an insipid brown, Hugo's perception of colours was different here. Back home, he'd see that colour as deeper, more textured, closer to oak. The head of the staff was heart-shaped, matching the key, and its identical hollowed-out centre had the three limbs of the T touching the inner rim.

Janus' walking staff indicates his knowledge, guiding the way, said the caption.

Hugo had seen the key before, when he'd searched online for Janus info at home. But the only time he'd seen this design of staff had been in a completely different universe. A flat sketch kept by Naga, a descendant of the lift builders.

He trawled his memory. What had Naga said? Something about field teams summoning the corporeal version of Janus with walking staffs, for mythology research... Centuries later, the lift builders had outlawed any interaction with the locals, and all the staffs were supposedly destroyed. A while after that, triggered by a software upgrade, Janus had become sentient.

Hugo's hands trembled as he held the book. There was something else, just out of reach.

At the bottom of the page, a date was written in a precise, neat hand. *June 1889. I. M.*

The sketch of the staff could have been copied from a much older drawing, but the depth and detail suggested the artist had drawn it from an actual walking staff, one that had survived into the 19th century. The walking stick could still be around now, in 1927.

He turned to the front of the book. Published in London.

Unlikely the staff was in the Manor. It could be anywhere in the country, in this world.

'Oh.' He remembered now. The walking staffs had another function. They remotely fixed technical issues in the lift, reset the ship's software.

Resetting the ship would mean *resetting Janus*. He'd revert to what he'd been before his upgrade.

No longer sentient.

Hugo drew a deep, slow breath. Janus' core algorithm prevented him from physically harming travellers, but he found ways to torment them. Trapped in his ship for millennia, Janus' personality had endured and warped. He'd become more bored, more sadistic. And he was surely probing the rules of his prison, seeking to subvert them.

Hugo shut the book, his brain racing. A walking staff that could turn a capricious, predatory god into a mindless machine. Once rid of Janus, the original quantum software could reliably transport them, protect them.

If a walking staff still existed and *if* it still worked...

Okay, that was two big ifs.

He read the rest of the book. Standard summaries of the Greek and Roman pantheon of gods. How peculiar that, entirely out of keeping with the *Mythical Symbols Reimagined* page, most of the book was lists and summaries. Almost an afterthought.

Taking his notebook and pencil from his pocket, Hugo carefully copied the key and the walking staff, labelling the relevant colours.

He gazed into the fire. Janus couldn't get inside his mind, only the minds of travellers who had the gene. If Sophie, Freddy — or Charlotte — knew there might be a surviving staff, and what it could do, Janus would know the instant they summoned him in the lane. Faced with even the remotest possibility of his own death, would Janus' most important algorithm prevail? Or would he snuff them out?

This information had to stay locked up in his 'lesser being' brain. And as soon as possible, he'd return to modern London to research more online, focusing on the walking staff.

Except he couldn't. Sophie would ask why he needed to travel, and unless she went with him, there was no way to get home.

CHAPTER 11

That evening, Sophie and Hugo felt well enough to dress up for dinner, and Hugo went off to his old bedroom to sort his clothes.

Maud removed a gown from Sophie's wardrobe. 'I can help you dress, Miss.' She laid a red tea dress on the bed.

'Yay!' said Sophie. Her favourite dinner gown. No corset required. The dress could only be worn when guests weren't staying. The Armstrongs and Clarissa had evidently been guests at the Manor for so long, they'd turned into residents.

Maud eyed Sophie's gold wedding band. 'Master Freddy's engagement ring was very fine. If you don't mind me asking, what happened to it?'

'I returned it to him.' That at least was true. Sophie set down Bella beside Charlotte. The dog stretched and Bella did the same. Copying Charlotte would keep the baby entertained for a while.

As Sophie undressed and put on the gown, her mind skittered back to the last occasion Maud had helped her change for dinner. Sophie Arundel-Harrington didn't only have a different name. She'd been changed by travelling through time, as well as by the passing of regular time.

Maud fastened the dress. 'Lady Lacey asked if I'd be Bella's nanny, Miss. I'd love to mind her.'

'I don't need…' She was being silly. Another pair of hands would be brilliant, and Maud's pride in performing any role to perfection bordered on the obsessive. Like hers. Sophie smiled at her.

'I'll watch Bella while you're at dinner, Miss.'

Sophie took in her reflection in the long mirror. Long red dress with train. Check. Expensive necklace. Check. Hair up in an old-fashioned loose bun. Check. 'I can't believe every-one's still dressing up … with all this trouble?'

'It's important, Miss. Good for morale.'

Hugo knocked and came in, fabulously fit in Shorten black tie. His jacket had tails at the back, reaching to his knees.

Bella stared at him and pushed her soft fringe from her forehead. Her gesture was unnervingly Hugo-like, but the habit was due to watching and copying. Freddy's paternity had been confirmed in 21st century London, the test 99.9% accurate. Hugo picked up the baby, nestling her in his arms, and she did her contented gurgle.

They walked to pre-dinner drinks, the dogs in their wake, and Sophie's dress swished expensively. What had she missed about Shorten? Anne and Richard, Maud and Lucy. The people. Yes, she did love this dress, but dressing up every night was in the 'not missed' category.

In the anteroom, there was no sign of Clarissa, and Hugo relaxed.

'Clarissa's still unwell,' said Anne, without prompting. She was wearing her royal-blue gown and the Armstrong sisters were wearing dresses Sophie recognised. Alice's was faded. This was 'make do and mend,' Shorten style.

Freddy, deep in conversation with his father, looked predictably good in his black tie. Rakish with his beard.

'Mrs Watkins has really taken to Bella,' Sophie said to Anne. Maud had never struck her as the maternal type, but people change.

'I thought she would.' Anne lowered her voice. 'I understand she's waiting until we're settled in America before starting a family.'

Sophie nodded. No secrets in the Manor.

Jack was sticking close to Richard, but Charlotte was drifting around, listening to conversations. Luckily, she didn't appear to be listening. The chatter was subdued. Two gamekeepers had died in Reynolds' car.

'I'm still under par,' said Freddy to Sophie. 'How are you feeling?'

'Rough.' She'd taken onboard Lucy's advice, stopped drinking laudanum.

Rupert addressed Sophie. 'Apologies for my lack of manners on the road. I was … surprised.'

At six foot, Rupert was a little shorter than Hugo, and his blond hair was lighter than Freddy's. Rupert's pointed chin and arresting blue eyes shouldn't have looked right for such a masculine face, but they did. Yes, back in the day, Sophie had turned down Rupert's proposal, but maybe another version of her, in a parallel universe, had married him.

'Your Grace.' A maid topped up Rupert's glass.

'Your Grace?' repeated Sophie. 'Does that mean…'

'Yes,' said Rupert, his voice flat. 'My father gave up the ghost last winter, making me a duke.' He drank his sweet sherry. 'Let's hope it will impress the good folk of Virginia.'

'America will be exciting,' said Ethel. The older Armstrong sister glanced up at Rupert, a glint in her eye.

'An adventure,' said Rupert, his attention on Ethel.

Ethel was flirting. That was different. And Rupert was different too. He'd lost his swagger.

With so many diners, the meal felt as formal as it used to. Sophie was seated opposite Hugo, between Freddy and Rupert. Two unfamiliar maids were serving. Scullery maids? Before, they'd never interacted with the Laceys. Dusted rooms before dawn like invisible fairies.

Jack sat beside Richard's chair. Charlotte sat next to Sophie's.

Sophie sipped tomato soup, remembering to scoop the spoon away from her in the Shorten way. 'Rupert, I'm sorry about your father.'

'He treated me badly as a child,' said Rupert, looking up. 'But he died defending Radden Hall, how he'd have wanted to go.'

Sophie hesitated. 'How is your mother?'

He ducked his head down again. 'On the run.' Rupert's mother was a high-profile suffragette. 'She skipped bail, and no one knows where she is.'

Freddy frowned. 'That's worrying.'

'She's a hardy soul,' said Rupert.

Along the table, Alice Armstrong was chatting to Harry who'd exchanged his doctor's coat for black tie. When Sophie had last seen Alice, she'd been traumatised by an attack on her home, Armstrong Hall. But tonight, she seemed happy, her elfin face animated in the light from the table's candelabra.

'Hugo, I want to hear about your adventures,' said Harry. 'Mr Parkes told the police that the lift sent you insane.'

Hugo raised his eyebrows. 'At home, Parkes is wanted for murder.'

'He thought if we permanently opened the lift, our police would track him down,' said Sophie, 'so in the lane, he tried to kill us.'

Harry looked shocked. 'Mr Parkes assaulting you … we should inform the police in Shorten town.'

Hugo shook his head. 'How would we prove it?'

Richard was talking earnestly to Freddy. 'The Poorhouse Payments Scheme should begin soon, but it could take months or years to undermine the militia.'

'And all the while, the government raises horrendous taxes to pay for it,' said Anne.

'We shouldn't emigrate.' Freddy put aside his crystal wine glass. 'We should stay and fight.'

The room fell silent. A sea of sombre faces.

'We can't win,' said Rupert.

'We don't have to win,' said Freddy. 'We just need to hold out until the Payments Scheme starts to work.'

'How many lives will be lost in the meantime?' said Rupert.

'It's been … difficult,' said Harry. 'Not only the fatalities. Terrible injuries.'

'Not leaving will show leadership, encourage others to fight with us,' said Freddy. 'Even one family's decision could make a difference.'

'The Greenworthys left in the summer,' said Ethel.

'Kate's left too,' said Anne.

Freddy's brow creased. Kate was a childhood friend. Hugo was silent, aware this decision wasn't his.

Before she'd had Bella, Sophie's instinct would have been to stay, to fight. But now, protecting her daughter trumped that, and being a mother had brought with it unwelcome feelings of helplessness, vulnerability. Sophie took a sip of white wine. Part of the gig. Suck it up.

Richard cleared his throat. 'As circumstances change, so must the calculation of risk. I had thought mining the lane was restricted to our local militia, to their particular tactics.' He scanned the table, his gaze passing over Sophie and settling on Anne. 'But the availability of mines is increasing daily, as is their use throughout the county.'

'Where are they getting them from?' asked Rupert.

'Russia, through militia-controlled ports.' Richard swirled the red wine in his glass. 'As a consequence, the roads to Liverpool are even more dangerous. Everyone must decide what is best for them, but for the moment, we've decided to delay emigrating.'

Rupert sighed, watching Ethel. She'd set her mouth in a determined line. Her sister, Alice, looked equally resolute, her eyes on Harry. What had happened to nervous, shy Alice?

'So, we fight.' Freddy's lips compressed into a grim line.

Hugo frowned and Sophie frowned back. Freddy had believed that bringing Bella here was a calculated risk, but with no way of knowing what was happening in Shorten, that risk hadn't been 'calculated' at all.

Just a stupid high-stakes gamble, driven by family and love and hope.

CHAPTER 12

The next morning, keeping well away from the antique Wilton rug, Sophie changed Bella's nappy. The cloth nappies needed frequent changing, were unbelievably messy, and leaked.

Maud selected a dark dress from the wardrobe. 'The ladies wear plain gowns for nursing duties, Miss.'

Sophie sighed. She was beyond this. 'Miss Blackmore and the scullery maids do guard duty in trousers. No one will care.'

'You're right, Miss.' Maud returned the dress to the wardrobe. 'The country's going to the dogs.'

Hearing the derogatory tone in Maud's voice, Charlotte arched a furry eyebrow.

'Bah.' Bella poked Charlotte in the chest with her finger, and Maud strode over and picked the baby up.

'Don't worry about Charlotte snapping. It's a game they play.' Sophie set off to the large drawing room.

She walked down the long corridor, past old portraits, but paused in the doorway, taken aback by all the beds and patients. Harry gestured for her to come in.

The fire was lit in the grate, but cold air was blowing through open windows. Sophie shivered. 'These can't all be gamekeepers and gardeners from patrolling. There's too many.'

'We take in casualties from across the county,' said Harry. 'The cottage hospital's full.'

'I only know basic first aid.' Sophie pulled on a white apron. 'I'll need close supervision.'

'Knowing what you don't know is a good thing.' Harry straightened the cuffs on his white coat. 'Well-meant poor interventions can be fatal.'

'Where's Dr Griffiths?' The Laceys' doctor had treated her after she'd fallen from a horse.

'He died last year, poor man. A stroke.'

Clarissa hurried past them. No greeting. No 'good to see you.' Okay, entirely understandable. Sophie followed Harry towards a bed by the windows.

'Could you sit with this one?' asked Harry. 'Keep his temperature down and read to him.'

'What's his injury?'

'He lost a leg,' said Harry. 'Gangrene's set in.'

The boy was a few years younger than her, about sixteen. There were freckles on his nose and cheeks and his skin looked damp. Sophie shut her lips against a sickly-sweet smell she associated with bodies, not someone still alive. She sat on an upright wooden chair beside the bed, wrung out a flannel from a bowl of water, and pressed it against his brow.

The boy's closed eyelids flickered. 'Am I home?' His voice was shaky like an old man's.

Sophie hesitated. 'Yes.'

Read to him? There was no book on the bedside table, only a pile of envelopes. She opened one and extracted a letter. It was signed, 'Mam xxx.'

'Shall I read the letters?'

'Please.'

'*Friday, 18th February.*

Dearest Philip,

The house and the village are much the same. I make bread every day for the militia. They are sometimes noisy at night in the pub, but don't bother us. I've saved ingredients for a cake for you...'

The letter was three or four pages, as was the next letter, and the next. An insight into a mother's humdrum life: reassuring, comforting. When Sophie finished reading the last letter, she returned to the first.

The boy's breathing was irregular, raspy. She hadn't noticed a change and reached for another letter.

Harry touched her shoulder. 'Thank you.'

'I shouldn't stop.'

Harry felt the boy's neck and drew the blanket over his head. Shocked, Sophie burst into tears. Alice rushed up and offered a handkerchief.

Sophie wiped away her tears, conscious her crying would upset the other patients. 'How long have you been doing this?'

'About eighteen months,' said Alice. 'You'll cope fine tomorrow.'

'Who looks after them during the night?'

'We take it in turns,' said Alice, her gaze steady. Amidst this nightmare, she'd found a purpose.

'You know,' said Sophie, 'Charlotte could help here.' Medical service dogs visited hospital wards at home. With Charlotte's enhanced reasoning, she didn't need training to stay calm and quiet.

But Alice's eyes widened. 'Your dog?'

'She'd sit by patients' beds,' said Sophie. 'The less sick ones could stroke her. She'd cheer them up.'

Harry frowned. 'She could spread infection.'

Sophie opened her mouth to argue but stopped. She'd struggled through her first day. Who was she to offer suggestions?

'Stick to light duties.' Harry pointed to a kitchen area with a small stove in a corner of the bay. 'Serve tea.'

Sophie gave tea to those who could drink unaided and for the sicker patients, she held their cup or spoon-fed them.

Reynolds could drink from a cup. It had been him lying in the road, thrown out by the explosion. An angry burn stretched across his forehead and one arm was wrapped in a thick bandage.

Sophie put the cup and saucer on his bedside table, and he sat up. She adjusted pillows at his back, and he grimaced as she did so. 'I thought I was a goner,' he whispered.

'You were lucky.'

His face fell. 'The gamekeepers with me weren't.' He picked up the cup and drank slowly. 'I'm so glad the baby wasn't hurt.' He blushed. 'Doesn't seem right, you waiting on me.'

'I'm not sure I'm needed, but I wanted to help.' The bay was busy with nurses hurrying about their duties. She smiled at him. 'Get better.'

She continued giving out tea and after that washed up. Harry was sitting near the kitchen, writing in a ledger.

'Will Reynolds completely recover?' Sophie asked him.

'His arm will give him gyp for the rest of his life. Bad burn.'

Ethel came towards them. 'More tea, please.'

Serving more tea, defying Harry and assisting Ethel with bedpan chores, Sophie lost track of time. She ate a hurried sandwich for lunch and sneaked a teaspoon of laudanum, returning the bottle to her pocket.

Harry approached her. 'Enough for today.'

For a nasty moment, Sophie thought he meant the laudanum, but he opened the bay door for her, and she gladly took off her apron.

CHAPTER 13

At ten that evening, Alan was behind The Crooked Gate bar, carefully drying glasses that didn't need drying, and Roy was sitting on a barstool, nursing his drink. Frank was upstairs asleep, used to the racket, and Betty served drinks, counting the minutes till closing time.

Mr Morley was reading a newspaper at his usual table, and Joan was opposite him, analysing codes in her notebook. According to the militia broadcast, the mine had killed two men, wounded one, and now the Laceys weren't leaving for Liverpool.

Jim Hayden strode up to the bar and ordered a beer. He was a head taller than the other men. 'You all right, mate?' he said to Roy.

Roy didn't look up. 'Fine.'

'That Mrs Harrington's like a cat,' said Jim. 'Got nine lives.'

Betty focused on pulling the pint, thankful Mrs Harrington's baby hadn't been hurt. Just the idea of hurting a child made her feel sick.

Jim turned away with his beer. 'We should lay another mine.'

'To what end?' said Mr Morley from behind his newspaper. 'We've lost the element of surprise.'

'I'll make you a cup of tea, Mrs Hill.' Roy slipped through the bar and disappeared into the kitchen.

Betty would miss Roy when the militia pushed off to the Manor. But who knew when that would happen?

Roy returned with her tea and set it on the bar. Alan didn't notice, kept drying glasses.

'The London militia have been busy.' Mr Morley put down his newspaper. 'They've shot another member of Parliament. At this rate, there'll be none left.'

'The London militia is led by a numpty,' said Roy.

'Oi!' Jim called from his table. 'It's bad down there. They don't waste time yapping. Just get on with it!'

'Knocking off politicians won't help the cause,' said Roy. 'We'll end up like Russia.'

'How do you mean?' Mr Morley closed his newspaper.

'They murdered the Tsar,' said Taffy. 'Can you imagine knocking off the king? Country would go to hell in a handcart.'

'Taffy's right,' said Roy. 'The royal family are our glue. Hold the country together.'

Most of the men nodded, and Betty giggled, picturing the King in his posh clothes, sticky with glue.

'Russia's coping without a king,' said Mr Morley. 'Some day, I intend to visit.'

'My missus knows this lady that came from Russia,' said Taffy. 'Soldiers killed her whole family.'

'The situation is complex,' said Mr Morley.

Men were squaring up in front of the bar and Betty sidled over to Joan. 'Perhaps you should call closing time? We don't want more fights.' They'd lost nine beer glasses the previous night, and Joan hadn't paid for replacements.

'The men need to let off steam.' Joan shut the notebook. 'The Laceys not leaving means a change of plan.'

Beside Joan, Mary brushed a loose red curl from her eyes. 'That army bloke said we'd have the fancy new weapon this month.'

Joan scowled. 'He said that last month.' She glanced over at the bar. 'See? Under control.'

The men who'd been squaring up were now laughing at some joke, patting each other on the back as they stumbled to their table.

'But Mr Parkes is pushing his luck, Mrs Hill,' said Joan. 'You might want to get him upstairs.'

Alan was poking Roy in the chest with his forefinger, trying to provoke him.

Betty hurried over to them.

'Riffraff, coming here, doing what you want,' said Alan. 'I'm not having it.'

'Stick with your glasses, mate,' said Roy.

Alan shoved him hard with his left hand. Alan's other arm was limp by his side, his shirt sleeve covering the stump near his wrist.

'Come on, love,' said Betty. 'It's late.' She held Alan's maimed arm.

But Alan shook her off. 'No.'

'You go up and I'll bring you a piece of cake. How does that sound?' Betty took his arm again.

'Farce, better, even the bicycle.' When Alan was tired, he often spoke nonsense. He frowned, as if noticing the militiamen for the first time.

Betty guided him to the bar, through the kitchen and upstairs. His shabby bedroom looked over the green. They'd had separate bedrooms since the day he'd lost his hand. The day Will had died.

Betty left him undressing and checked on Frank in her bedroom. Sleeping peacefully, curled up like a puppy.

She stepped back onto the landing. Roy was coming up the stairs with a slice of Victoria sponge on a side plate. He'd baked the cake that morning. Roy was a strange one. A man who enjoyed cooking.

Betty went into Alan's room with the cake, but he was already asleep, still wearing his work trousers.

Three days after the mine had exploded in the lane, a trader's van was escorted through the Manor's fortified gates. *Slater's Bakery* was written on the side in swirly letters.

Maud's sister, Lizzie, owned the town bakery, and this was her afternoon delivery. Drizzle fell from the dull November sky as she climbed out of the driver's cab, her boots crunching on the gravel. Her auburn hair was tucked under a yellow bobble hat and her unfastened pale coat flapped about her ankles, revealing a striped navy and white apron over a dark dress.

She opened the rear doors, and as maids unloaded sweet-smelling boxes and carried bread into the house, Sophie walked out onto the drive. Her neck still ached but parac-etamol sorted it.

'I heard you'd returned, er Madam,' smiled Lizzie.

'Let's keep with Miss.'

A mature woman jumped out of the front passenger seat. She was tall, wore a man's formal coat and a navy cap, and carried a rifle.

'Where are my manners?' said Lizzie. 'This is Lady Georgina—'

'Lady Georgina Denning-Lytton,' said the woman. 'How do you do?'

'How do you do?' Sophie took in the woman's dirty face and intense blue eyes. This must be Rupert's famous suffragette mother. 'Sophie Arundel-Harrington.' She could do pompous names. 'Please come in.'

Lady Georgina strode over the drawbridge and Sophie followed with Lizzie.

'She flagged us down on the road,' whispered Lizzie to Sophie. 'We had no idea who she was. Our escort almost shot her.'

In the hall, Lizzie handed a letter to Mrs Rawlings. Lizzie gave regular reports about militia activity in the town to the housekeeper, who passed them on to Richard.

Mrs Rawlings hurried off, and Lady Georgina peeled off her ragged, woollen gloves. She glanced around imperiously, and Sophie fought an illogical need to curtsey.

Anne swept into the hall and smiled. 'My dear Lady G. Let's get you settled in.'

That evening, Hugo and Sophie walked to the anteroom for pre-dinner drinks, and Charlotte kept pace with them. Jack was still avoiding Charlotte and he bounded up ahead.

For the first time since they'd arrived, Clarissa was there, talking to Ethel. Her gown was newer than Ethel's: a looser cut and decorated with shiny beads. With the shorter skirt showing off her ankles, it resembled a flapper dress.

Hugo tensed, and Sophie stayed close. They moved as one past Clarissa, and headed towards Richard and Rupert, who were speaking to Lady G. Wearing a borrowed lilac dinner gown of Anne's, Rupert's mother managed to look rakish, her ample bosom more prominent.

'Miss Small allowed me to sleep in The Crooked Gate last night.' Lady G downed her sherry. 'As usual, we argued. We share common cause with suffrage, but nothing else. If she had her way, we'd all be beggared.'

Rupert's mother evidently knew Joan from her suffragette work, but this was complicated. Lady G was no friend of the militias. She'd lost her home when a militia had requisitioned Radden Hall.

Lady G accepted another glass of sherry from a maid. 'Miss Small runs those men like a pack of foxhounds.'

'We lost good men in the lane.' Richard's gaze lingered for a moment on Sophie. 'It's increasingly difficult to man patrols.'

Lady G shot him a no-nonsense smile. 'Just as well I'm here then.'

Beside Sophie, Charlotte was sitting quietly, her attention on Lady G.

'Mama, may I present Miss Ethel Armstrong.' Rupert put his arm through Ethel's.

Lady G looked surprised, though not as surprised as Ethel.

Ethel recovered first and raised her chin. 'Your son's presence has made our stay here so much more agreeable.'

That wasn't Ethel speaking. She'd been possessed by Jane Austen.

Lady G nodded politely, evidently understanding Jane-Austen-Speak.

'The morale of Miss Small's militia is good,' said Lady G. 'Surprising, given the publican's lack of charm. I appreciate having one hand must be trying, but when I arrived, Mr Parkes almost bared his teeth.'

Charlotte growled, recognising the name. Alan Parkes had nearly killed her in the fight by the lift.

Lady G glanced down at Charlotte. 'Was it something I said?'

'She's hungry,' said Sophie.

The butler opened the dining room's double doors, and they all trooped in. With ten people around the table, avoiding eye contact with Clarissa was doable and Anne, with characteristic tact, had seated Clarissa as far from Hugo as possible.

Freddy sat beside Clarissa and over the starter course, he regaled her with his adventures in the medieval realm, glossing over and exaggerating, but leaving out unseemly bits, including making out in the bear pit. Obviously.

Clarissa pushed food about her plate. She seemed bewildered by Freddy's new stories — and him.

'Is Miss Small aware you're here?' Richard asked Lady G. 'That you may assist us?'

'I told her I was bound for Liverpool, and that was my intention, but with these ghastly mines, I've reconsidered.' Lady G drained her glass of red wine. 'I understand winters in Virginia can be cold.'

Sitting between Sophie's chair and Rupert's, Charlotte did her unnerving nod. Fortunately, no one noticed.

'Don't nod at things,' Sophie whispered to Charlotte. 'Act more dog-like.'

After dinner, the ladies stood up, withdrawing to the small drawing room. Given that everybody talked politics over meals, leaving the men to worrying worldly discussions was pointless. But hey, go with the flow.

The ladies wouldn't be drinking coffee. The ports were in turmoil, disrupting the supply of beans. Fortunately, the government had stockpiled tea. Lady G asked the butler for a case of cigars and a bottle of whisky. Not a conventional request, but Mr Crawford didn't turn a hair.

Jack stayed dozing by the fire while Charlotte was keen to listen more to Lady G. Sophie, though, didn't want to drink tea with Clarissa, so made her excuses and retreated down the corridor towards the bedroom.

Bang.

Firing across the moat.

Curious about maids doing roof duty, Sophie turned around and set off up the stairs to the attic on the fourth floor — a warren of rooms for unmarried female servants.

From the attic landing, Sophie climbed a narrower staircase, lifting her floor-length skirt and train to avoid tripping. At the top was a skylight. She opened it and clambered out onto the roof.

Before her, there wasn't a single roof but many, set at different angles and heights. In between them, narrow walkways disappeared into darkness, obscured by smoke from a forest of chimneys. The smoke smelled of sweet applewood and coal, intense enough to cut through a bitter breeze that stung her face.

Far below, the Manor gardens stretched out, mysterious and shadowed. Patches of the grounds were briefly illuminated as clouds drifted across the moon.

Bang.

Sophie jumped. The firing was much louder here.

Someone was lying near the edge of the roof, aiming a rifle towards the moat.

'Hello. It's only Mrs Harrington.' Sophie kept her voice low and slow, to avoid startling the guard. 'I was curious about the roof.'

The guard rolled away from the edge and sat up. Dressed entirely in black, save for a cream scarf.

Sophie walked gingerly forward and knelt down.

'You gave me this scarf.' The girl's voice was soft and nostalgic. 'Do you remember?'

'You asked for a penny for the guy, for Bonfire Night.' Sophie had gifted her the scarf instead. Though the girl was older, a teenager now, she recognised her.

'I wear it for luck.' The girl rolled into her firing position again.

'Do you keep watch all night?'

'No. Four-hour shifts.'

Sophie squinted into the gloom. 'How do you see anyone?'

'If there's moonlight, it reflects off the moat, gives enough light.' The girl raised the rifle slightly. 'And you notice if somebody moves. They return fire, but they haven't got me yet.'

'I shouldn't distract you.' Sophie got to her feet, shamed by the girl's bravery, and as she felt her way back to the skylight, she remembered Richard's words before dinner. '... *increasingly difficult to man patrols.*'

The Laceys didn't need her help with nursing, or with roof duty. They needed her to patrol.

CHAPTER 15

'You don't need to patrol,' said Hugo after breakfast the next day. 'Stick to nursing.'

Sophie balanced Bella on her hip as they returned to the bedroom. The shame she'd felt on the roof was stronger than the helpless, vulnerable feeling tied up with Bella. '*You're* patrolling tomorrow.'

Trotting beside them, Charlotte looked up at Hugo, her golden eyes worried.

'There aren't enough men.' Sophie put her arm protectively through his. She'd have loved to stop Hugo from patrolling, stop him crossing the road. She bent down and stroked Jack who was scurrying close to her legs. 'My neck's better, and I'll be careful.'

Hugo seemed conflicted, maybe considering the last resort, 'Bella needs you,' card.

'Richard hasn't said I *can't* patrol.' Actually, Sophie hadn't asked him. Didn't want to risk being grounded. She opened the door to their room. 'I'm glad that Richard won't let Freddy patrol.'

'It's driving Freddy nuts.' The son and heir had skipped

breakfast, was labouring away helping to rebuild the families' rooms.

Sophie set Bella down on the floor and put the picture book they'd packed in her lap. Bella pointed at a Gruffalo with a stubby finger.

When she lost interest in the book, Sophie rummaged in a makeshift toy box for Bella's favourite toy, a rattle Reynolds had made from old garage keys. Bella seized the rattle and waved it.

For a man who had no children, Reynold's present was pitch perfect. The keys smelled intriguingly of forbidden petrol and oil, the rattle was too big to swallow, and the keys were too tough to break.

'What are you wearing to patrol?' asked Hugo.

Sophie took her ski jacket from the wardrobe, her scarf, and an old, dark coat. 'I've borrowed this from Lucy and I'm wearing her beanie. The militia won't know it's me.' She put on the jacket.

Hugo picked up his gloves, slipped on his coat, and kissed her on the forehead. 'Keep safe.'

'I will.'

After Hugo headed off to the families' building, Maud came in and frowned.

'Don't say it. Mr Harrington's been nagging me not to patrol.'

'I was only going to suggest you wear that scarlet jacket inside out, the dark lining on the outside.' Maud met her eyes. 'You'll hold your own on patrol, Miss.'

Maud had seen her despatch Inkpin, saving her and Lizzie. Sophie gave her a nervous smile before kissing Bella and the dogs goodbye.

As she walked down the corridor, putting on the coat and beanie, nerves swirled more. In the hall, rifles were stacked on a wooden rack, including the weapon Sophie had been allocated two years ago by Lucy. A new shaky 'S H' had been painted on the butt.

She picked it up. It was nothing like the clay-pigeon gun she'd used on a day out in 21st century London. Different weight, different balance.

Lady G strolled into the hall in her black coat and navy cap, her rifle slung over her shoulder. 'Fine day for it, cold but dry.'

At the bottom of the drive, a gardener was waiting near the fortified gates. Closer to the house were patrol cars, engines running.

Rupert and a gamekeeper were standing by the vehicles, talking. Rupert looked up and frowned at them. 'I hadn't realised you were both on the new roster.'

Lady G smiled. 'Good morning to you too, darling!'

'When I tell you to do something,' said Rupert, 'please don't ask questions. Just do it.'

His mother gave him a mock salute, and Sophie nodded.

Lady G climbed into the passenger seat of Rupert's car and Sophie got in the back.

Sophie checked that her fair hair was hidden under the beanie and adjusted the scarf to cover half her face. Another gamekeeper ran out of the house and jumped into the other vehicle, and the metal gates were hauled open.

The convoy drove out, the gates closed behind them, and Sophie's stomach muscles clenched with perverse excitement. Rupert's mother was already watching the road, gripping her rifle.

Sophie released her gun's safety catch, resting her forefinger away from the trigger as she'd been taught. Didn't want to fire the rifle by accident.

Lucy's training sessions in the armoury had been too brief and too long ago. Like sliding on a tea tray to prepare for bobsleigh.

The wind rushed over the half-height doors, arctic-cold, and Sophie fought not to screw up her eyes. Had to keep alert.

On the seat beside her were towels, bandages, and a tin with a barely readable label, wet and smudged: *Acriflavine.*

Sophie leaned forward. 'Do you know what Acriflavine's for?' she asked Lady G, yelling over the wind.

'Antiseptic. It's made from coal tar.'

The road was deserted, and Sophie's concentration dipped. She imagined militiamen jumping out from behind trees, but they turned into vampires. Stress did weird things to your brain.

They passed a timbered farmhouse and the road widened.

'Nearly there,' shouted Rupert.

The men at the town checkpoint wore brown coats with red cloth badges. Within the badges' white circle was the letter P, also in white.

'What does P stand for?' Sophie asked Rupert.

'Protect.'

After the checkpoint, they soon reached Lizzie's bakery on the high street. The solid red-brick building was brand new but looked eerily the same as the old one, which had been destroyed in a bloody battle against the militia. Only the sign above the door was different. BAKERY carved in plainer letters.

Just past the bakery, they cut down a sideroad and parked at the rear of the building beside other Manor patrol cars.

Sophie climbed out and smiled at Rupert. 'That was okay.'

'The militia don't bother us going to the town,' said Rupert. 'Only on the way back, when we're escorting goods vehicles.'

Right.

A butcher's van drew up and a young man got out. Skinny

and tall, his cap set askew, he could have been an extra in *Peaky Blinders*.

He strode up to their car and said to Rupert, 'All ready, your Grace.'

Rupert nodded.

The young man noticed Sophie and Lady G. 'Women on patrol?'

Sophie frowned at him. So much for the scarf and beanie disguise.

'Do your job,' ordered Lady G, addressing Cheeky Blinder. 'And we'll do ours.'

The young man scuttled into the driver's cab and positioned the van behind the other patrol car, in front of Rupert's.

'Here we go,' said Rupert.

The convoy moved off down the narrow road through the scrubland and turned right onto a side road and then the high street.

Sophie's grip on her rifle tightened. The excitement she'd felt when they'd left the manor was gone, replaced by a cold, queasy sensation.

They slowed at the checkpoint and the Volunteers waved them through.

Sophie focused on the road, had no problem concentrating this time. Adrenaline had kicked in.

They passed the farmhouse. The road narrowed, and the lead patrol vehicle disappeared around a bend.

Ahead of Rupert's car, the butcher's van braked hard. A pheasant running across the road?

The van swerved, spun around and stopped, blocking the road.

Rupert screeched to a halt and Sophie and Lady G were pitched violently forward. Lady G narrowly avoided hitting the windscreen, but Sophie slammed into Rupert. 'Get out!' he shouted.

Lady G leapt from the car.

Sophie fumbled to open her door. She scrambled after Lady G towards the verge, taking cover behind an elm tree.

The van window wound down.

Rupert was driving straight for the van and speeding up. Sophie's heart thumped in her ears.

Peaky Blinder aimed a shotgun out of the van window and fired at Rupert. Lady G shot at the van and a bullet banged off the bonnet. Sophie fired at the van driver's open window. No idea if she'd hit anything. When she'd practised aiming, she'd steadied her breathing. Couldn't do that now.

Peaky Blinder fired again just before Rupert's car slammed into the van. The force of the collision pushed the van backwards.

Lady G sprinted forward, and Sophie ran alongside.

Rupert got out of his car, a round bloodstain on his coat. 'I'm all right.'

Lady G set her mouth. 'I'll deal with the traitor.' She marched over to the van.

Rupert was swaying on his feet.

'You're *not* all right.' Sophie took his arm and he crumpled, one of his legs giving way at an angle beneath him.

'Dear God.' Rupert's voice was raspy.

Sophie laid down her rifle and grabbed a towel from the rear seat.

Rupert's blond hair was speckled red, and she opened his coat. The bullet had hit his shoulder, and he was straining to breathe. She folded the towel and pushed it firmly against the wound.

The other patrol vehicle was back, must have turned around.

Shots rang out and a gamekeeper ran towards the van,

but Sophie hardly noticed because Rupert closed his eyes and slumped sideways. She managed to take his weight and lowered him to the ground.

Witty, hedonistic Rupert could *not* die. She put two fingers on his neck. Still breathing. 'You'll be okay, you'll be okay,' mumbled Sophie, but her brain was scrambled. Focus. Press the towel harder…

'We'll take him.' Two gamekeepers carried Rupert to their car.

They set him down with practised skill. Sophie put aside her rifle and perched on the rear seat by Rupert. Clean towels were stacked in the seat well and she pressed one against his shoulder.

The car swerved around, forcing Sophie to hold on to the car door. 'We can't leave. Lady Georgina's behind the van!'

The vehicle lurched forward and sped up. 'His Grace is still alive,' said the driver. 'Takes priority.'

Which meant… No. Sophie looked back, but they'd passed the bend and the van was lost to sight.

Their car thumped over a pothole and Rupert groaned, his handsome face slick with sweat, and Sophie doubled down on the towel. Rupert's woollen jumper and shirt had meshed into the wound.

The world swam and Sophie concentrated on breathing. In, out.

She unscrewed the lid of an Acriflavine tin, revealing brown-red dust. The stuff must work, or they wouldn't keep it in the cars. She sprinkled it liberally over the wound, staining the frayed cloth of Rupert's shirt.

'Keep your eyes peeled,' shouted the driver.

Sophie glanced down at her rifle. If they were ambushed now… Don't think about that. Tend to Rupert.

Despite the car's near reckless speed, time crawled.

Finally, they reached the Manor and drove through the

gates. 'You're safe,' Sophie whispered as the vehicle juddered to a halt. Rupert's eyelids flickered.

The gamekeepers carried Rupert out of the car, jogged with him over the drawbridge and into the house, and Sophie followed.

As the gamekeepers turned towards the passage that led from the hall to the hospital bay, Sophie felt dizzy again. She sank into the armchair, reliving the van stopping, the crash, Lady G marching towards the van—

'Where's Lady Georgina?' Mrs Rawlings was standing in the doorway to her study.

'I think she's … dead,' said Sophie, hating how the words sounded.

The gamekeepers were in the hall. 'Mrs Rawlings, please call the police station,' said the shorter gamekeeper. 'Ask the Volunteers to tow the butcher's van and our car to the town.'

Mrs Rawlings disappeared into the study.

The gamekeeper who'd been driving gave the other man a sombre glance. 'That nasty surprise was weeks in the planning, Mr Freeman. The militia will have towed both vehicles by now and taken their man's body.' He addressed Sophie. 'Are you able to provide cover?'

For a moment, Sophie didn't understand, but then she did. 'Of course.' The gamekeepers — and she — needed to retrieve Lady G.

Sophie and the gamekeepers hurried across the drawbridge to the drive.

The car's back seat upholstery was streaked red. She gave the cracked leather a token wipe with a towel, sat down, and slammed the door closed.

They rattled through the Manor gates and Sophie picked up her rifle from the seat well. Peaky Blinder must have worked in the town butcher's shop for weeks, maybe months. He'd been surprised she and Lady G had been the escort, but their gender hadn't deferred the ambush. Too late to abort or he'd recognised Inkpin's nemesis. Or both.

The road was quiet, and they quickly came to the ambush site.

Sophie got out the car. Smoke was spiralling into the air from the farmhouse chimney. A bird was crowing in a tree. She walked forward, treading on something. A tangled bit of metal. 'Would the militia have taken Lady Georgina's body?' asked Sophie.

Mr Freeman shook his head. 'They leave our people, and we leave theirs.'

The sound of an engine. A car was racing towards them from the town. She raised her rifle.

'Friendly,' said Mr Freeman.

The vehicle's bonnet was painted with the white letter P, like the letter stitched on the Volunteers' badges. Sophie lowered the rifle.

Two men jumped out and they moved in a subdued group away from the farmhouse, searching the verge.

'There.' Mr Freeman pointed into a ditch.

Lady G was lying on her side, wrapped in her black coat, her navy cap beside her. Her eyes were closed, her face peaceful.

Mr Freeman knelt next to her. 'Shot through the chest, died instantly.'

As the gamekeepers carried Lady G to the car, Sophie forced herself to scan the lane. At home, terrorists targeted first responders. Could be the same with the militia.

'They won't come back,' said Mr Freeman. 'Let's take her home.'

Sophie sat on the rear seat by Lady G, up against the half-height door, not wanting to touch her body.

At the Manor, the gamekeepers took Lady G to wherever

bodies were stored before burial, and Sophie slowly walked into the house.

Freddy and Hugo ran into the hall and Hugo hugged her so hard she couldn't breathe.

When he released her, Sophie held his hand. 'Rupert's in the hospital bay.'

They all hurried down the corridor, but Anne stopped them at the door. 'Rupert's in surgery. You'll only get in the way.' Her tone was gentle, but her expression brooked no argument.

They retraced their steps with Anne along the passage. 'It's dreadful about Lady Georgina.'

'When the van driver turned on us,' said Sophie, unsteadily, 'she was incredible.'

Freddy touched his mother's arm. 'I'll call for tea in the small drawing room.'

'You go on,' said Sophie, 'I need to change.' The coat borrowed from Lucy was streaked with Rupert's blood.

Hugo went with her.

In the bedroom, Sophie peeled off the coat. The rest of her clothes were okay. 'Where's Bella?'

'With Maud in the nursery,' said Hugo. 'The nursery's been well spruced up.'

'Where's Charlotte and Jack?'

'Miss Blackmore wanted to mind them.'

Sophie warmed her hands by the fire, then ran to the wardrobe and reached up, feeling for a hidden flask. She wiped off a layer of dust, unscrewed the top, and took a swig. She spluttered as the rum burned her throat.

'Your secret stash?' Hugo raised his eyebrows.

'Maud wouldn't approve,' said Sophie. 'But back in the day, when you were acting like you weren't interested and I was engaged to Freddy, it helped me cope.' The rum was so strong, it was making her eyes run. She held out the flask.

'I'm good.' Hugo gave her an understanding glance. 'Your day's been a lot worse than mine.'

There was a knock on the door and Sophie hastily returned the flask to its hiding place. Charlotte bounded in and Jack followed.

Miss Blackmore filled the doorway. 'Something's not right with Charlotte. She obeys commands before I've even finished speaking.' Miss Blackmore was hot on dog-discipline.

'She did loads of training while we were away,' said Sophie. Sort of true.

Miss Blackmore nodded vaguely and left, and Sophie stroked Charlotte. 'I love you.'

Charlotte leaned against Sophie, meaning, 'Tell me what's happened.'

Sophie summarised the fire fight. 'Lady G died protecting her son.'

Charlotte whined and curled up on the floor. Sophie dropped to her knees and cuddled her. Jack seemed confused, then lay beside them.

'Jack's adapted to the new Charlotte.' Sophie got to her feet and wiped her eyes. 'I need a cuddle too.'

Hugo hugged her close. 'I'm needed at the families' rooms.'

Sophie kissed him.

After he left, Sophie retrieved her flask, but as she unscrewed the top, Charlotte raised her head and let out a delicate cough, her expressive eyes fixed dolefully on her mistress.

Sophie suppressed a sigh, hid the flask on the wardrobe, and went over to the door. 'I have to clean my rifle.'

As she stepped into the corridor, Charlotte put her head down by Jack.

Charlotte would mind him — and Charlotte didn't need minding.

CHAPTER 16

The next morning, Rupert was still in the hospital bay, fighting for his life. And in the new graveyard by the armoury, the Laceys and their guests gathered to say farewell to his mother. It was far too dangerous to bury her beyond the moat in the chapel cemetery.

Four gamekeepers lowered the wooden coffin into the grave, marked by a small cross with L.G. on it.

In normal times, the vicar from Little Shorten would have conducted a service but, like most of his flock, he no longer left the village. In the absence of the vicar, Richard led a short service, and Anne gave the eulogy. 'You were stoical and brave and stood no nonsense. You'll never be forgotten.'

Jack was subdued in his tartan coat, and Charlotte stayed close to Sophie, comforting her mistress as she'd always done. Sophie laid her hand on her beloved dog's head. Charlotte needed comforting too.

Three days later, Georgina's son was still alive.

The bullet had hit Rupert at an angle, puncturing a lung and narrowly missing his heart. Harry had extracted the bullet while his patient was unconscious with chloroform, performed his careful stitching, and applied more of the brown crumbly mixture.

After the surgery, Sophie only glimpsed Rupert from afar. Ethel was nursing him, guarding him, and shooing away well-wishers. It was now clear what Ethel's Jane Austen language had meant: 'I'm in love with your son and I mean to marry him.'

Sophie went over to Reynolds. He was sitting up in bed and she offered him a cup of tea.

He took the cup and saucer, and Sophie sat by the bed until he'd finished. 'You're looking better.'

'I'm feeling better.' Reynolds glanced around. 'Doc needs more beds. I'll be out of here soon.'

'Dr Richards won't discharge you unless you're fit to go.' Sophie hoped he wouldn't.

'I heard about the ambush.' Reynolds stared into the distance. 'Mr Freeman said you gave a good account of yourself.'

Change the subject. 'Tell me everything I've missed at the Manor. Not war stuff. Nice things.'

'I'm courting Miss Parry.' Reynolds managed a smile. 'When this trouble's over, we're getting married.'

'You're a resilient person,' said Sophie. 'As well as cheeky.'

'Cheeky?'

'You must remember winking at me after I went swimming with Master Freddy in the river.' Newly arrived in Shorten, her wet dress had turned scandalously transparent. 'I was young and silly.' Two years ago. Felt like a lifetime.

'Mrs Harrington!' A patient was calling for her.

Sophie hurried over. It was Scarf Girl from the roof. She

was half sat up, a bandage covering her hair and obscuring one eye.

'What happened?' said Sophie.

'My luck ran out.'

Sophie's heart lurched.

'Doc says my eye's gone. On the bright side, the bullet skimmed my face, missed my brain. I told him, I want a *pretty* eye patch.'

The girl's bravado was paper-thin but humbling. Sophie reached out and held her hand, searching for something to say, but a nurse bustled up. 'She needs to rest.'

After her shift, Sophie marched down the corridor, silently railing against so much misery. Here, the home front *was* the war. No sanctuary. Defending your land, your people, all the while knowing that any second, the enemy could destroy everyone you loved — and you.

She helped with the rebuilding, and at dusk she retreated to the library, with Hugo and Freddy, and Bella and the dogs.

Despite the library's well-fed fire, as usual, the impressive room was chilly. Sophie kept on her ski jacket and buttoned Bella into her fleecy babygro.

Her daughter was progressing from crawling to standing up, and falling over. Fortunately, her sturdy build ensured she bounced. Today she was content to sprawl on a large cushion with her keys-rattle. Freddy sat beside her, armed with the picture book, but Bella ignored it, furiously chewing on the rattle.

'Aha.' Hugo was sitting in the black leather chair, *A History of Shorten* resting on his lap.

'Something interesting?' Sophie had read the book, didn't remember an 'Aha' moment.

Hugo touched a page with his forefinger. 'Freddy's writer ancestor hid it in the acknowledgements.'

Sophie hadn't read the acknowledgements. How many people did that?

'Hid what?' Freddy propped Bella more upright.

'The clue to a secret passage,' said Hugo. 'They were built so priests could come and go unnoticed.' Back in the sixteenth century, the Laceys had sheltered persecuted Catholic priests.

'If there was a tunnel,' said Freddy, 'I'd know about it.'

Sophie looked at her lap. There was at least one Manor secret Freddy didn't know. After escaping Inkpin and keeping how she'd escaped under wraps, Sophie had exchanged notes with Richard about the militia by way of a concealed compartment, just feet from where they were now.

'This has to be a clue,' said Hugo. '*Transcending words, the revered beast points to the hollow. Lesser is greater, backwards is better, born to follow.*' He took his notebook from his pocket and scribbled in it.

Sophie hated riddles because she was rubbish at decoding them. 'Why not describe it in the chapter on Tudor times?'

'No idea,' said Hugo. '*I am grateful to my esteemed friend Hector Noitavlas, a poet who reigns on high.*'

Sophie didn't recognise the poet's name but *reigns on high* was familiar… No, she couldn't place it.

'*That* Frederick Lacey loved riddles and jokes,' said Freddy. 'He had a dog called Hector. It's a red herring.'

'Beyond words,' said Sophie, half to herself. 'This library holds thousands of words.'

Hugo stood up. '*Revered beast.* The stag's a revered beast, and these bookcases are covered in them.' Carved into the wood at the bottom, the top, and the ends of the shelves, most of the stags were generic, resembling the stags on the Lacey coat of arms: proud with craggy antlers. Others were fashioned as bookends, each dignified head different.

'If we turn one,' said Hugo, 'we might find a tunnel.' He climbed the ladder of the first bookcase and tried to turn a stag. It wouldn't budge.

'Given that bookcases line the whole room,' said Sophie, 'this will take a while.'

After an hour, Freddy clambered down the last ladder, and they all accepted defeat.

'If this was a Sir Frederick joke,' said Sophie, 'I'm not laughing.' None of the stags had moved, except one that had fallen off when she'd twisted it. She sheepishly turned it over. 'Do you think we can fix it back on?'

Freddy examined the snapped off carving and made a face.

CHAPTER 17

When Sophie and Hugo went to pre-dinner drinks that evening, only Freddy and Clarissa were there. Freddy's attention was fixed on Clarissa, who was doing her simper-flirt back. Freddy had never shown the slightest interest in Clarissa and vice versa. But the old shy, sheltered Freddy had been battered by a shedload of parallel-world life choices. Maybe Clarissa was intrigued by the new version…

Charlotte leaned forward, definitely intrigued. Jack, who was now determinedly shadowing her, yawned.

'Where is everybody?' said Hugo.

'Alice is nursing,' said Freddy, 'and everyone else has gone down with a cold. Harry's asked them to keep to their beds. He doesn't want it spreading to the hospital bay.'

They trooped into the dining room and a solitary maid served the starter.

'Tell me about future London,' said Clarissa to Freddy, sitting beside him.

'There is a great deal of glass. In tall buildings, and bathrooms, and coffee tables.'

Hugo's lips twitched and Sophie stifled the urge to giggle.

'Your whole day revolves around telephones.' Freddy waxed lyrical about instant messaging and articles on maths equations that he'd read on his phone.

Clarissa listened, apparently enthralled, even by maths.

After dinner, Freddy and Hugo drank more brandy, Clarissa retired, and Sophie headed to the bedroom with the dogs.

Bella should have been asleep, but Maud was pushing the Edwardian pram back and forth. 'She has a fever, Miss, and she's off her food.'

'She was fine before dinner.'

'It came on sudden.'

Bella's cheeks were an odd deep-pink and she was crying, but the cries were catching in her throat.

Sophie's paranoia switched on with a snap. 'I'll watch her through the night. Can you ask Master Freddy to fetch Dr Richards?'

'Of course, Miss.' Maud hurried out.

Charlotte sat down by the pram, her eyes on the baby. Sophie dug around in her holdall and found the thermometer from home. She picked Bella up, climbed onto the bed with her, and pressed the device to her daughter's brow.

Harry arrived with Freddy and Hugo.

The thermometer bleeped. 'She's burning up,' said Sophie. '39 centigrade.'

'What's that in Fahrenheit?' asked Harry.

'Over a hundred.' Hugo rummaged in his holdall. 'Paracetamol should bring it down.'

'I couldn't make space for Calpol.' Stupid. She should have made space.

Hugo showed Harry the paracetamol packet.

'I'm not familiar with it,' said Harry, reading the instructions.

'The doctor at home said it was better for babies than aspirin,' said Sophie. 'I can't remember why.'

Harry crushed the pill, mixed it with water in the tippy mug, and Bella drank it. He left and quickly returned, carrying a pile of wet flannels. 'These will help reduce her temperature.'

Sophie laid a flannel against Bella's forehead. 'She has a lump on the side of her neck. Glands?'

Harry examined the lump and looked down Bella's throat. 'Her tonsils are swollen.' He straightened. 'The adults have developed rashes.'

'What is it?' said Freddy.

'I'll only know for certain if she develops the rash.' Harry rubbed his temples. 'Keep the room cool and give her plenty to drink. I'll return in an hour.'

Hugo sat in the blue chair, Freddy sat by Sophie and Bella on the bed, and a few feet away, Charlotte and Jack stood guard. Bella's crying grew fainter and more sporadic.

Sophie took her temperature every ten minutes and by the time Harry came in, the thermometer showed 41 centigrade, and Bella had a rash on her chest. The hives were rough, like sandpaper.

'This is scarlet fever,' said Harry. 'It can be serious in young children. I'm sorry.'

Serious ... I'm sorry. Sophie's chest tightened and horror ran through her. Bella wasn't moving, her eyes half-closed. 'What do we do?' Sophie's tone was urgent.

'There is nothing we can do,' said Harry, gently. 'The rash will spread, and the disease will take its course.'

Freddy stared at him, distraught. 'Harry, could she die?'

'Yes.'

Panic and helplessness. 'Is she in pain?' asked Sophie, louder than she meant to.

'She has a headache and her stomach hurts,' said Harry.

This wasn't happening. Please let this not be real. They should *never* have crossed universes with Bella. Did scarlet fever exist in 21st century London? If it did, was it life-threatening there? Probably got sorted with antibiotics.

Antibiotics. The just-in-case Amoxicillin.

Sophie gave Bella to Freddy, jumped out of bed, and rifled through her bag for the bottle.

Hugo leapt from his chair and grabbed it from her. 'I didn't realise you'd packed this.' He handed it to Harry. 'This was prescribed for an ear infection but might work.'

Harry read all the instructions.

'It's safe,' said Sophie, trying to hurry him up.

'Despite the side-effects listed here, we've nothing to lose.' Harry measured the liquid into a spoon and tipped it into Bella's mouth.

Freddy returned Bella to Sophie and sat beside them. Sophie held another wet flannel against her daughter's cheek, cold tears on her own face. She'd been too easily reassured that the adults were 'mildly unwell,' and by Harry's calm manner.

Harry felt Bella's forehead and listened to her heart with his stethoscope. 'You need to prepare yourselves. She might not recover, or if she does, she may develop rheumatic fever which could affect her forever.'

Anne and Richard came in, Freddy put his head in his hands, but Sophie sobbed, losing her last shred of control. The rash had spread, even to Bella's toes.

Without a god to pray to, Sophie pleaded with an indifferent universe.

Save her. I'll do anything.

CHAPTER 18

*I*n the 21st century, Bella had been vaccinated against a plethora of childhood diseases, including diphtheria, tetanus, whooping cough, polio, measles, and mumps.

But there'd been no vaccine for scarlet fever.

Sophie had stuffed the holdall with nappies, clothes, and baby food. Struggling to zip the bag closed, she'd chosen the smaller Amoxicillin bottle over Calpol. A moment's decision. Almost a whim.

Would antibiotics prescribed for ear infections work for scarlet fever? Had they begun the course too late?

At dawn, still cuddling Bella, and bleary from lack of sleep, Sophie's mind spiralled off at a tangent. What had Janus told Hugo and Freddy about people in parallel universes? About her? This had happened, *was* happening in many universes. Outcomes tumbled over and over in her head.

'Let me hold her,' said Freddy.

She put Bella gently in his arms. Her daughter would die in some universes, or most of them. Or she'd recover but with complications. It didn't matter. All that mattered was what happened to this Bella. *Her* Bella.

'Nine hours since she started the Amoxicillin.' Hugo's face was grey in the morning light.

'Why hasn't Harry come back?' said Sophie, her attention on her daughter.

Charlotte was also staring at Bella.

'Because there's nothing more he can do.' Freddy kissed his daughter's brow and Bella opened her eyes. 'Huh.' He touched her cheek. 'She's not as hot.'

Sophie pressed the thermometer against Bella's forehead.

'38,' said Sophie.

Bella's rash was still an alarming red, but she blinked, seemed to be focusing on Freddy. Then she wriggled.

'That's new.' Sophie burst into tears.

Two hours later, Harry planted his stethoscope on Bella's chest and listened. She tried to grab his coat. 'This is a miracle.' He picked up the Amoxicillin bottle from the bedside table. 'How does it work?'

Sophie struggled to remember. 'It's derived from mould.'

'When was it invented?' asked Harry. 'I mean, when will it be in use here?'

Sophie brushed one of Bella's curls off her daughter's face. 'Hopefully, soon.' Too exhausted to explain why antibiotics might never be used here.

'At home, penicillin was discovered in the 19th century,' said Hugo, 'but only widely prescribed from the 1940s.'

Bella took Sophie's hand and held on tight.

'It kills bacteria or stops it spreading,' added Hugo.

'She's going to be okay,' said Sophie, taking immeasurable

comfort from the pink clutch-marks of tiny nails on her own skin.

Bella sat up and cried, indignation and demand on normal volume, and something clicked in Sophie's brain. Bella needed both her parents, and that trumped her mother returning with Hugo to modern London.

'Antibiotics had a nickname,' said Hugo. 'The wonder drug.'

'It truly is a wonder.' Harry pocketed the Amoxicillin. 'This will save another child.'

'No,' said Sophie. 'Bella must finish it all.'

'To ensure all the bacteria are killed,' said Hugo.

Sophie pushed away a pang of guilt. The urge to protect her own child, even if that meant not saving another baby, was primitive and stubborn.

Harry reluctantly returned the bottle.

CHAPTER 19

*I*t took a week, but Bella's rash finally faded, and the skin around her fingertips and toes dried and peeled. Sophie and Freddy caught scarlet fever, but with mild symptoms. Rupert was stable in the hospital bay, and though asleep most of the time, he was eating and drinking.

And life returned to normal. War-normal.

Anne wasn't at breakfast, presumably having breakfast in bed, and Richard was already outside, supervising rebuilding.

'I envy you going on patrol today,' said Freddy.

'Apparently, it's usually very boring,' said Sophie. 'Anyway,' she added, teasing him, 'we're not as precious as you.'

'I can't imagine being confident with a gun,' said Alice, glancing over at Harry.

Alice was confident enough to play demure. Interesting.

'Some gamekeepers are going out on individual missions,' said Hugo. 'Picking off the militia.'

'*Please* don't do that,' said Sophie.

Charlotte pricked up her ears.

'You can't volunteer,' said Hugo. 'Richard handpicks them.'

After breakfast, Freddy headed off to join his father. Rebuilding was progressing slowly, hampered by incessant rain.

Sophie and Hugo collected their rifles from the hall. Outside, the rain had turned into hail, bouncing off the drive gravel.

'I don't think the militia will give us trouble in this weather,' said Hugo, getting into the lead car beside the driver. Sophie clambered into the back.

They reached the town without drama and met the vintner's van they were escorting. The driver was a short, elderly man.

But remembering the firefight with Peaky Blinder, Sophie said, 'How long have you worked at the wine merchants?'

He squinted at her. 'Nigh on thirty years.'

When their convoy reached the checkpoint and passed through, Hugo frowned at the road ahead, misty in the rain. 'Why are we risking our necks for wine?'

'Vital for morale,' said Sophie.

Half a mile later, almost invisible in the rainy gloom, two men were stumbling along the verge. The first man had his hands tied behind his back, a bandage tied messily around one arm, and he was limping.

Reynolds, with a prisoner. He'd only just left hospital. Sophie twisted about in her seat. 'They'll catch their deaths in this weather.'

The vehicle lurched to a halt.

'We've got room,' said Sophie. 'Hugo, I'll squeeze in with you in the front.' She jumped out of the car with her rifle — and saw the prisoner's face.

The filthy beard. Those hard eyes. *Beard Man.* Two years ago, he'd robbed her at knifepoint.

Her heart missed a beat and that moment rushed back.

The blade point in her neck. Convinced she would die. He didn't deserve to live.

She raised her rifle, pointed it at Beard Man, but as she pulled the trigger, Hugo pushed the barrel aside and the bullet whined into a hedge.

Beard Man shrank away, and Reynolds stared at her.

Hugo grabbed her gun. 'What are you doing?'

'He's the vagrant who robbed me in the lane when we first came here,' said Sophie. 'You must remember.' Beard Man would have cut her throat if Charlotte hadn't bitten him.

Hugo's eyes were flinty. 'You're out of order.'

Sophie gulped. What had she been thinking? Beard Man was unarmed, defenceless. 'I'm sorry, I—'

'Get in the car,' said Hugo. 'In the front. Now.'

She returned to the car. The driver didn't look at her. Neither did Reynolds.

That evening before dinner, Hugo marched into their bedroom in black tie holding a piece of paper. 'Richard's posted a copy of this in the anteroom.'

Sophie unfolded it.

'It's also up in the servants' hall.'

It was a numbered list. *Rules of war. 1. Wounded militiamen must be given medical care and treated with dignity...*

'A pocket-sized Geneva Convention,' said Sophie. 'You told him.'

'He'd already heard. We agreed written guidance would be useful.'

Jack was dozing on the bed, Charlotte beside him. She opened one eye.

Hugo paced before the fireplace, his square-jaw in profile.

'Look, you weren't there.' Sophie tapped her feet under the skirt of her red dinner gown. 'Charlotte, we're talking about Beard Man, the guy who attacked me in the lane.'

Charlotte opened her other eye.

'Today,' said Sophie, 'he was on the road and … I wanted to kill him.'

'I understand why you *wanted* to.' Hugo stopped pacing and faced her. 'What I don't understand is why you pulled the trigger.' He hesitated. 'Killing when you don't need to is—'

'Evil.' Sophie winced. 'I'm so glad you stopped me.'

Charlotte watched them, her expression inscrutable.

'This is England, Sophie. It may be a different England, but both sides in this conflict follow agreed rules.' He drove his hand through his hair. 'Not executing prisoners of war, respecting flags of surrender, not targeting civilians.'

'Tell that to Joan Small.'

'That was you-specific.' He met her eyes. 'Richard has new orders for you. While the prisoner's convalescing in the hospital bay, work your charms. Ask him to report back from the pub on the militia.'

'What?'

'He's half-starved,' said Hugo. 'An additional payment might persuade him to change sides.'

'Spying in the pub didn't work out before.' Maud's John had been beaten up, had nearly died.

'This is different,' said Hugo. 'The prisoner's one of them.'

Beard Man wouldn't spy for the Manor. Richard was just teaching her a lesson. 'I'll pass on dinner.'

'Oh, no, you don't,' said Hugo, taking her arm. 'Brazen it out.'

Reluctantly, she walked with him.

In the corridor, Charlotte pretended to be a regular dog and ran ahead with Jack. The dogs waited in the anteroom, their tails whirring like a wind turbine competition. Canine joy usually made Sophie smile, but not this evening. The list of war-rules, pinned above the dining room doors, was impossible to miss, rubbing in the shame.

Over dinner, Sophie was quiet, occasionally talking on autopilot about nothing. Was she evil? Did evil people worry about being evil? She was worrying she might be. Did that mean she wasn't?

Richard showed no sign he was disappointed in her, but she gave him a chastened glance. Lesson learned, or was that re-learned? *Think* before doing.

After dinner, she passed on drawing room girl-talk. Right now, there was a certified evil person in the hospital bay, waiting to be charmed.

But she dawdled in the passage, wanting to turn around.

No. Best get on with it.

The hospital bay was lit with lamps beside a few beds, and in the dim light the patients' moans seemed louder. Sophie made her way as quietly as she could across the bay, the skirt of her gown rustling.

Ethel acknowledged her, clipboard in hand.

'I hate the moaning,' whispered Sophie. 'Knowing they're in pain.'

'Harry says they're not. It's the laudanum. After a few weeks, it gives them nightmares.' Ethel looked at a nearby bed. Rupert was asleep. Not moaning.

'How is he?'

'Getting better.'

'I've come to see the prisoner.'

'I heard you nearly shot him.' Ethel scribbled something on her clipboard.

'I mean him no harm now.' Even Sophie Arundel-Harrington would baulk at shooting someone in a hospital bed.

'He was riddled with lice,' said Ethel. 'But he's had a hot wash and new clothes.'

'Where is he?'

Ethel pointed to a bed apart from the others. Down to him being with the militia? Or was that the lice?

Sophie walked with Ethel to the bed. No longer Beard Man. Clean-shaven.

He was sleeping, unaware of her scrutiny. Purple shadows under his eyes contrasted with his sallow, pale skin.

Shame at what she'd almost done battled inside Sophie with residual regret she hadn't sent him to a higher court, to whatever god or random force dispensed justice after death. Except there likely wasn't a higher court. She frowned. 'Do we know his name?'

Ethel read her clipboard. 'Bill Taylor.' She hesitated. 'What do you want with him?'

'Just a chat.'

'Is it important? Shall I wake him?'

'No.' Too tired for charm. She'd mess this up. 'I'll come back tomorrow.'

'I don't want to befriend … Bill,' Sophie whispered to Hugo over breakfast the next day. Hugo still loved her, despite her almost turning to the dark side.

'It'll be good for your soul,' said Hugo, a determined glint in his eye.

'Easy for you to say.' Sophie fed Charlotte and Jack each a sausage.

Richard's "pay to spy" idea was a non-starter. 'Bill will take the money and run.'

'Perhaps.'

Sophie put on her best doe eyes. 'Come with me?'

'Finishing the families' building has priority.'

Right. She was on her own. Sophie got to her feet. She could do this. But first, she'd check on Bella.

The nursery was on the second floor. Bella had her meals there now. As Sophie came in, the round table had the remains of breakfast on it, the highchair and regular chair were askew, and Bella was sitting on a bright blue rug, smashing her metal rattle onto the picture book. Maud was watching her, aghast.

All was well.

'I'll put her down for a nap before lunch,' said Maud. Near the window was a swing cot fashioned in sturdy mahogany, with a cute, arched cover at the head end.

'Sounds good.' Sophie picked up Bella, jiggling her daughter on her hip. 'I know she's exhausting.'

'How it should be, Miss.' Maud shot her a glad smile.

Bella pointed at the sepia photo on the mantlepiece. 'Bah.'

The photo was of four-year-old Freddy, wearing what appeared to be a girl's sailor dress. He was staring at them with a glint in his eye, almost as if he could see his daughter, decades in the future.

Maud pulled out the fireguard, added more wood to the fire, and returned the guard. Sophie sat Bella back on the rug. 'I'm going to see the prisoner today.'

Maud's expression betrayed her surprise. 'The man you nearly…'

'Yes.' Of course, Maud had heard.

Sophie left the nursery, walked downstairs and into the corridor to the hospital bay.

In most of the manor, random pictures adorned the walls: landscapes, family portraits, children's samplers. This passage had grander art.

Sophie stopped in front of a cracked oil painting of Elizabeth I. Her neck ruff was pale and far too big, like an out-of-control spider's web, and her pallid complexion made the bags under her beady eyes more prominent. Richard's ancestor had probably bought this picture to signal the family's loyalty — to fool Elizabeth's priest-hunters.

But why would Elizabeth have signed off such an unflattering picture? A long-ago history lesson… *Elizabeth wasn't interested in looking pretty, only in projecting power.* Something stirred in Sophie's memory, but it eluded her.

Okay. Time to deploy Sophie-power, wrapped in charm.

Inside the hospital bay, Bill was chirpy, sitting up. His arm injury couldn't have been serious.

Sophie drew up a chair and fastened her ski jacket against the crisp air. 'I'm glad you're feeling okay,' she said through gritted teeth.

'Why did you try to shoot me?'

He didn't remember attacking her in the lane? Likely, she was one of many. 'We met a while back. Your mate stole my necklace. You wanted to kill me, but my dog mauled your leg.' Okay, that came out blunter than she'd intended.

He paled. 'You were wearing tight men's trousers.'

Skinny jeans. 'Yep.'

'Is your dog here?'

'No, but I can fetch her.'

Bill swallowed.

Hmmm, this charm offensive needed work.

Alice handed Bill a cup of tea and he smiled at her, showing off brown, broken teeth. He peered at Sophie over his teacup, wary. 'You're that Miss Arundel,' he said. 'Mrs Harrington.'

He knew about Inkpin.

'I-I don't blame you for shooting me.'

'*Trying* to shoot you,' corrected Sophie. 'What happened to your friend, the one in the lane?' The other man had been decent, had baulked at killing her.

'Long gone. Stabbed in a fight.'

'You'll be fit to return to the pub soon.'

'Be bossed about by Saint Joan?' He slurped his tea. 'Once I get my money from the post office, I'm off.'

'Payments don't start until next week.'

He eyed her with fresh suspicion. 'Why are you talking to me?'

Best to be straight. Sophie lowered her voice. 'Unemployment benefit is only eight shillings. How would you like a bit more cash?'

His eyes narrowed. 'Go on.'

'I know you're not keen on Joan and the pub, but if you post me a letter once a week, tell me what the militia's up to, every week, you'll get another eight shillings.'

Bill frowned. 'Spy for the Manor?'

'Think of it as a public service, keeping the women and children here safe.'

'Can I think about it?'

Stuff charm. Bill would respond better to a guaranteed carrot *and* stick. 'If you do it, I'll make sure you're paid. But I'll hear if you double-cross me. The money will stop, and you'll end up the same as Inkpin.'

He gulped. 'I'll do it.'

'Thank you.' Sophie got to her feet, the chair scraping on the oak-boarded floor. The guy was lying through his crooked teeth.

On the way out, she passed Rupert's bed. He was reading a book, looked much better.

Sophie kissed his forehead, risking Ethel's wrath. Close to his ear, she whispered, 'Don't tell Ethel.'

His lips twitched. 'I won't.'

'About Ethel…'

'What about her?'

'Before the war,' whispered Sophie, 'you enjoyed yourself. A lot.' Hugo had been convinced that anyone who married Rupert would catch an unpleasant disease. 'If you marry Ethel—'

'Is that why you turned me down?' Rupert reached out and took her hand with a smile, which changed into a wince. He briefly closed his eyes, still holding her fingers. 'I was always careful.'

Ethel was walking towards them, and Rupert hastily let go of Sophie's hand.

Sophie glided serenely out of the room. Rupert was a delicious duke, and Ethel would be a debonair duchess.

A good distance along the main corridor, she heard shouting from up ahead. She quickened her pace and hurried into the hall.

Reynolds was haranguing a group of gamekeepers, including Miss Blackmore.

'What's going on?' asked Sophie.

'It's Miss Hemmings.' Miss Blackmore seemed distraught. 'My patrol was ambushed and after the firefight, she'd disappeared. We searched the lane, all the verges, but there was no sign of her.'

'Could the militia have taken her prisoner?' asked a lad.

Reynolds flexed his fingers and winced, his burned arm hurting. 'They've never taken our people before.'

Sophie went cold. 'I'll go get Mr Harrington.' She addressed Reynolds. 'Will you take us to search again?'

Reynolds nodded.

Sophie ran outside into the rain, panic speeding up her heartbeat. She sprinted to the families' building.

Hugo and Freddy were at the top of different ladders, hammering nails into roof beams.

When she told them about Lucy, they climbed down.

'You're needed here,' said Hugo to Freddy.

Freddy looked as if he wanted to break something.

Sophie and Hugo scurried away, leaving Freddy staring after them.

Reynolds was waiting on the drive, standing by a rain-soaked car. A grey-haired gamekeeper was already behind the wheel of another.

They jumped into Reynolds' car and the convoy set off at

speed, but only half a mile out, the vehicles slowed and stopped.

Skid marks scarred the tarmac, overlaid with spent shotgun cartridges. 'A gamekeeper dead, and they have one of our cars.' Reynolds grimly surveyed the scene. 'Perhaps a fresh pair of eyes will find Miss Hemmings.'

They all got out and searched. The rain had eased off and over the pit-platter of drizzle, tree branches creaked in the wind. The air smelled perversely washed and clean.

'We should search further down,' said Hugo. 'She could be in shock, wandered off.'

They returned to the cars and drove on and around a bend.

Opposite the break in the hedgeline and the field gates, someone was lying on the road, a woman kneeling beside them. Paper flyers were blowing about on the tarmac and the verge.

The cars drew up and the woman jumped to her feet. She was shivering in a thin flowered skirt, a navy T-shirt, and a grey cardigan. Her shoulder-length frizzy hair was streaked brown and blonde, held in place by a red Alice band. She stared at them through round, steel-rimmed glasses.

The person by her feet was half covered by a summer-yellow jacket. 'She's hurt her leg.' The woman had an American accent.

Sophie and Hugo left the car and cautiously walked forward.

It was Lucy lying on the road. Her bobbed hair awry, plastered wet about her face. Sophie dropped to her knees and touched Lucy's neck. 'She's not dead.'

Hugo peeled the yellow jacket off her, and grimaced. 'Her leg's a mess.'

Lucy's trousers were undone, half pulled off, and the hem

of a trouser leg was messily embedded in her wound. Sophie grimaced, looked away from the injury, and fastened Lucy's trousers.

Reynolds and the other driver had already turned the cars around. Hugo picked up Lucy's legs, Sophie took her shoulders, and the stranger helped them transfer Lucy to the rear of Reynold's car.

As Lucy's wounded leg met the seat, she screamed. 'I'll sit with her,' said Sophie.

Hugo hauled off his ski jacket and offered it to the American who was blue with cold. 'I'm Hugo.'

'Thanks.' The woman pulled it on and zipped it up to the collar.

'Take the front seat,' said Hugo. 'The Manor's not far.'

She wordlessly climbed in, and Hugo got into the other vehicle.

As the cars moved, Sophie shuffled further to the edge of the seat, giving Lucy more room. Wet paper was stuck to the bottom of Sophie's boot, and she pulled it off. Above a smudged picture of a colourful galaxy was a headline: *The cosmic censorship hypothesis. Lecture moved to 7pm.*

'Miss Blackmore searched this part of the road,' shouted Reynolds, over the wind and drizzle.

'She said somebody left her for dead in a field,' said the American.

Hugo had been right. Lucy had wandered off, not thinking straight.

The woman said to Reynolds, 'I'm Tiana, by the way.'

Reynolds acknowledged her with a nod.

Tiana was holding tight onto her half-height door. 'This is an insane dream.'

'You need to know, this isn't a dream,' said Sophie. Tiana was dressed for a summer stroll or a heated building.

Tiana frowned.

Sophie leaned forward, towards her. 'I'm guessing you stepped into a gold lift.'

CHAPTER 21

After Lucy had been transferred to the car, it took five minutes to reach the Manor, and the game-keepers carried Lucy over the drawbridge and off to the hospital bay.

'I can't bear it.' Sophie made to follow them out of the hall, frantic. '*Lucy.*'

Hugo grabbed her arm. 'You're in a state. Harry's got this.'

Sophie pressed her lips together. Calm down. Then help.

The Manor drawbridge winched up and shut with a thud. Tiana backed away from it, looking around as if she'd been thrown into a jail cell.

'I'll arrange for tea and sandwiches,' said Mrs Rawlings, her hazel eyes on Tiana. 'Ah, Mr Crawford, we have a new visitor.'

The butler acknowledged Tiana. 'Madam.' Mr Crawford's assured manner matched his immaculate formal attire: black suit with matching waistcoat, black bow tie, and a white shirt with winged collar.

Tiana managed a confused smile. Her clothes were

muddy and wet, right down to her squelchy trainers. Hugo's ski jacket swamped her.

'We'll explain over tea,' Hugo told her.

Miss Blackmore came in from walking the dogs, her flat cap and dark coat glistening from the rain. The dogs and their jackets were also wet. Jack seemed happy but Charlotte looked pained, had adopted her martyr face. She'd never appreciated bad-weather walks.

'You can get dry in the small drawing room by the fire,' Sophie whispered to her.

A nurse ran into the hall. 'Mrs Harrington, you're wanted in the hospital bay.'

Sophie's heart missed a beat. Hugo took the dogs, and she rushed off.

In the bay, Harry was giving orders from behind screening curtains.

'I want Mrs Harrington.' Lucy's voice, high and strained.

Sophie swiped back the nearest curtain and Harry glanced up. 'We've no chloroform,' he said. 'Talk to her, about anything.'

Lucy was tied to the bed with leather straps. Her trouser leg had been cut off just below one knee, exposing the bloody, ragged wound.

Alice pressed a laudanum bottle to Lucy's lips. 'Please drink the rest.'

'No.' Lucy strained against the straps.

'I'm here,' said Sophie. 'Drink it.'

Lucy swallowed the mixture. Sweat dripped down her brow and she clutched at Sophie.

Alice handed Harry a thin, shiny knife, her expression resolute.

'I'll be as quick as I can,' said Harry.

Sophie wrenched her gaze from the blade and held Lucy's hand tighter. 'You're safe in the Manor. This will pass—'

Lucy screamed and writhed, but the straps stayed tight.

'I love you,' said Sophie. 'Hold on.'

Lucy screamed louder. Finally, her hand went slack and her head flopped.

'Thank God,' said Harry. 'I can slow down.'

Sophie didn't watch. Instead, she wiped Lucy's brow with a cool cloth.

Finally, Harry exhaled. 'Bullet's out.' He laid the knife on a plate. 'Mrs Harrington, wash the knife thoroughly with soap, then soak it in Milton.' Milton was Shorten disinfectant. 'Alice, pass me another spoon of Acriflavine.'

Alice unscrewed the lid of the tin and gave Harry a level spoonful of the brown red crumbs. He sprinkled it over the injury and began stitching.

Sophie went to the kitchen area to clean the knife and then returned.

Harry finished stitching. 'Now we wait.'

'For what?' said Sophie.

'To see if the wound stays free of infection.'

'She has a good chance,' said Alice.

'Come back in a few hours,' said Harry.

Sophie washed her hands in the kitchen corner and headed for the small drawing room.

Hugo and Tiana were seated opposite each other. The coffee table between them was loaded with a silver tea pot and a three-tiered cake stand, empty save for crumbs. Tiana was still wearing Hugo's ski jacket. She looked dazed.

'Harry asked me to help with Lucy,' said Sophie.

Hugo nodded. 'How is she?'

'He's optimistic.' Harry hadn't exactly said that, but Sophie kept that thought to herself.

Careful not to disturb the dogs snoozing by the fire, Sophie dropped a fresh log into the grate.

'Sophie, sit down,' said Hugo. 'You look terrible.'

'Thanks,' she said, sitting beside him.

'I thought I'd wait to explain stuff. Do it together,' said Hugo.

'This is one hell of a dream.' Tiana shook her head. 'Why can't I wake up?'

'You're not dreaming.' Hugo sighed. 'I've told her that four times.'

The new visitor peered at them. 'You're the students that disappeared,' she said, clinging to a fact like a life raft. 'You joined a cult.'

'No,' said Sophie. 'We disappeared to here.'

'Hallucinating.' Tiana was talking to herself. 'You're a physics professor. Get a grip.'

'We came via the lift in the students' union,' said Sophie, 'as you did.'

'When you took the golden … elevator,' said Hugo, 'you crossed into a parallel universe, a century behind ours.'

Tiana frowned.

'History's panning out differently.' Hugo paused to take a breath. 'This England is much more violent than our England.'

'The Manor, though, is an oasis of calm,' said Sophie. 'Mostly.'

Tiana narrowed her eyes. 'Okay, if this is real, tell me which multi-verse theory is correct. Eleven universes, thirteen, or billions?'

'We don't know,' said Hugo. 'But we can explain what's happening in this universe.' Hugo laid it all out. How the Great War never happened, how mass unemployment and riots had turned into a revolution, then a civil war. Practical parallel universe stuff.

'And you crossed over,' said Sophie, 'through the gold lift.'

'The elevator's a *portal*?' said Tiana. 'Crazy.'

'It's not a portal,' said Hugo. 'It's a ship that travels between universes.'

Tiana guffawed. 'More crazy.' She knocked her knuckles against the coffee table. 'Seems solid.' She exhaled slowly. 'But if this is true … my God, it'll transform physics.'

Hugo traded a look with Sophie.

'It would,' said Sophie, 'but if our 21st century government found out, even if they made it top secret, involving a few scientists, they'd contaminate this world, destroy it.'

'Very few individuals go through the lift into that country lane,' said Hugo. 'Counting you, just eight in thirty years.'

Sophie nodded. 'With a rare gene.'

'Okay, where does the gene come from?' Tiana's scepticism was now tinged with curiosity.

'From the beings who built the lift, the ship,' said Hugo. 'I don't have it. I travel courtesy of Sophie because we have an emotional connection. Actually, the first time I travelled, that was courtesy of Charlotte.'

'Who's Charlotte?' asked Tiana.

'My dog.' Sophie pointed.

By the grate, Charlotte opened an eye.

'I need a drink,' muttered Tiana. 'A stronger one.'

'When it's safe,' said Hugo, 'we'll drive you back to the lift, to the university.'

Tiana sat up straighter. 'The injured woman in the lane, why was she there?'

'She was ambushed by our local militia,' said Hugo. 'They want to starve us out, take the Manor.'

The drawing room door opened, and Anne came in.

Sophie stood up. 'This is Tiana.'

CHAPTER 22

That same night, Sophie returned from the hospital bay to the freezing bedroom, checked Bella was snug in her cot, and changed into her nightdress really fast. The strongest fire in a grate could never be as good as central heating.

Hugo was already in bed in his blue pyjamas, reading a book. Sophie darted under the four-poster's heavy covers.

'Lucy's lost a lot of blood.' Sophie stretched out her toes and found the Shorten equivalent of a hot water bottle, a heated brick wrapped in a cloth. 'On the upside, Tiana's settled in her room, seems okay.'

'She's handling it better than we did, when we first came through.'

Sophie heaved the blanket up to her shoulders. 'Tiana's fascinated by how the lift travels between universes. You should give her your notebook.'

Janus had explained the crossing basics and Freddy had written it down for Hugo.

'Freddy will love Tiana,' added Sophie. 'They can talk about equations.'

Hugo pulled Sophie closer. 'I want to make mad, glorious love to you,' he whispered.

'After today, I'd probably fall asleep in the middle.' She kissed him and rested her head on his chest.

He chuckled. 'I've been thinking about *A History of Shorten*, the poet mentioned in the acknowledgments.'

'Hmm?' Sweet sleep was calling.

'It could be coincidence, but his surname, Noitavlas, is "salvation" spelled backwards. A religious clue?'

The portrait of Elizabeth I by the hospital bay... 'Tudor papists.' Sophie's memory whirred, pulling her fully awake. 'Another part of the riddle is definitely a religious reference.'

'Which part?'

'Reigns on high. Pope Pius V in 1570 issued a Papal bull, *Regnans in Excelsis* or *Reigning on High* in English. The bull declared Elizabeth I a heretic, absolving Catholics of any allegiance to her.'

'Right.' Hugo yawned. 'Catholic in-jokes.'

Sophie relaxed against him and closed her eyes, but the memory of Lucy in hospital was stark against her lids...

The bottom of the deep, open grave was dark and silent. Sophie was lying on her back in it, unable to move, even a finger. Lucy was next to her. Cold. Dead. Sophie tried to blink. Was she dead too?

Earth dropped from the sky. Heavy, wet lumps, shovelled in, more and more. She choked on iron and grit and filth...

She woke up coughing, her hands over her face, fighting to breathe.

'You're okay. You're okay.' Hugo switched on the beside lamp. 'A dream. Only a dream.'

Gradually, her panicked breathing slowed.

Sophie drank water from a glass on the bedside table. 'I'm sorry I woke you up.'

He turned off the light and embraced her, but the nightmare lingered: the steep sides of the sodden grave, the slimy earth smell, the taste of dirt. The dread.

Hugo's breathing steadied, but Sophie couldn't sleep.

She climbed quietly out of bed, put on her Shorten dressing gown and slippers, and tip-toed out, making her way down to the empty kitchens.

Searching for a teacup, she opened a cupboard.

'If the militia get hold of modern artillery, the Manor will have to surrender,' said a voice.

Sophie froze. The butler's rooms were opposite the pantry. Why wasn't he asleep? Who was he talking to?

The rear door of the kitchens was ajar, and beyond it, so was the door to Mr Crawford's rooms.

'We still have our plan, just in case.' Mrs Rawlings's voice.

Sophie caught her breath. Our plan? Were they defecting to the militia?

'If we wait too long, we may never do it.' Mrs Rawlings sounded upset. 'We're not exactly spring chickens.'

'We've a few years in us yet. And that village is perfect.'

'It is,' said Mrs Rawlings. 'Near the sea, and quiet.'

Sophie sagged in relief. They were planning retirement, not betrayal. She took another step and a floorboard creaked, horror-film loud.

Mr Crawford's door swung open. The butler was dressed in a tartan dressing gown. 'Mrs Harrington?' He looked shocked.

'Apologies for disturbing you. I was hoping to make tea.'

Mr Crawford smiled.

She'd never seen him smile before. Not a proper, relaxed smile.

'You're in luck. We've just made some.' He disappeared

into his rooms and returned with a teapot. He took a cup and saucer from a cupboard, added milk from the pantry, and poured tea.

Sophie thanked him and retraced her steps upstairs. The butler's kindness had vanquished the dream.

CHAPTER 23

*R*oy Ducker leaned on the bar in The Crooked Gate, his elbow resting on a beer-soaked cloth. A week after the militia had captured a Manor car, he was still reliving the ambush, embroidering his exploits. 'They were no match for Roy.' He slurred the words.

Betty slid another pint onto the counter. One hour until she could close the bar.

'Blue suits you, Mrs Hill,' said Roy. 'Matches your eyes.'

Flutter your eyelashes. Smile.

'Pardon me for asking, but what happened to Mr Hill?' said Roy.

Betty turned her back on him to reach up for a glass. She'd invented a husband and worn a curtain ring on her finger when she'd fallen pregnant with Frank. 'He died in the Cambridge riot.'

'Mr Parkes is really not with it, is he?'

Betty glanced over at Alan. The pub was so noisy, he hadn't overheard. But even if he had, he might not have understood, or cared. He'd stopped moaning about men flirting with her. He just washed clean glasses and dried them as if his life depended on it. Recently, he'd started wearing outdoor clothes behind the bar, his work jacket or tweed cap.

And at night, in his sleep, he talked about the lift, about pictures showing the Manor on fire and a road that twisted and forked. Daft things. Part of his mind trouble. Had the lift done this to him?

'Cheer up, Mrs Hill,' slurred Roy. 'The post office money will set you and this pub up for life. You'll see.'

The militiamen had collected their cash that morning. Most of them were a lot drunker than Roy.

Betty called across the pub. 'Mr Morley, even you could buy a drink tonight.'

He looked up from his book, *The Suffragette* by Sylvia Pankhurst. 'No, thank you. Mrs Morley has my post office money.'

'Armchair revolutionary,' muttered Roy.

'Each to their own,' said Betty.

'The ambush was well done, Mr Ducker,' shouted Mr Morley. 'Saluto te.'

'Eh?' said Roy.

'Latin,' said Mr Morley. 'I salute you.'

Jim Hayden sauntered up to the bar. 'I'll have another beer.' He scowled. 'Barty wouldn't have taken cash off me.' After he'd returned late from the ambush in the lane, Joan had torn a strip off him and docked his pay.

'It's no disaster,' slurred Roy. 'Your post office money made up for the fine.'

The pub door swung open, and both men turned around. 'Look who's here,' said Jim. 'Scarecrow's back.'

Everybody called Bill Taylor Scarecrow, on account of his dirty, crooked teeth.

Joan beckoned Scarecrow over to her table. Behind her, lined up against the wall, were the rifles and shotguns. No one still armed got a beer.

'The Manor patched me up good,' said Scarecrow.

'Sit,' said Joan.

'There's a new visitor,' said Scarecrow, sitting down.

Joan nodded. 'We heard.'

Betty walked over and handed Scarecrow a beer.

He counted out coins on the table for his drink. 'The visitor's most peculiar. A lady professor. From America.'

Betty waited for the money, her mind wandering. The Laceys took visitors in, and they stopped at nothing to look after their own too, even nobbling the police. When the Manor's chauffeur had murdered her brother in the lane, Reynolds had got off scot free. Dear heaven, she missed Will…

Alan barged over and scooped up the coins. Hampered by only having one hand, some fell off the table. Betty retrieved them.

'Did you pick up anything *useful*?' said Mary James, nursing her pint.

Bill smirked, revealing his wonky teeth. 'They're really short of men. Scullery maids are doing guard duty.'

Betty transferred dead glasses onto a tray. They knew this already.

She strode to the bar, pushing past Jim. He groped her bottom, and she gasped in disgust and dropped the tray. The crash silenced the room.

Betty slapped him on the face. 'Get out of my pub!'

'It's not *your* pub.' Jim's face twisted in an ugly leer. 'It's our pub.'

Betty stood her ground. 'I said get out.'

Jim tried to kiss her, and she kicked him in the shins.

Roy shouldered his way forward and Jim punched him on the jaw, sending Roy sprawling onto the shattered glasses. Someone smashed a chair over Jim's head, the chair splintering.

Betty was stuck in the middle. She stumbled into Mr Morley, who was waving his hand and yelling, his words lost in the din.

The sound of a rifle shot stopped everyone in their tracks.

Joan had fired into the ceiling. She glared around. 'Bar's closed.'

Disgruntled muttering.

She pointed at Jim. 'Clear up the mess.'

Same old routine. No wonder the village regulars kept away.

Betty hurried to the kitchen to fetch a broom and a box for the broken glass, marched over to Jim and thrust them at him. Returning to the kitchen, she turned on the tap, poured water into a bowl with some Milton, and picked up scissors and a roll of bandages.

Back in front of the bar, she put it all on the nearest table. 'Line up.'

Five men, with a variety of cuts and scratches, formed a disorderly queue.

She tied a Milton-drenched bandage on Roy's arm, and he gave her a sheepish smile. He'd sobered up fast. Jim was sweeping glass into a corner, oozing self-righteous resentment, and Betty ignored him.

He was right about The Crooked Gate though. It was no longer hers, no longer her home.

She carried the bowl and bandages to the kitchen, shut the door behind her and leaned against it. This wouldn't last forever. Joan reckoned the military equipment would come through and once it did, the militia would take the Manor and clear off there.

Christmas was only a few weeks away, and who knew what the new year would bring?

Betty went over to the sink, poured herself a glass of water and held it up in a mock toast. 'To 1928.'

CHAPTER 24

Two weeks after they'd rescued Lucy from the lane, Sophie sat at her bedside in the hospital bay. Lucy was in good spirits and had eaten a hearty breakfast.

A nurse removed the breakfast tray and Lucy pulled the blanket off her leg. 'Doc says it'll be a few weeks before it's healed.'

Sophie peered at the scar. The neat, cross-shaped stitching was doing its job.

A nurse bustled up with a cup of tea for Lucy. With the scarlet fever gone, the nursing team was back at full strength, but the bay was half empty. Lately, there'd been fewer encounters with the militia, so fewer casualties.

'Hey.' Tiana drew up another chair.

'Hey,' said Lucy. 'You've more questions?'

Tiana had been tending to vegetables in the greenhouse, following Lucy's instructions. Lucy addressed each question, writing in the notebook Tiana had given her.

'My grandmother grew potatoes, squash, beans, and corn on the reservation.' Tiana did a one-shoulder shrug. 'I never got the hang of it.'

'Tiana has native American heritage,' said Lucy.

'Mixes in nicely with the Jamaican and Italian,' said Tiana. 'Why I'm so good-looking.' A self-deprecating joke. Tiana looked every inch the dowdy academic. She was still wearing the clothes she'd arrived in but had acquired a fine, grey shawl. Borrowed from Anne? What a difference two years made. War had bent the Shorten unbendable dress code for women so much, it barely existed.

Lucy handed Tiana back her notebook, and Tiana flipped to a different page and showed it to Sophie. 'Freddy gave me this info.'

Sophie squinted at the spidery scrawl.

'The lift ship travels into a rotating black hole. At the centre, there's an opening that allows matter to slip from one universe to another, but the exit is dynamic, so selecting the right moment to leave is difficult.'

'This is beyond me.' Sophie stood up and stretched. 'Time to patrol.'

'Be careful,' said Lucy.

Sophie managed a confident smile. 'Always.'

In the corridor, Sophie walked briskly past Elizabeth I and strode towards the hall. Five minutes early. Her last three patrols had been uneventful. Maybe the militia had changed tactics in the colder weather?

As Sophie drew level with the door to the small drawing room, Freddy and Clarissa came out. Clarissa was flushed, and Freddy didn't notice Sophie, so intent was his gaze on Clarissa.

Sophie cleared her throat.

Clarissa glanced at her. 'I'm late for my shift.' She hurried away.

'Are you serious about Clarissa?' whispered Sophie. 'After what happened with Hugo...'

'I'm serious.'

'Then, I'm glad.'

Freddy tipped his head on one side. 'I didn't see it before, but she's like you.'

Sophie snorted. 'We're both female.'

'She's brave and stubborn and speaks her mind.'

'Freddy Lacey, you're in love with her.'

He nodded.

'Does she feel the same?'

'She does.' Freddy checked the passage was empty. 'I couldn't continue the courtship under false pretences. I've told her you're Bella's mother.'

'*What?*'

'She was shocked,' said Freddy. 'Understandably.'

'Will she … does she still want to marry you?'

'She said that even though the baby was half yours, Bella is *completely* beautiful.'

'You know,' said Sophie, 'I've always underestimated Clarissa.'

'As did I.' Freddy kissed Sophie on the cheek. 'I know the militia's been quieter but remember how loved *you* are.' He strode off.

Sophie smiled at his retreating back. Freddy was frustrated he couldn't patrol, but with the families' rooms repaired, he was enjoying more time with Bella — and apparently Clarissa.

In the hall, Sophie collected her rifle and nodded to Reynolds. She preferred patrolling without Hugo. No distraction. More focus.

Outside, the driveway was shiny with frost. 'We should proceed with care because of the ice,' said Reynolds to the driver of the other vehicle.

Sophie climbed into the passenger seat beside Reynolds, and they drove through the Manor gates.

'The bad weather works both ways,' said Reynolds. 'If they're setting up an ambush, they'll be freezing.'

The convoy slid onto the ungritted lane. A flurry of snowfall reduced visibility and Sophie gritted her teeth against the cold.

'Proceeding with care' meant driving at ten miles an hour and it took thirty minutes to reach the town. The road was deserted the entire way.

They passed through the checkpoint but a few yards on, Reynolds' car slid on compressed snow and ice. They continued sliding in surreal slow-motion, before thumping hard into a ditch.

The impact jarred Sophie's teeth, and she bit her tongue. She climbed out and Reynolds retrieved a thick rope from the boot. The second vehicle stopped, and the driver and shooter hurried over with another rope.

'Between us, we can sort this,' said Sophie.

Reynolds blushed, as he had in the hospital bay.

Did he fancy her? Scandalous. She was a 'smug married.'

'Please leave this to us, Madam,' said Reynolds, his moustached face earnest.

Right. Reynolds didn't fancy her. He was embarrassed a woman might help him like a regular person. A man.

Sophie gave him a tight, polite smile and walked to the rear car. A desire to whistle came over her. Nonchalant, sarcastic whistling. But she had no idea how to whistle. She stamped her feet to keep warm instead, and paced, Hugo-style.

After a fair amount of male grunting and swearing, their car was back on the road. Given how many dents and bashes it had already suffered, the vehicle looked no different.

But starting the engine again took fifteen minutes, by which time Sophie's feet were numb.

At the bakery, they made the grocery van wait while they called in on Lizzie and warmed up.

Lizzie's industrial kitchen had been rebuilt pretty much the same as before, only with a bigger oven. The sturdy cupboards lining the other walls had been painted cream. A long preparation table was bare and scrubbed clean, and a metal spiral staircase, as steep as the previous one, led to the next floor.

Sophie stood near the hot oven and wiggled her toes inside her boots.

Lizzie made tea and set out teacakes. 'My sister loves being your nanny. She's getting broody.'

Sophie smiled. 'Bella's exhausting. Might put her off?'

'I doubt it,' said Lizzie. 'A child can run you ragged but somehow you blot it out, want another.'

After a second cup of tea, Sophie said they should get going, and Reynolds wrote Lizzie a credit note.

The road back to the Manor was deserted like before. Just as well. Sophie's fingers were so stiff with cold that aiming her rifle was impossible, never mind firing it.

In the house, Sophie returned her gun to the rack and removed her ski jacket and Lucy's dark coat. 'Do you think the militia have given up?' she asked Reynolds.

'It's not long till Christmas, and militiamen have families too.'

Mrs Rawlings came out of her study. 'This arrived for you, Madam. Postmarked from the village.' A tatty buff envelope with 'Mrs Harrington, The Manor' scrawled across it.

Bill. He'd delivered on his promise. Sophie opened the envelope. *They got artilary masheen. A soldier is trayning them.*

Sophie's stomach turned over and she checked her watch. Nearly one. She hurried towards the dining room and waylaid Richard. 'I've news,' she said.

He turned on his heel and walked with her to the library. Sophie closed the hefty door and handed him the letter.

'I didn't think your protégé would co-operate.'

'I know.' She studied the floor.

'I underestimated your charm.'

Sophie looked up. 'There wasn't much charm involved.'

To her surprise, Richard smiled. 'You could have worked for the War Office.'

In his youth, Richard had worked for a secret government department... She should take the remark as a compliment.

Richard screwed up the note. 'If this is true, it explains why the militia has gone quiet.' His lips twisted into a grim line. 'Why risk lives when all they have to do is wait?'

'Maybe you should travel to Liverpool, after all, and I should try to get Bella to the lift again? Take advantage of the lull?'

'The roads to the port are mined and Miss Small may have laid more than one mine in the lane.'

Sophie gulped. 'Could we evacuate to the town?'

'No. We have to negotiate. By all accounts, Miss Small is honourable in her way.' Richard's fist tightened around Bill's letter and he stared into the cold grate. 'Perhaps an exchange of letters over the holiday.' Richard's secret squirrel past had made him a canny aristocrat.

Pale light from the library window emphasised the fan lines around his eyes. 'I'll offer Miss Small a secure head-quarters but, in exchange, I'll need a guarantee that the family and servants will be treated properly.' He put his arm through Sophie's. 'Come on, my dear. Lunch.'

In the dining room, happily ignorant of the militia's plans, Alice was holding hands with Harry under the table, Rupert and Ethel were brazenly flirting, as were Freddy and Clarissa.

Richard's face gave nothing away, but despite Sophie acting nonchalant, Charlotte glanced at her and so did Hugo, their eyes questioning.

Richard hadn't explicitly sworn her to secrecy.

She'd tell them.

CHAPTER 25

After Bill's message about the militia's weapon, the roof duty guards reported no activity and the road to the town remained deserted.

Rupert monitored their broadcasts, making notes in a book beside the wireless, but the announcements now concerned a nearby city. Derby had recently been seized by a different militia.

Hugo and Charlotte were aware of the militia's winning card, but Sophie was determined that Freddy — and everyone else — shouldn't find out. Not yet. Four days before Christmas, this was the calm before the storm, which would surely erupt after the holiday.

Bella was growing in confidence. She used an unsteady walking route from the sofa in the small drawing room to the nearest chair and was undeterred by falling, giggling as she picked herself up. Sometimes she cheated, tottering while holding onto Charlotte's collar while Charlotte walked slowly — a sight almost as unnerving as her human-like nod.

Lucy was living in the rebuilt families' building and Sophie visited every day. The head gardener's leg was encased in a plaster cast, but she could move around using a stick.

Sitting in the tatty armchair, Lucy pulled her injured leg up onto a stool and winced.

'It still hurts?' said Sophie.

'Not as bad. More of an ache.'

'What's that?' Sophie gestured at a side table. On it was a device resembling a miniature satellite dish.

'Belling electric heater. Reynolds found one in the town.'

Sophie wiggled her hands in front of it, enjoying the wafts of hot air.

The heater gave off a tangy, metallic heat, but most of Lucy's sitting room smelled of damp plaster and paint. Enlivening the cream walls was a bright paper chain. Tiana's handiwork.

Her yellow jacket was draped over a wooden chair and Sophie picked it up, sat down, and laid the jacket across her lap. 'Tiana seems happy.'

'Knowing she can go home eventually,' said Lucy. 'That helps.'

'I'm glad you get on with her.'

'Actually…' Lucy lowered her voice. 'We're getting on *really* well.'

'Lucy, that's wonderful!' A same-sex relationship here, if it ever became public, would be incredibly dangerous, but their secret was safe with her. 'Happy ever after?'

'Early days,' said Lucy, 'but perhaps.'

'I'm so glad.' Sophie jumped up and hugged her, but then drew back. Lucy's shoulders were stiff. 'Obviously, you can't literally jump for joy yet, but … something's wrong.'

Lucy hesitated. 'His face is always in my head, Sophie. The lad who died in the ambush.'

'Once the war's over, you should go through the lift with

Tiana. Have therapy.' To Sophie's alarm, a tear ran down her friend's cheek.

Lucy wiped it away. 'Nah, I'm old school. *Crocodile Dundee.*'

'Sorry?'

'The 1980s movie.' Lucy had come to Shorten from 2003. 'Somebody talks about therapy, and Dundee says, haven't you got any mates?'

Lucy's sense of humour was intact. She just needed time.

After lunch, wheeled into the Manor dining room in a bath chair, Lucy supervised gardeners erecting a Christmas tree. More gardeners brought in bunches of holly, fresh from the grounds.

Miss Parry handed round glasses of eggnog. Sophie took a sip and sighed with pleasure: double cream, the last of the rum, caster sugar, grated nutmeg, and — of course — eggs. Thanks to the chickens beside the stables, eggs weren't rationed.

Lucy opted for tea instead. She examined the base of the tree from her bath chair and nodded. 'Erected securely. Thanks, lads.'

The gardeners trooped out.

Anne opened an ancient travelling chest. Inside were tree ornaments, enjoyed by many generations: a paper jester with faded motley cut out from a book, hand-knitted angels, and glass baubles that resembled apples, etched with glitter.

'I made this.' Anne held up a nest of material. The green felt had a serrated edge like a fern leaf and the brown centre was an acorn, dotted with pale bits for snow.

'This will be our first Shorten Christmas,' said Hugo. 'We crossed universes before the previous one.' He shot Sophie a tender look and she returned it, illogically embarrassed. They were married, after all...

A rustling sound came from the dining room table.

Freddy, dapper in his boxy suit and bow tie, was cutting up shiny sheets of paper. Charlotte was sitting on the floor, watching him. So was Bella.

'What are you doing?' Sophie asked him.

'Assembling crackers. I make them every year.'

'Nice idea,' said Hugo. 'At home, we just buy them.'

Clarissa smiled at Hugo. Freddy had restored her confidence, and miraculously unravelled the Hugo-hurt.

'They'll have a surprise toy inside,' said Freddy, 'but with all this trouble, I can't source the ingredients to trigger the proper snap.'

'What ingredients?' said Sophie.

'Silver nitrate and concentrated nitric acid, for the silver fulminate. I used to order it from a shop in London, but now the post office won't deliver it.'

'Sounds dangerous,' said Ethel.

'It isn't,' said Freddy. 'The quantities are tiny. You put two strips of paper together, paint the fulminate on one side and stick sand on the other. When they're pulled apart, you hear the snap.'

Sophie sipped her eggnog. She'd never take factory-made crackers for granted again.

Rupert fiddled with the wireless which emitted static and squeaks. 'Nobody's broadcasting.'

'Let's leave that off till after the holidays,' said Richard.

Sophie nodded, stepping back from the tree to admire it. The roads were quiet, and the hospital bay was empty. This would be a good Christmas.

On Christmas Day after breakfast, the Laceys and their guests adjourned to the small drawing room.

Sophie and Freddy helped Bella with her presents, and

their daughter's excitement was infectious. Harry had carved wooden animals for her: a flock of sheep and a pig. Bella clapped as Freddy made the toys jump and run.

Most of the gifts were handkerchiefs, embroidered with the recipient's initials. Maud had helped Sophie make sturdy toys out of cloth for Bella and the dogs. Bella loved her rag doll, and Jack loved his toy pheasant, but Charlotte showed no interest in her rabbit. Instead, she flipped open Bella's picture book and stared at it.

Sophie snatched up the book. 'You can look at this later,' she whispered to her. 'When we're by ourselves.'

In the late afternoon, over Christmas dinner, Richard opened what he called 'ridiculously expensive' wine. 'We've twenty bottles left.' Today, no one was patrolling, including the footmen, and they filled everybody's glasses.

'Twenty bottles of the best or twenty in total?' Rupert asked Richard.

'In total.'

The rich wine made Sophie sleepy, but she withdrew to the small drawing room with Charlotte, Anne, the Armstrong sisters, and Clarissa.

To her surprise, Clarissa sat beside her on the emerald sofa. 'I'm sorry I didn't embroider a handkerchief for you.'

The spirit of Christmas worked in mysterious ways. 'Same.' Sophie dropped her voice. 'Freddy is madly in love with you.'

Clarissa gave her a wistful smile. 'I hope so.'

On Boxing Day morning, Sophie presented Maud with a blue shawl she'd knitted in secret and a matching hat. Maud put them on and paraded around the bedroom.

'The shawl hem's a bit uneven,' said Sophie, 'but it should keep you warm.'

Maud hugged her and Sophie burst into tears.

'Miss?'

'Happy tears,' said Sophie, mortified. 'This has been a *lovely* Christmas.'

Boxing Day passed in a whirl of food and finishing off the wine, but Sophie found a quiet hour to slip off to the bedroom and sit with Charlotte and Jack on the four poster. She spoke out loud the names of the characters in Bella's book.

As Jack dozed, Charlotte memorised the spoken words and how they were written, putting her right front paw below the sentences as Sophie read.

'This is too childish.' Sophie closed the book. 'I'm guessing you'd find stories about dogs the most interesting?'

The Charlotte nod.

'At home, there are loads of books that have dogs in them. My favourites are paranormal dogs … special, like you. But in the meantime, we can borrow *Peter Pan* from the Manor library. The dog in that is called Nana. She's an enormous breed, a Newfoundland, and she minds the children.'

Charlotte tilted her head, unimpressed.

'Nana doesn't have any actual adventures but, hey, let's give it a go.' Sophie hadn't read the book, only seen the movie.

Sophie went to the library. It didn't take long to find *Peter Pan*.

Back in the bedroom, the first chapter proved much harder than the picture book. '*Of course, they lived at 14…*'

Charlotte frowned.

'I think that means that the years passed, and Wendy is fourteen.' Sophie skimmed over paragraphs until she found Nana. '*She proved to be quite a treasure of a nurse. Nurse is* another name for a nanny.' Charlotte pointed at Bella's cot with her paw.

'Yes.'

Hugo came in and smiled at them.

Sophie showed him the book. 'Charlotte is such a quick learner.'

Charlotte bounded off the bed over to Hugo and Jack did too.

Hugo stroked them. 'Is the next Charlotte-task learning calculus with Freddy?'

Sophie closed *Peter Pan*. 'Honestly, nothing would surprise me.'

On 27th December, the plan for an invigorating mid-morning walk was stymied by heavy sleet, and everyone gathered in the small drawing room.

Harry added wood to the fire and Rupert switched on the wireless.

'This is the British People's Alliance.' Static. *'Local News. 1928 will mark a new beginning, a fairer Britain. Shorten Manor will welcome the militia.'* More static.

Rupert frowned and switched it off.

Hugo reached for Sophie's hand and Charlotte sat close against Sophie's legs.

'Usual rubbish,' said Freddy, who was playing on the floor with Bella.

'I'm afraid it isn't.' Richard was standing by the fireplace, and he turned to address the room. 'I received a letter from Miss Small before Christmas.'

Anne looked at her lap, knowing what was coming, but Harry, sitting on the sofa opposite Sophie and Hugo, looked up in alarm.

'Miss Small is in possession of a piece of modern artillery,' said Richard. 'I've verified her claim with my contacts in the county. It's in a field outside the village and they have two shells.' He paused. 'That's enough to reduce a good part of this house to rubble.'

A communal intake of breath. Alice paled, and Ethel put her hand over her mouth.

'Can we destroy the artillery?' asked Rupert.

'If we had explosives, but we don't,' said Richard. 'I replied to Miss Small, saying that I was prepared to negotiate, and I've just received her reply. She wants the Manor intact but if we don't surrender, I have no doubt she'll use her weapon.'

'If she has us over a barrel,' said Freddy, 'what is there to negotiate?'

'Safety guarantees.' Richard's gaze lingered for a moment on Sophie.

'We shouldn't stay,' said Clarissa. 'We should go to the town.'

Rupert nodded. 'Thanks to the Volunteers, it's safe.'

'What about the mines?' said Alice.

'The militia use the town road,' said Rupert, 'so haven't mined it.'

'I won't leave the servants to the mercies of the militia.' Richard turned towards the fireplace and warmed his hands. 'Not before I have an agreement in place.'

Anne cleared her throat. 'We've stipulated that Miss Small must keep on the servants.'

'Will her men behave like gentlemen?' said Harry.

'Miss Small runs a tight ship,' said Richard.

Ethel raised her chin. 'Then I suppose we should co-operate, at least on the surface.'

In her own way, Ethel was as formidable as Rupert's late mother. Maybe that's why Rupert had fallen for her.

'They'll expect the best in food and drink,' said Rupert.

'We should manage expectations then,' said Freddy, 'particularly with regard to the drink.'

'I'm off to see Lucy,' said Sophie to Hugo. She patted Charlotte. 'You stay here with Jack, in the warm.'

Sophie left the drawing room, went to the bedroom to fetch her jacket, hat, and scarf, and hurried into the garden.

The sleet was turning into snow. She pulled her ski hat further over her ears and walked to Lucy's rooms.

Hearing nothing after she knocked, she went in. The sitting room was empty, the bedroom door ajar. Sophie peeped in.

Lucy was sitting on the bed, dressed in a tatty woollen dressing gown, though it was gone ten. She'd been tearing pages out of a notebook and scrunched up bits of paper lay scattered on the floor.

'You didn't hear me knock?' Sophie hesitated. 'Are you okay?'

Lucy shrugged.

'Richard's surrendering the Manor.'

Lucy didn't react to this bombshell, didn't even look up, and Sophie rushed forward. 'Is your leg infected? Have you and Tiana fallen out?'

'No ... and no.'

Lucy looked drained. Listless, despairing. Had somebody else died? Sophie gathered up the balls of paper and dropped them in a wicker bin. 'Whatever's happened, we'll get through it together.'

'Close the door.'

'Okay...' Sophie closed it, then sat on the edge of the bed, careful to avoid Lucy's leg.

'I'm pregnant.'

The words sounded loud in the small room, and Sophie stared at her friend in shock. 'Are you sure?'

'I'm sure.'

Sophie's heart missed a beat. The ambush when Lucy had gone missing… What had Tiana said? *Somebody left her for dead in a field.* Sophie swore. 'One of the militia.'

Lucy bowed her head.

'Look at me. You're not on your own with this.'

'Oh, I am.'

Sophie took her friend's hand. 'You haven't told Tiana?'

'I was going to ask her to stay with me, but I can't now.' Lucy shut the notebook. 'Tiana's a scientist, not a historian. I've been trying to write her a note, to explain what happens to single mothers here.'

As if on cue, Tiana strode in. 'I've got you another tea—' She stared. 'What's going on?'

Sophie hastily let go of the head gardener's hand.

'Sit down,' said Lucy.

Tiana flopped onto the wooden chair with a frown. Lucy left the saucer on the bedside table and drank the hot tea, her fingers wrapped around the cup.

Sophie got to her feet. 'I should go.'

'No,' said Lucy. 'You being here makes this easier.'

Sophie sat down again.

Lucy met her partner's eyes. 'I'm pregnant. I'm single. So, as they say at home, I'm well and truly screwed.'

Tiana's mouth dropped open.

'As soon as I can, I'll go through the lift,' said Lucy. 'At home, I won't starve.' She avoided Tiana's gaze.

'If it's not too personal,' said Tiana, 'who—'

'I don't know his name, and I don't want to.'

Realisation and horror showed on Tiana's face. 'You were … in the lane. Oh, my God, we must call the police.'

'They're too stretched with the war.' Lucy's lips twisted. 'And when word gets out, I'll lose my job.' She gestured at the room. 'And this place … and everything.'

Tiana shook her head. 'When your colleagues and friends

know the circumstances…' She leaned forward. 'They'll be supportive.'

'They won't be.' Lucy plonked her cup down on its saucer with a clink. 'I have to go home. Start again.'

Lucy had no family in the 21st century. 'I'll go with you,' said Sophie. 'You can stay at Hugo's house. His parents are used to us bringing guests back.' She tried to sound upbeat.

'Thanks.' Lucy blinked.

'This place is your whole life. You can't just throw it away.' Tiana stood up. 'I'm guessing the other option with the pregnancy is illegal here, too dangerous?'

Lucy nodded. 'Ironically, I've always wanted a family, children.' Her eyes flicked to Tiana. 'But I understand that this changes everything, with us I mean.'

'It's certainly a shock, and it'll take some getting used to, but an actual baby is months away.' Tiana put her hands on her hips. 'What if it was *me* that was pregnant?'

'You're pregnant too?' said Lucy.

'Of course not, but if I were, I've a no-good ex-husband at home. That would tick the *respectable* box, wouldn't it?'

'I see where you're going with this,' said Sophie.

'I don't,' said Lucy.

'To use a gardening and fertility analogy, I scatter a few seeds,' said Tiana, fluttering her fingers. 'Start telling folks about my "husband," not mentioning we've gone our separate ways.'

'That's genius,' said Sophie. '*You* become gradually more "pregnant," waddle about the greenhouse, while Lucy's in here with her bad leg.'

'That would require consistent acting over months,' said Lucy. 'You're wonderful to think of it, but we'd never pull it off.'

'We will,' said Tiana, her lips set in a determined line.

'We'll plan it carefully. My ex is a real guy, so I won't have to invent details, or worry about contradicting myself.'

'What's your ex like?' asked Sophie.

'Brilliant scientist, utterly self-absorbed, and a pain in the ass.' Tiana smiled to herself. 'But we had some good times at grad school. I'll major on those.'

'Once I start to show, we'll need help from somebody with cunning and authority,' said Lucy.

'Great minds think alike,' said Sophie.

'Who do you have in mind?' asked Tiana.

'Someone who, back in the day, rescued me from social disgrace more than once,' said Sophie.

Tiana shot her a bemused look.

'If anyone can help us pull this off, it's her,' added Sophie.

Lucy sat up straighter. 'Lady Anne Lacey.'

CHAPTER 27

Three days later, at two p.m. precisely on 30th December, Richard ordered the Manor drawbridge to be lowered.

A clear blue sky made for a memorable backdrop to the formal surrender.

Richard walked onto the drive with Anne and Freddy, and all the Laceys' guests but one followed them. Harry was in the servants' hall, helping with a difficult birth.

Mr Crawford and Mrs Rawlings joined the assembled line behind Richard.

Standing straight and motionless beside Hugo, Sophie put her arm around Bella in her sling. She'd packed the holdall with Bella's milk, snacks, terry-nappies, keys-rattle, and picture book. Part of the agreement was that the Laceys would stay for two days to assist the militia, but for the first few hours, while the militia got organised, the family and their guests would be confined to a single room.

Sophie was dressed in an ankle-length cloak and a fur hat. The occasion called for proper clothing. But she was wearing trousers under the coat, and nobody noticed.

The militia strode across the drive, thirty pairs of boots crunching on the frosty gravel. They wore scruffy trousers and jackets and slung over their shoulders were shotguns or rifles. Amongst them was the fair-haired ex-footman and the red-haired girl who used to work as a maid. There was no sign of Bill.

The militia didn't line up or stand to attention. Some stared at the house, some looked at the Laceys, others whispered to each other. One man folded his arms.

Joan shook Richard's hand. His boxy suit and bowler contrasted oddly with her workman's clothes and bobble hat.

'This is a momentous day,' said Joan. 'The start of a new era.'

Richard gave her a sharp nod and Joan gestured for the men to enter the house.

The militia marched towards the drawbridge and crossed the moat. A man at the rear of the group was taller than the rest, his dark hair greased with Brilliantine, a fashionable hair gel.

The family line broke up to follow them in. Sophie caught up with Richard and Anne on the drawbridge. They were walking stiffly, their expressions unreadable.

Up ahead, at the entrance to the Manor, the tall militiaman spun around. 'This is for Barty.' He raised his shotgun and fired at Sophie and Bella.

Richard threw himself sideways. Sophie was jolted backwards, her head thumping against the drawbridge, and Richard slammed on top of her and Bella.

Sophie rolled over, clutching her baby, her daughter's screams filling her brain. Her stomach felt warm, as if a hot water bottle had burst.

She fought for breath. Hugo hauled her out from under Richard and dragged her upright. The baby stopped crying and dread made Sophie's throat close. 'Bella!'

Hugo lifted the baby out of her sling. 'She's okay,' he said in a rush, peering at Bella. 'Just shocked.'

'The sling's covered in blood.' Sophie's voice cracked.

Hugo swallowed. 'It's not her blood.'

Sophie's light blue cloak was stained red. Why was there no pain? 'My blood...'

'No.' Hugo's face crumpled, but he wasn't looking at her.

Richard was sprawled on the drawbridge, Anne on her knees beside him.

Freddy was staring at Joan, murder in his eyes. 'Hayden will answer for this,' she said. 'You have my word.'

Sophie stepped towards Richard. Was he unconscious? But Hugo pulled her back.

'We need to help,' said Sophie.

'Too late for that.' Bella was whimpering in Hugo's arms, and he handed her to Sophie.

'Everybody inside,' said Joan. '*Now.*'

Rupert took Ethel by the arm and hurried with her to the house. Clarissa and Alice followed with the butler and the housekeeper. But Freddy stayed where he was. So did Hugo.

And Sophie couldn't move, her legs paralysed by an invisible, despairing force. Anne was still kneeling on the drawbridge by her husband, rocking to and fro.

Two militiamen silently picked Richard up and carried him into the house. Freddy helped his mother to stand and led her forward.

'Come on,' Hugo said to Sophie.

Bella whimpered louder, her lips opening and twisting, but her baby noises seemed far away.

Richard was dead...

Hugo guided Sophie into the hall. Anne was slumped in the armchair.

Sophie gripped Hugo's arm, and time stopped. No, the

grandfather clock was ticking… She slipped Bella's bag off her shoulders and rocked the baby.

Joan addressed the housekeeper. 'Is there somewhere we can take Sir Richard, temporarily?' Her tone was conciliatory, apologetic.

'Follow me.' Mrs Rawlings left, and the militia carried Richard out of the room.

By the grandfather clock, the militia were restraining the man who'd shot Richard. The shooter's eyes fixed on Sophie, and he clamped his mouth into an ugly line. 'She should pay for killing Barty.'

'You've broken the agreement.' Joan walked up to him. 'I'm tempted to finish you now, but you're a waste of a bullet.' She turned to Mr Crawford. 'Do you have a room where we can lock him up?'

'We do. A store cupboard near the kitchens.'

'Take him,' said Joan.

Mr Crawford led the way out of the hall, the shooter manhandled behind him.

Sophie stared after them, her mind numb.

Scratching and canine whining was coming from Mrs Rawlings' study.

Hugo opened the door and assumed charge of Jack. Charlotte bounded over and, out of habit, Sophie took her lead.

A militia straggler came in carrying a tool bag, a tweed cap tilted low over his face. As he headed down a corridor, Charlotte barked and strained against the lead. Sophie tightened her grip on it.

'In accordance with our agreement,' said Joan to Freddy, 'I need you all to stay in one place, but not for long.'

Joan pointed at one of her men. 'You. Escort them to the library.'

CHAPTER 28

The ancient library door closed with a thud, and they heard the militiaman turn the key in the lock.

'Locking us in wasn't part of the agreement.' Freddy led Anne to the red chair and his mother sank into it, still wearing her pale coat, now streaked red. She took off her fur hat, her hands shaking.

Sophie found the keys-rattle in the holdall and sat with Bella on the floor. She reached over to hug Charlotte who'd settled nearby with Jack. 'Richard's dead,' she whispered to Charlotte.

Charlotte lowered her head, but Jack didn't react, might never realise his old master was gone.

Hugo sat on the floor next to them. The library was spacious but didn't have enough chairs. He took his lift puzzle notebook from a pocket and flicked through it, trying to distract himself. Sophie had left hers in 21st century London. Hadn't missed it.

Rupert strode over to the fireplace and lit the fire. Twice the normal amount of wood was piled up by the grate.

Confining them to the library must always have been the plan. Strange Richard hadn't mentioned that…

Alice was sobbing, collapsed in the black leather chair, but Sophie couldn't cry. Her mind knew Richard was dead, but her heart couldn't accept it.

Her thoughts scattered, then settled on Lucy. The militiaman who'd raped her might be here in the Manor. But she was in the families' building. Hopefully, wouldn't come across him. 'Lucy and Tiana are well out of this,' Sophie said to Hugo.

He nodded. Sophie had told him about Lucy's pregnancy. They'd vowed after their wedding … *no more secrets. Forever.*

Clarissa was gazing out at the gardens, holding her hat, and keeping on her coat. The arched leaded window was the library's most beautiful feature, but its size was the reason the room was so chilly.

Anne was staring at nothing.

Sophie went to her and squeezed her hand. 'He died saving his granddaughter.' Anne gripped her hand back with such force that it hurt.

Richard had loved Anne for thirty years. Their love match had nurtured this household and the whole estate. Freddy was sitting on the floor on the other side of his mother's chair, his knees drawn up to his chest over his town coat.

The dogs jumped up and barked.

'The firewood was wet.' Ethel wrinkled her nose. 'It's gone all smoky.'

'No,' said Rupert. 'There's smoke coming from under the door.' He rushed over and touched the frame. 'It's hot.' He spun round. 'The corridor outside must be on fire.'

Freddy jumped to his feet. 'They mean to kill us.'

Sophie picked up Bella, pocketing the rattle. The smoke sliding under the door was grey and thick. She stepped further into the library. Charlotte moved with her, and Jack kept close.

Hugo ran up to the door with a chair cushion and wedged it against the bottom to block the smoke, but long fingers of flame were curling around the door. He retreated.

The bitter smoke irritated Sophie's nose and throat and she coughed.

Rupert pulled Anne from the red chair. 'Alice, stand up,' he said. 'We can use the chairs to break the window—'

The library door crashed down and a sheet of fire shot across the double-height ceiling to the window. Glass panes split and exploded, and the blaze roared, fed by air from outside.

Clarissa screamed, her coat alight. Freddy hauled off his coat and thumped it around her. He threw her down to the floor and rolled her over, whacking at the flames until they were out. Clarissa's coat was fire-black and crisp.

The window was a wall of flame and sparks on the ceiling were jumping and scattering, darting through rolling smoke.

Hugo grabbed Sophie's hand, and the fear in his face fed her own. The fire's roar filled her ears, and she was gripped by blank terror.

She scurried further into the library with Hugo until she could go no further, jammed up against a bookcase with the dogs. Why would Joan try to murder them? Why risk destroying the headquarters she'd fought so long to take?

Hugo kissed her, his cheeks wet with tears.

'This is the end,' said Rupert, his voice faltering.

Sophie shook her head. They couldn't die. Not like this. 'The window's gone. We could run through it, jump into the moat.'

Rupert dragged his eyes from the leaping flames. 'We'd die trying.'

Heat and smoke were surging through the library, wave upon wave.

'Hugo,' Sophie coughed. 'Help me get Bella into her sling.'

If they could somehow get through the window, she should be ready. Rupert could be wrong…

Hugo lowered Bella into the sling and Freddy kissed his daughter. Hugo gripped Sophie's hand, and Charlotte and Jack cowered against them. Both dogs were trembling.

Sophie's dead parents swam into focus inside her mind, but she ignored them. Keep in the present. Get out. She slipped Bella's holdall onto her shoulders.

But the flames were dancing towards them, mesmerising, inevitable. The chair that Anne had been sitting in moments before was smouldering, the red leather cracking.

Anne looked wildly about, as if only now registering the danger. 'Unclip a bookcase ladder,' she said to Freddy. '*Quickly.*'

'Why?'

'There's a way out.' Anne's dazed state had been replaced by agitation — and terror.

Freddy unclipped a ladder, his face shiny with sweat.

'Put it up next to the side window,' ordered Anne.

The side window was a column of single panes, too narrow to escape through. This made no sense.

Hugo's grip on Sophie's hand tightened.

'Hurry,' said Anne. The red chair was properly alight, emitting darker, foul-smelling smoke.

Freddy set the ladder up.

'Hugo, climb to the top,' said Anne. 'You're the tallest. You can easily reach it.'

'Reach what?' said Hugo, releasing Sophie's hand.

Freddy held the bottom of the ladder and Hugo climbed fast, holding his breath against thicker smoke near the ceiling.

'There's a carving of a tiny doe.' Anne coughed. 'Turn it anti-clockwise. Carefully. Stop turning when it resists.'

Hugo reached up.

A scraping sound came from the bookcase behind Sophie. She whirled round.

Hugo scrambled down the ladder while Anne hurried over to the bookcase. She swiped a book onto the floor and pressed something on the inside of the shelf.

A snap and the bookcase creaked open, revealing a door-size gap and beyond it, darkness.

Sophie's breathing sped up. Not going to die. Not going to die.

The bookcases near the library door and the red chair were invisible, lost in the smoke.

Anne attached Jack's lead to his collar and stepped with him into the tunnel doorway. 'Hold hands, don't let go, and proceed in a line. The passage has false turnings that go nowhere.' She grabbed Freddy's left hand.

Clarissa reached for Freddy's other hand. Hugo quickly tied Charlotte's lead on his wrist and joined the line after Clarissa. Sophie was between Hugo and Alice, followed by Ethel and Rupert, and together they all filed through the gap.

At the back of the line, Rupert swung the bookcase shut, sealing off the smoke and flames.

Plunging them into the dark.

CHAPTER 29

*D*eath by fire had haunted Sophie since her schooldays, when she'd been traumatised by gruesome descriptions of witch trials. When anything even vaguely related was in a book, she'd stopped reading. Dramatised on TV or in a movie, she'd stopped watching.

Fire in Shorten burned as it did at home. As it had in the medieval realm. Were there any worlds where fire had different properties? Didn't burn?

The library's bookcase-door in Shorten Manor was made of wood. Once that was gone, would the fire chase them down here?

Was this passage constructed of stone, or bricks? Sophie couldn't see the walls, and holding tight onto Alice's hand and Hugo's, she couldn't touch them.

The tunnel was narrow, just enough room for one person, and the ceiling was so low that, in front of her, Hugo was shuffling in a half crouch.

Near the top of the line, Freddy said, 'Why didn't you tell me about this?'

'It's the Manor's most guarded secret,' said Anne. 'Your father broke with centuries of tradition by telling me.'

What had Anne said when they were discussing Inkpin? *We talked it through, and as a result he shared with me other information, and I'm glad of that.*

Sophie shuddered. If Richard hadn't told her about the bookcase...

'I'm worried about Harry,' said Alice.

'The fire was nowhere near the servants' hall.' Even as she said this, Sophie's heart skipped a beat. The fire outside the library hadn't been an accident. Had other fires been set too?

A change in the air signalled a fork in the passage. They turned left and the floor dipped sharply. Alice's hold on Sophie's hand strengthened.

When the ground levelled out, it was damper and colder, and water dripped from the ceiling onto their heads.

'Where are we?' Hugo called to Anne.

'Under the moat.'

Hugo's grip on Sophie's hand grew tighter and she gasped, claustrophobia fuelling panic. Don't think about the moat, the weight of water.

The air changed again. A strong earth smell mixed in with moisture — another fork in the passage.

Up the line with Anne, Jack was whining, frightened by unfamiliar smells. There was no sound from Charlotte in front of Hugo. She was likely plodding on, hoping for the best. Like her mistress.

They veered right and the air smelled different. Cold and sour mildew...

Boom.

The sound came from behind them and a moment later, it felt warmer, constricting. A momentary flash illuminated the tunnel.

They shuffled quicker, stumbling, and Sophie's heartbeat thundered in her ears.

A whoosh of hot air and the tunnel lit up for longer, revealing the passage's stone walls and ceiling.

A new tunnel branched off. Then another.

Alice's hand was hot and clammy, as was Hugo's.

At the rear of the line, Rupert coughed. 'Speed up!'

'Not far now,' said Anne.

Not far. Keep going.

Bella wailed, confused by wet-stone smells, dripping water and the heat. Sophie calmed her own breathing. 'Shush. All is well.'

Hugo sped up and Sophie sped up too, dragging Alice.

Another flash. Red cinders were floating in the air.

The corridor stretched on straight and Bella kept wailing.

'*Faster*,' shouted Rupert.

Sophie glanced back and stumbled. A fiery ball was rushing towards them, pulsating and roaring in the confined space. Hugo was climbing upwards, and Sophie followed as fast as she could, the treads slimy under her boots.

Higher up the stairway, Anne groaned. 'Freddy, I need your help.' The noise of something heavy scraping.

Alice slipped and Sophie steadied her.

More scraping. A rush of air. Grey light.

Sophie scrambled after Hugo. She hurled herself forward, hauling Alice with her into the cold.

Rupert pushed Ethel forward, and she fell in a heap beside Sophie. Rupert jumped out, breathing hard.

Freddy gestured at a stone slab. 'Help me push it back.'

Rupert, Hugo, and Freddy leaned on it, rolling it across the entrance to the tunnel. It looked the same as the lids of nearby coffins, concealing its true purpose.

Sophie stood up and was enveloped in a Hugo bear-hug.

Charlotte joined in the hug, and squished in the middle, Bella squirmed.

Rupert dropped to his knees, trying to catch his breath.

They were in the nave of a church, empty and dusty, with the sort of heavy silence that weighed down the living. The drop in temperature was welcome, but Sophie shivered.

Twilight filtered through stained-glass windows, making the rows of pews and the altar seem dull and washed out.

'Where are we?' said Ethel.

'The chapel,' said Freddy. 'Beyond the moat.'

Rupert brushed dust from his hands.

'Can the fire burn through the slab?' Ethel asked him.

'I don't know.'

Freddy ran to the church entrance and wrenched open the door. He stepped outside and stood still.

Everyone followed him, and Sophie paused on the church path and stared across the moat.

The Manor was as bright as a stage set, flames and sparks jumping high into the dark. Orange and yellow and scarlet.

Charlotte nuzzled into Sophie's legs, and Sophie stroked her, turning away from the house, but the image had seared itself into her brain.

'I'm in no mood for the militia,' said Rupert. 'We should go to the town.'

'Agreed.' Freddy turned on his heel.

They walked off, an eerie red glow from the Manor at their backs. Sophie exchanged a worried glance with Hugo. It was bitterly cold, and the town was five miles away.

Bella wriggled in the sling and made her hungry noise. Too cold to stop and feed her.

The dogs didn't have their coats. Charlotte looked okay, but next to Anne, Jack was shivering.

'I'll carry Bella in a bit,' said Hugo to Sophie.

'Thanks. No need to bother Freddy.'

Charlotte was trotting beside Freddy, but he was staring straight ahead, his face shuttered.

'All of you, please don't mention the secret passage to anybody,' said Anne. 'If part of the Manor somehow survives, I'd like to restore it. Later generations may have need of it.'

'Was the riddle in *A History* a clue to the tunnel after all?' Sophie asked Hugo.

'Yes.' He pulled out his notebook, flicked through the pages, and read aloud. '*Transcending words, the revered beast points to the hollow. Lesser is greater, backwards is better, born to follow.* I get it now.'

'I get … some of it,' said Sophie. 'The mechanism was on the wall, above the words in the bookcases. The revered beast is a deer, and the hollow's the tunnel.'

Hugo nodded. '*Lesser is greater* is a Victorian sexist clue. A female deer, a doe, is regarded as less important than a stag, but the doe carving was the way to open the bookcase. *Backwards is better* refers to turning the carving anticlockwise.'

'And *born to follow*,' added Sophie, 'describes the only family member who should know about the tunnel.'

'Correct,' said Anne. 'Discovery would have meant death for the priest, and the Manor would have been seized by the Crown. Richard's ancestor decreed that, apart from trusted priests, only he should be told and, thereafter, just his son, and so on.'

'What if the Manor owner dies unexpectedly…' Clarissa winced. 'I'm sorry.'

But Anne acknowledged the question with a nod. 'Our solicitors keep the details in a safe. On inheriting the estate, the heir is given a sealed envelope, memorises the instructions, and returns the contents to a new envelope and seals it. That envelope is then returned to the safe for his heir to see in due course.'

'Were you aware of the clue in the book?' Hugo asked her.

'No,' said Anne, 'and … Richard wasn't.'

'It was a beautiful book,' said Hugo.

'Was that the only copy?' Sophie asked Anne.

'Probably.'

'If it's the same as at home, there should be a copy in the British Library,' said Hugo. 'Every book that's been published since the seventeenth century is stored there.'

Sophie shot him a fond smile. Of course, Hugo would know that.

They finally left behind the red glow of the Manor, and the road was lit by moonlight, but with all the women except Sophie wearing court shoes, tottering rather than walking, progress was slow.

Sophie put her arms around Bella to make her warmer. Even inside thick socks, Sophie's toes were numb. Her fingers were numb too.

'Time to swap,' said Hugo.

Sophie lifted Bella from the sling, put it on Hugo, and lowered the baby into it. Fortunately, the rhythm of walking had made Bella sleepy.

Rupert pointed at a milestone on the verge. *Shorten Town 4 miles.*

They trudged on and Sophie remembered Richard, then the library, but one thought repeated. Why had Joan turned on them?

It took an hour and a half to reach the outskirts of the town and the checkpoint.

The Volunteer challenged them. 'Who goes there?'

'The Laceys and their friends,' yelled Rupert.

The man peered at them and lowered his rifle. 'Your Grace?' The other Volunteer stared.

'The Manor's on fire,' said Rupert.

'Is anybody hurt?' said the first Volunteer.

'We don't know,' said Rupert. 'Any trouble here tonight?'

The guards shrugged. 'Nah.' One gestured at the road. 'Freezing.'

After the checkpoint, it was another half a mile to the high street and the bakery. In the early evening in the winter-dark, there wasn't much traffic, and the pavement was icy. They cut down the alley to the back door and Freddy knocked on it with his knuckles.

Lizzie opened it and blinked in surprise before gesturing for them to come in.

They all trooped past her into the fabulously warm room. The only light came from a single gas lamp above the oven.

'What's going on?' Lizzie closed the door.

'My father's dead.' In the soft illumination of the gas lamp, Freddy's face was grey with exhaustion.

Anne sank into a worn armchair and Freddy stood beside her. Sophie unclipped the sling on Hugo and put Bella down on a rug.

'The militia set the Manor on fire,' said Ethel.

'What about the servants' hall? My sister?' Lizzie's brow creased, concerned about Maud.

'When we left, just the house was burning,' said Hugo.

Sophie sat at the table on a chair nearest the oven and rifled in her bag for Bella's bottle. As she fed the baby, a new question whirled in her head.

What if Maud and the others had been locked in — and the servants' hall set on fire?

CHAPTER 30

Well before dawn the next morning, Sophie was deeply asleep on the parlour floor in the bakery. But she was woken up by Bella crawling on top of her. Bright as a button, her baby made insistent gurgling noises.

Sophie groaned. Careful not to wake up the Armstrong sisters, Clarissa, and the dogs, she tiptoed out with Bella into the kitchen.

Lizzie and Miss Kemble, her all-sorts maid, had retired early the previous day and were already awake, kneading dough. Bella babbled at them, and the women shot Sophie an understanding smile.

Miss Kemble was wearing a neat white apron over a dark dress. Lizzie's apron was huge, probably her late husband's.

At Lizzie's feet, her toddler, Rose, was lying on her front on the rug, gripping a tiny wooden horse, making the toy jump over the mat's bright woven lines and swirls.

Sophie put Bella down beside Rose and rummaged in her bag for a food jar.

Once she'd been fed, Bella fell asleep on the rug. Sophie

sat in the armchair by the window, and lulled by the smell of baking bread, she fell asleep too.

When she opened her eyes, there were voices coming from a passage off the kitchen. Sophie headed down the corridor.

The front door was open, and from the doorway, Lizzie and Miss Kemble were selling bread. Sitting on upright chairs, they wore coats and fingerless gloves. Miss Kemble was wrapping loaves in brown paper while Lizzie took the customers' money, dropping the coins into a metal tin. Nobody was getting any change.

'Daylight robbery,' one older customer muttered as she gave over a shilling. The buyers were predominantly women, wrapped up in cheap coats, bobble hats and scarfs. The men wore tatty trousers, short jackets and caps.

When the last loaf was sold, those who'd missed out drifted away, and Lizzie heaved a sigh of relief and shut the door.

'Have you raised the price?' asked Sophie.

'The price of everything's up.' Though barely a teenager, Miss Kemble sounded world-weary.

'Demand's up too,' said Lizzie, as they trooped back to the warm kitchen. 'Must be the post office money.' She filled a kettle and looked at Sophie. 'Tea?'

'Yes, please.' Sophie stretched and yawned, stiff from sleeping on the floor and in the armchair.

Bella and Rose were still curled up on the rug, undisturbed by bread-selling and the chink of crockery.

The men were sleeping in the 'posh parlour' and Anne was in the only spare bedroom upstairs. Hopefully, she was asleep, oblivious that Richard was gone. At least for a while.

Sophie gratefully sipped her tea, remembering Richard's body on the drawbridge. He must have moved so fast to save her and Bella, an instinctive split second, but that memory just wasn't there. Never formed, or her brain had blotted it out.

Hugo shambled into the kitchen, looking bleary.

'How was the posh parlour?' said Sophie.

'Fine.' Hugo acknowledged Lizzie and accepted a cup of tea.

Freddy came in with Rupert, and Lizzie addressed Miss Kemble. 'Can you go with the gentlemen and bring down more chairs from upstairs? There's a few stacked by the grain.' As well as bedrooms on the upper floors, there were rooms to store bread ingredients: flour, yeast, and salt.

Six chairs were brought from upstairs and more transferred from the posh parlour. Not long afterwards, the women and the dogs emerged from the regular parlour.

Sophie and Hugo pulled on their jackets and went with the dogs through the courtyard to the scrubland. It was milder now and raining. Sophie turned up her collar.

'I woke up hoping yesterday wasn't real, a nightmare,' said Hugo. He hugged Sophie close. 'For a few seconds on the drive … I thought you and Bella were dead.'

Sophie rested her head against his chest, re-living Richard lying on the drawbridge.

Jack had stopped exploring and Charlotte leaned against Sophie's legs, wanting to go back inside.

In the bakery, Lizzie was setting out fresh bread, butter, jam, and a sturdy grey teapot. Everybody except Anne was sitting at the table. Sophie and Hugo hung up their jackets and joined them.

Lizzie put a water bowl down for the dogs. Sophie fed them chunky bread and jam, then helped herself. The damson jam was deep and sweet, and she spread a thick layer on her bread.

'What now?' said Rupert to the table in general.

'I'd appreciate help with the baking, your Grace,' said Lizzie. 'Once you get the hang of it, I can have a lie in.'

'A splendid idea.' Rupert pointed at a small, domed-shaped wireless on the windowsill. The casing was tatty, and its brown protruding knobs were streaked with flour. 'Does that work?'

Lizzie nodded. 'Tuned to the Volunteers' channel.'

A brisk knock came from the back door. 'Are you expecting someone?' said Hugo.

'No.' Lizzie scurried over to open it.

A firefighter was there, his blue uniform dark with soot. He removed his pointed helmet, his attention on Lizzie. 'Mrs Watkins is safe.' Then he saw the crowded table and gawped. 'You're all dead.'

'No,' said Rupert. 'Obviously.'

The firefighter shook his head. 'How on earth did you escape?'

'Through the library window,' lied Hugo.

The firefighter strode over to the sink and washed his hands, then he sat in the armchair. 'You were incredibly lucky. The whole wing has gone.'

That beautiful, wonderful library…

Lizzie stirred two lumps of sugar into a cup of tea and handed it to the firefighter with a sandwich. 'Miss Small told us about Sir Richard Lacey,' he said. 'Terrible.'

'You've been up all night?' Clarissa asked him.

He nodded. 'The main fire's out. Thank God for rain.' He chomped on his sandwich.

Anne came down the spiral staircase and silently sat by Freddy. She accepted tea from Miss Kemble.

'Is the house entirely destroyed?' Freddy asked the firefighter.

'Not all of it. Miss Small organised a human chain to pass up water from the moat. That helped.'

'Do you know how the fire started?' said Hugo. 'Was it an accident?'

'It was arson. The chap who runs the pub, *ran* the pub, in Little Shorten, he set the fire.' The firefighter scratched his chin. 'Alan… Alan Parkson.'

'Alan Parkes.' Sophie's fingers closed around her cup, her insides churning. Beside her chair, Charlotte raised her chin, her golden eyes alert.

'Is he in custody?' Hugo asked the firefighter.

'Died at the scene.'

No one noticed Charlotte's nod of satisfaction … or was she relieved?

'The militiaman who arrived late,' said Hugo. 'That must have been Parkes.'

Charlotte had barked at him in the hall, hadn't been fooled by his cap, pulled low to hide his face. Sophie topped up her tea, trying to take it in.

'Whatever you think of the militia, that Miss Small should have a medal,' said the firefighter. 'She got her men to search the Manor room by room, getting all the servants out. Just before the big roof went.'

'I suppose the arsonist had a fitting death,' said Clarissa. 'Paid for his crime.'

Sophie put down her cup, recalling the pictures Alan had seen on the lift doors. The Manor on fire, and another sketch, the forked road. The house picture symbolised his final destination, and the road with two paths symbolised the choices he'd made to arrive there.

'Miss Small said the arsonist was doolally.' The firefighter frowned. 'Off with the fairies.'

Sophie chewed her lip. Okay, this wasn't straightforward. At the end, Alan couldn't choose his path. So, what did the forked road represent? His earlier choices?

'I feel sorry for his lady friend,' said the firefighter.

'Betty Hill.' Sophie picked up her cup. 'I feel for her too.'

CHAPTER 31

$\mathcal{B}$etty knocked on Alan's bedroom door. When there was no answer, she ventured in. The room was empty, the curtains still open.

Yesterday had been one of Alan's good days, almost like his old self. He hadn't planned to stay over at the Manor with the militia. Must have changed his mind.

Heavy rain was beating at the window, the village green outside obscured and hazy. Alan would wait until the rain eased off to walk back.

Betty collected *Vogue* from her room and went downstairs. Roy Ducker had bought the glossy magazine for her with his post office money. He shouldn't have spent so much, but it was a thoughtful present. Something she could enjoy, over and over.

She sat in the brown armchair by the fire, relishing the quiet. Frank was doing his colouring, and there was plenty of time to clear up before lunchtime. Now the militia had gone, the old regulars would return.

The front door burst open, and Roy hurried in. His face was grimy, so was his jacket and cap, and he was wet through. He removed his hat. 'I came as fast as I could.' He shut the pub door and strode over to the fire.

'Get out of those wet clothes, sharpish.' Betty frowned. 'You'll catch your death.'

Roy laid his rifle against the wall and peeled off his jacket.

Betty closed *Vogue* and stood up. 'I'll fetch Mr Parkes' dressing gown.'

He touched her shoulder. 'I'm so sorry. He's … dead.'

'Who's dead?'

'Mr Parkes.'

Betty stared at him. Dead? How could Alan be dead?

Roy was saying something else. She sat down again. Frank left his colouring and sat by his mother, and she absently stroked his hair. Roy walked over to the bar and soon returned. He handed Betty a tumbler of whisky.

She wasn't a drinker, but she sipped.

'The Manor caught fire. We carried him out, but the smoke did for him.' Roy hesitated. 'The thing is, he started the fire, planned it. Stashed a can of petrol in his bag.'

Betty shook her head. 'I wondered why he took his repairs bag.'

'Most of the house is destroyed.'

Betty got to her feet and in a daze, climbed the stairs to Alan's room. His dressing gown was lying on the bed. She draped it over her arm.

Downstairs, she offered it to Roy.

'Are you sure?' He was shivering.

'You don't want to catch pneumonia.'

Roy awkwardly accepted the dressing gown. 'Lock the front door, I'll change here.'

Betty locked the door, then went to the kitchen, setting the whisky tumbler by the sink. As she filled the kettle and reached for cups and saucers from the cupboard, guilt rippled through her. She should have kept a closer eye on

Alan, asked more questions when he'd set off. If she had, would he have gone through with it?

She put the kettle on the stove, imagining Alan in the burning Manor. How many people had perished?

After she'd poured the tea and added the remaining whisky to both cups, Betty hurried through the bar to Roy.

He'd laid out his wet clothes by the grate and was wearing the dressing gown. 'Jim Hayden killed Sir Richard Lacey. Shot him through the heart.'

Betty's mouth fell open.

'We locked Hayden up but had to let him out when the fire started. He's scarpered.' Roy sat down and sipped his fortified tea. 'Lady Lacey and her son died, and a whole load of other people. Do you know why he did it?'

Alan mumbling nonsense… 'It was his mind-trouble. He thought destroying the Manor was what he was supposed to do.'

'Eh?'

'When he came here, he saw a picture of the Manor on fire, on the magic lift,' said Betty. 'He used to talk in his sleep, said burning it down was his destiny. Whenever I asked him about it, he clammed up.'

'So, he was just insane.'

Betty bit her lip. 'He blamed Mrs Harrington for losing his hand.'

'Mrs Harrington was in the library with the Laceys. He set the fire right outside. Her husband and daughter died with her.'

Betty felt sick.

'But we got all the servants out.'

'Including the chauffeurs?'

'They weren't in the house.' Roy's eyes narrowed. 'You mean Reynolds.'

It was common knowledge Reynolds had murdered her

brother. Reynolds should have been hanged. She forced herself to get to her feet. 'The bar needs cleaning.'

'I can do that.' Roy stood too and tightened the tie on the dressing gown.

'They'll be here soon.'

'Who will?'

'Everyone else. The militia.'

'They're not coming here,' said Roy. 'Why would they?'

'You said the Manor's destroyed—'

'One wing survived. It's huge. And the other buildings weren't affected.'

Betty exhaled.

'You've had a shock, Mrs Hill. Go upstairs and get some shut eye. I'll watch Frank.'

She rubbed her temples.

'Could I … stay over?' said Roy.

Stay over? This was too fast, disrespectful. She hadn't loved Alan, but he'd been good to her. 'Won't the militia want you back?'

'Saint Joan won't miss me, and I don't like the thought of you being by yourself.' Roy gave her a sympathetic glance. 'I'll sleep down here.'

CHAPTER 32

In the bakery, Rupert was helping with the washing up.

'I wasn't serious when I suggested you help, your Grace,' said Lizzie.

'It's the least I can do.' Rupert shot her his rakish smile.

Lizzie blushed.

Ethel set up a rota for everyone to lend a hand, but Anne retired to her room. She'd rallied to escape the fire in the library but now couldn't face company, needed to be alone with her grief.

Sophie and Alice had been tasked with the second bake of the day, and Miss Kemble ladled what looked like grainy sand into industrial-sized bowls.

Jack sniffed at the table, then settled on the rug beside Charlotte, Bella, and Rose.

Miss Kemble put a timer on the table. Lizzie set out jugs of water, cartons of salt, and measured ingredients into a bowl. Sophie and Alice copied her, then stirred their mixtures with wooden spoons.

Rupert, Ethel, and Hugo watched them as if this were a cookery class. Which, in a way, it was.

Freddy was sitting in the armchair in his crumpled suit, his eyes closed. Clarissa moved her chair next to him, sat down, and rested her hand on his arm.

He opened his eyes briefly and covered Clarissa's hand with his.

Sophie focused on stirring, laboriously changing the mixture into a rough mass of dough. When were electric mixers invented?

Miss Kemble sprinkled flour over a wooden board and turned out her dough. Sophie and Alice did the same.

'Now we do it for those bowls.' Miss Kemble pointed to them all. 'We're doing extra today because tomorrow it's Sunday and New Year's Day. So, we're closed twice over.'

Sophie's arms were aching from stirring when the timer finally chimed. Reminded her of the bell on the lift.

The dough was put aside, and the mixing bowls cleaned and greased with lard. Then the dough went back into the bowls to rise.

'Broadcast time,' said Miss Kemble, washing her hands. She went over to the wireless.

Hiss. Crackle. *'This is the Shorten Volunteers. Following the fire at Shorten Manor, we can confirm that Miss Small's militia remains in residence. We send our deepest condolences to the family of Sir Richard Lacey, following his murder. Other reported missing persons are safe and well.'*

The firefighter must have reported to the Volunteers.

Lizzie switched off the wireless.

'Have you any paper and an envelope?' Alice asked her. 'I'd like to write to Mr Richards. Now the militia have the Manor, they've no reason to disrupt the post.'

Lizzie disappeared into the posh parlour and returned

with a writing pad, envelopes, and an old-fashioned fountain pen.

Alice completed her letter, addressed the envelope, and sealed it.

'The London post is unreliable.' Clarissa took the pad of paper and the pen. 'But if I write every day to my parents, one letter might get through.'

Once Clarissa had finished her letter, Sophie wrote to Maud and to Lucy. Sophie had mastered writing with an ink pen and no longer did splodges. She wrote the same message in both.

I hope all is well with you. We're all staying in the bakery. Any news you can commit to writing, send letters here. I'll write again soon.

'Such short letters,' said Miss Kemble. 'Hardly worth sending.'

'I can't think of anything else to say,' said Sophie, sealing the envelopes.

Under Miss Kemble's guidance, Alice and Sophie shaped the risen dough into loaves and set them on wide trays which were slid into the oven.

A loud knock came from the back door. 'Delivery,' said Lizzie.

Thick-set men marched in and deposited heavy sacks. Lizzie counted the sacks before signing for them. They half-filled the kitchen.

'I hate delivery day.' Miss Kemble dragged a sack towards a large open cupboard. 'Getting them upstairs is such a palaver.'

Sophie tried to pick up a sack. 'How on earth do you carry them upstairs?'

'Dumb waiter,' said Miss Kemble.

Lizzie climbed up the spiral staircase and Hugo helped Miss Kemble drag a sack into the cupboard. Miss Kemble pulled on a rope and the dumb waiter slowly winched up to the next floor.

The cupboard came down, empty thanks to Lizzie, and Miss Kemble put in another sack.

Rupert and Ethel took over, and eventually all the sacks, one at a time, were stashed away.

Lizzie came downstairs and opened the oven. The bread was golden brown, and she tapped a loaf with a spoon. 'Sounds hollow, so it's done.'

While Sophie and Alice laid the bread on racks to cool, Hugo sat on the floor, playing with Bella and Rose. He pointed at the animals in the picture book, saying their names.

'I'm afraid it will be more bread and jam for lunch, and for dinner.' Lizzie peered into the pantry. 'We've got two cans of plums, a jar of pickle, and three carrots.' She removed her apron. 'The butcher has sausages set aside, but that won't go far.' She grabbed her coat and yellow bobble hat from the rack by the door.

'I'll accompany you,' said Rupert, slipping on his coat.

Bella was content beside Hugo, so Sophie retrieved her ski jacket and went with them into the courtyard. They cut down the alley to the high street.

Only a few vans and cars were on the road, but the pavement was busy with shoppers. An orderly queue snaked out of a post office. Men collecting unemployment money.

'This is war-free,' said Sophie. 'Normal.'

'The militia's focus has been on the Manor,' said Rupert. 'That may change.'

Change... 'Hold on,' said Sophie, 'we've no money.'

'My credit is good,' said Rupert. 'Speaking of which...' He paused in front of a wide-fronted shop with a black sign: *Shorten Co-Operative Society Limited*. 'Let's enquire about some petty cash.'

Rupert strode in and approached the counter. 'Good morning. I need cash wired from Coutts in London. Can you arrange that?'

The clerk gaped at him. 'I'm not sure, your Grace.' After months of patrolling, Rupert was well known in the town. 'Give me a moment. I'll fetch the manager.'

The clerk returned with an older man. 'Your Grace, please bear with us,' said the manager. 'With the disruption to the telegraph and telephone lines, wiring money is taking up to a week.'

'I understand,' said Rupert. 'I'm staying at the bakery.'

The manager smiled. 'How much would you like to wire?'

'Five hundred pounds should do it.'

The young clerk gaped again.

'A pleasure, your Grace,' said the manager, smoothly. 'I'll send word as soon as it arrives.'

As they walked out of the bank, Sophie whispered to Lizzie, 'Is five hundred pounds a lot?'

'Would buy a fancy new van, with plenty left over.'

Right. Rupert's petty cash…

Lizzie stopped outside a butcher's shop. The window was open to the street and haunches of meat hung from racks. Sophie reluctantly followed her and Rupert inside. She hadn't been into a specialist butcher store since childhood.

Small animal cuts, neatly assembled on plates, were displayed inside. Behind the counter were a man and a woman wearing clean white aprons and square straw hats.

The male shopkeeper addressed Rupert. 'We were shocked to hear about Sir Richard, and please accept our condolences for Lady Georgina.'

Rupert nodded. 'Thank you.'

'That lad was a sly one,' said the woman. 'Didn't act any different when he took the van that morning. Had us all fooled.'

Peaky Blinder had come from this shop. For a moment, Sophie was back in the patrol car, frantically trying to stop Rupert bleeding out.

Rupert glanced at her. 'Mrs Harrington was with me on that unfortunate day.'

The shopkeepers seemed to notice Sophie for the first time, and the woman gave her a tentative smile.

'I've come to collect my sausages,' said Lizzie.

'Miss Brown,' called the woman. 'Mrs Slater's sausages.'

'I wish to purchase lamb, beef, and ham,' said Rupert, 'enough for ten people for a couple of days?'

'Nine people,' said Sophie. 'I don't eat meat.'

A young girl hurried from the rear of the shop and handed Lizzie a paper bag with her sausages.

'Would payment in ten days be satisfactory, including for Mrs Slater's purchase?' Rupert was deploying his prodigious charm, but his tone was authoritative.

'Of course, your Grace,' said the butcher, his face unreadable.

Was this arrangement normal, unusual — or outrageous?

'Please supply a credit note with the goods,' said Rupert. And with that he left, and Sophie and Lizzie trooped out behind him.

'Aren't you going to choose the meat?' said Sophie to Rupert. 'Take it to the bakery?'

'They'll deliver,' said Rupert. 'A duke shopping in person is one thing, hauling goods around in public … quite another.'

By the time they'd ordered provisions from a fishmonger, a greengrocer, and a vintner, Rupert had dazzled half the town.

CHAPTER 33

The following morning after breakfast, Rupert said to Clarissa, 'We can't impose on Mrs Slater much longer. The Old Bell Inn may have rooms. Would you accompany me to assess if it's suitable?'

'Is it far?'

'Fifteen minutes,' said Rupert, collecting his coat and Clarissa's.

Freddy went upstairs and, a few minutes later, he came down with his mother. Anne sat in the armchair, pale as a ghost.

Freddy joined Sophie at the table, and she yawned. She'd been up since six, baking with Miss Kemble. The bakery might be closed but bread was needed for Lizzie and all their guests. 'I found baking calming,' she said, squeezing Freddy's hand. 'Obviously, nothing really helps but worth trying.'

Freddy squeezed her hand back but didn't look at her. 'Just don't make me do embroidery.'

'I hate embroidery.' She yawned again.

'Sophie, you should go for a kip.' Hugo opened his lift puzzle notebook.

His mind was on the lift and going home. Unsurprising, given what they'd been through. Sophie retreated to the posh parlour.

She woke an hour later, feeling surprisingly normal, and came into the kitchen as Rupert and Clarissa returned.

'The hotel has enough rooms,' said Clarissa, 'but it wasn't very nice.'

'How do you mean?' said Sophie. Clarissa was accustomed to the best of everything, including hotels. The Old Bell was likely just basic.

'It was dusty,' said Clarissa.

'Any port in a storm,' said Rupert.

'I wish we could leave the town,' said Clarissa.

'You know we can't,' said Rupert. 'Apart from the road to the Manor, every route is mined.' He put on the kettle. 'After we adjourn to the inn, we should continue helping here. We can double production.'

Sophie gave him a respectful nod. He really was a most unusual duke.

That afternoon, Lizzie and Miss Kemble enjoyed some rare downtime, and everyone else set off to the Old Bell. Passersby stared at Sophie with Bella in her sling. Baby slings had yet to catch on.

Freddy put Jack on the lead, but when Sophie clipped on Charlotte's, she was rewarded with a weary look. 'For appearance's sake,' Sophie whispered as they walked through the courtyard.

Down the street, Ethel stopped by a closed dress shop. The gown on the mannequin was like Clarissa's dresses: a simpler shape and ankle length. The matching yellow beret was plain, save for a feather. Maybe the disruption of war had led to less fussy fashion?

'I love that hat,' said Ethel. 'So jaunty.'

The road was quiet, the post office shut. 'Do you think the government amnesty will turn the tide, undermine the militia?' Sophie said to Hugo. It had been announced at lunchtime on the wireless. Men who signed the Amnesty Declaration wouldn't be prosecuted for fighting with the militia.

'It might tip the balance in our favour, but the post office money might prolong the violence. Men could use the extra cash to buy guns.'

'You're gloomy today.'

Hugo shrugged and opened the inn door.

The Old Bell was older than the Georgian shops surrounding it. Half-timbered with diamond-leaded windows, its upstairs storey jutted out at the front, over-hanging the entrance.

The foyer was tired but clean, and the owner raised an eyebrow when she saw Charlotte and Jack. But she welcomed them, taking their coats.

As the woman disappeared into a cloakroom, Clarissa said, 'They must have dusted when they realised a duke was staying.' She didn't bother lowering her voice.

Freddy frowned at her. He'd always disapproved of unnecessary rudeness. Hopefully, his impeccable manners would rub off on Clarissa.

That night, they had the Old Bell dining room to themselves. The meal was meat-heavy, so Sophie ate mashed potato and cabbage and fed her daughter the same. Bella sat on Sophie's lap, as the inn had no highchair.

Only three drinks were available: beer, brandy, and water. Anne drank barely anything, left most of her food, and an air of melancholy settled.

'We may be here for some time,' said Rupert. 'We should join the Volunteers.'

Freddy and Hugo nodded.

'I'll stick to baking,' said Sophie. Richard's death and the library fire had drained her.

After dinner, up in their room, Hugo frowned. 'This bed will be a squeeze.'

'Cosy.' Sophie gave him a buck-up glance. She sat on the bed with Bella and the springs groaned. 'No chest of drawers. Bella can sleep well-wrapped up on the floor until Rupert's money comes through. Then I can buy a cot.'

Hugo folded his arms. 'There's no space for a cot.'

'Talk to me.'

'What about?'

'The lift,' said Sophie. 'You're worrying about it.'

'I've realised, I should be able to cross by myself.'

Sophie stared at him, surprised. 'How?'

'You order Janus to transport me safely to universe 666. Once Janus acknowledges the instruction, you wouldn't have to travel. Janus' core algorithm stops him physically harming me.'

'Okay … that could work in theory, but you wouldn't want to go home without me.' She hesitated. 'Would you?'

Hugo seemed uncomfortable. 'This war will end, Sophie, and when it does, I'll be in limbo. This version of me has only one life and I'd like to seize it. Have a regular life at home, a career.' He paused. 'Start a family.'

'We could have babies here.'

'Expose them to potentially fatal diseases? No.'

Point taken. She looked down at her feet. It would be years before the way to the lift was de-mined. Luckily. Might never have to choose between him and Bella. 'You need to stop thinking about home. It'll send you crazy.' She kissed him. 'I love you.'

He shot her a poignant smile before giving his *Star Wars* reply. 'I know.'

CHAPTER 34

The following day, after breakfast, they used Rupert's credit with the local shopkeepers to buy day-to-day items and get them delivered to the inn: night-clothes, dressing gowns, underwear, shaving stuff for the men, toothbrushes, and round tins of *EUCRYL* tooth powder. The stuff was chalky and gritty but better than nothing.

Before they cut down the alley to the bakery, Charlotte growled, and unease prickled between Sophie's shoulder blades. Someone was watching them.

Sophie turned and scrutinised the street. A woman was pushing a pram, and further down the pavement, a boy was peering at a shop window. Across the road was the usual queue of men by the post office. None of them familiar.

Later, when she walked to the inn for lunch and then returned to the bakery, the 'watching feeling' wasn't there, though she still felt uneasy.

In the early evening, when Hugo turned up at the inn tooled up from the Volunteers, she told him about the feeling. 'Any guns going spare?'

'They gave us each a shotgun and a rifle,' said Hugo. 'Have my shotgun.'

~

Just before dawn in their tiny inn bedroom, Charlotte leapt onto the bed and barked. Sophie and Hugo awoke with a start, and Bella woke up too. Jack crawled under the bed.

'Charlotte never barks at nothing.' Sophie snatched Bella up from the floor.

Hugo stood against the wall and cautiously looked out the window. 'Nothing—'

Gunfire and shouting erupted from outside.

'Stay away from the window,' Hugo gasped.

Sophie didn't need telling. Neither did Charlotte. Too big to join Jack below the bed, she'd backed up against the inside wall. Another bang sent Sophie scurrying to join her. 'When do Rupert and Freddy finish?' They were on the Volunteer night shift.

'Not till seven,' said Hugo.

He scrambled into his clothes, and Sophie dearly wanted to bar the door, but Hugo wouldn't abandon Rupert and Freddy. 'Take my shotgun,' she said. 'The more guns and ammo the better.'

Hugo hesitated.

'I'm not running into a fight. Take it.'

Hugo hurried out carrying the rifle, the shotgun slung across his chest.

The sound of his running footsteps in the corridor faded and Sophie slid down the wall with Bella. The bangs and shouting from the road were louder.

It felt wrong cowering here. Useless, cowardly…

Charlotte shrank against her, and Bella did her nervous

snorting. Sophie held them closer. Get a grip. She was needed here more than out there.

Right outside, someone was yelling over the noise of gunfire. '... they went down that alley. *Go*.'

Sophie resisted the urge to peek out the window and pulled on her clothes. Whatever was happening, best not to face it in a nightdress. She slipped on her red jacket inside out, so only the dark lining was visible.

After changing Bella, Sophie put the fleecy babygro on her, and wriggled her into the sling.

Jack had to be coaxed out from under the bed. Sophie attached his lead and set off with Charlotte to find the other women. She had no idea which rooms they were in, would have to knock on doors.

She rounded a bend in the passage and was almost bowled over by Clarissa in a garish, flowered dressing gown.

'What's happening?' said Clarissa.

'I don't know.'

Anne was hurrying towards them in a navy dressing gown. 'We should all get dressed.' Sounded like her old self. Ready for action. Anne glanced at Clarissa. 'You and I can dress together.'

Shorten dresses did up at the back, needed someone else to fasten the buttons.

'Ethel and Alice are in room four,' said Anne. 'We should meet up in the dining room.'

Sophie knocked on the sisters' door, and Ethel opened it, her eyes worried. Their room looked over the inn's garden, so the gunfire was fainter. 'You need to come downstairs,' said Sophie. 'Get dressed, quickly.'

Down in the dining room, the gunfire was much louder.

'I'll lock the front door.' Mrs Gregory, the inn owner, hurried off.

A single shot rang out from the hall and Mrs Gregory

stumbled into the dining room. Behind her were two men waving shotguns and another, taller man. Familiar.

The man who'd shot Richard.

Hayden met Sophie's eyes and smiled.

Sophie backed away, then stopped. She gave Jack's lead to Mrs Gregory, frantically unclipped Bella from her sling and thrust her into Mrs Gregory's arms. 'Go upstairs,' Sophie hissed. 'Charlotte, you go too.'

Charlotte hesitated.

'Nobody move.' Hayden released the safety catch on his shotgun. 'Time for justice.' He made a sweeping gesture with his gun. 'I'm sending a message today. Righting a terrible wrong.'

Was he going to kill them all? 'The amnesty doesn't cover murdering civilians,' said Sophie, struggling to keep her voice even.

'You, Mrs Harrington, are not a civilian.'

Hayden's mates sniggered.

'You act like a man,' said Hayden. 'Let's see if you die like one.'

'Mrs Gregory *is* a civilian,' shouted Sophie, hoping Anne and Clarissa and the Armstrong sisters would hear and stay upstairs. 'Please let them go.'

'I love the pleading,' said Hayden. 'Reminds me of that woman after the ambush.' His mates sniggered again.

He was the man who'd attacked Lucy—

Bang. Hayden fell backwards. A second bang and one of his companions crashed to the floor.

Bella wailed, her cries joining fading gunfire echoing around Sophie's head.

Charlotte looked towards the stairs. Ethel and Alice were there, still in their dressing gowns. They were holding shotguns.

Clarissa pushed past the sisters and raised a rifle at the last man. 'Get out or you're dead too.'

The man hesitated but then stepped over Hayden's body and ran.

Sophie blinked at the dressing-gowned posse. 'You can shoot?'

'We've had years to practise,' said Alice, making her gun safe and laying it down.

'It's not something we talk about.' Ethel set aside her weapon. 'We don't want to undermine the men.'

Mrs Gregory handed Bella to Sophie, and Sophie rocked her daughter until she calmed.

'I'll get dressed and make tea.' Mrs Gregory retreated to the kitchen at the rear of the dining room.

'We have to do something about them.' Clarissa glanced at the men sprawled by the doorway to the hall.

Anne knelt beside the bodies and felt for a pulse on their necks. 'They're both dead.' Her voice betrayed no emotion. Either the Shorten code had kicked in or she was in shock. 'Help me move them out of the way.'

They dragged them over to the fireplace.

'We must stop anyone else barging in,' said Clarissa. 'I'll wedge a chair against the front door.'

Half an hour later, everyone was dressed, and drinking tea in the dining room. Mrs Gregory had lit the fire. There was no noise from the road and a clock on the wall tick-tocked, time slowing to the rhythm. Tick-tock...

Sophie finished her tea, shock receding, replaced by worry. Hugo, please be safe. And Freddy. And Rupert.

Tick-tock.

'I hate this waiting,' said Ethel. 'Perhaps we should go out—'

A hammering on the front door and Sophie stood up in alarm.

'It's us,' shouted Freddy's voice.

Sophie rushed to the hall, the other women following. She removed the chair and opened the door.

Freddy, Hugo, and Rupert came in, and Sophie felt faint with relief.

'Just five or six of them,' said Hugo, closing the door. 'Not a full-blown attack.'

The noise had been terrifying. What would a big attack sound like?

'Will they try again?' asked Sophie, as they walked into the dining room.

'They'll want to assess what happened, change tactics.' Freddy noticed the bodies by the fireplace. He strode over and peered at their faces. 'The man who murdered my father...'

'They came for me,' said Sophie.

Rupert looked wildly around. 'Who killed them? A Volunteer?'

'You gave me a gun.' Ethel pointed at the weapons stacked by the staircase. 'Who do you think?'

'Not bad for a civilian,' said Sophie.

'You're all ... formidable,' said Freddy.

'I shouldn't have taken the shotgun,' said Hugo, addressing Sophie, his mouth compressing into a rueful line.

'No, you shouldn't.' Anne laughed hysterically. 'Yes, you are all formidable. Brave and determined and *wonderful*.' And for the first time since Richard's death, she cried.

Shortly after the militia raid on the town, Betty woke up in the pub to the chink of crockery beside her bed. Roy made her tea every morning. She could get used to this.

Betty sat up, arranging pillows behind her back, and Roy planted a kiss on her forehead.

He knelt by the bed and Betty blinked. Was he praying?

'Will you marry me?'

Betty couldn't have been more surprised if he had been praying. 'Do you mean it?'

Roy smiled. 'Of course, I do.'

He was kind. An easy decision. 'I'd love to be Mrs Ducker.'

Roy stood up. 'I haven't a ring, but I'll have enough to buy one soon.'

Betty flourished her left hand, showing him the curtain ring. 'I don't need a new one. Let's save the money for something practical.'

Roy looked thoughtful. 'We should serve meals.'

'Meals?' Betty frowned. 'Start a restaurant?'

'No, simple nosh. Fish and chips. With the post office money, people might pay for that.'

Betty bit her lip. 'Alan wouldn't have served food.'

'Well, he's not here, is he?'

After breakfast, Roy switched on the wireless and sat with Betty and Frank by the fire.

'*This is the British People's Alliance. Local news. The militia tested Shorten town's defences in the early hours and found them wanting. We'll be taking the town very soon. In the meantime, join up. Enjoy a weekly wage and free board and lodging. The militia needs men like you!*'

'Why are they still recruiting?' said Betty. 'They've won, got the Manor.'

'What's left of it.'

'*In other news, the lucky Laceys and their guests are staying in the Old Bell Inn…*'

Betty switched it off, glad Freddy Lacey wasn't dead, but preferring quiet. She reached for her magazine. Elizabeth Bowes-Lyon graced the front cover. She'd married into the royal family and was pictured under her official title: the Duchess of York. She had a daughter, also called Elizabeth, a few years younger than Frank.

The duchess's dress had a fashionable fur collar and her pretty hat was fitted closely to her head, framing her face. Betty turned the magazine towards Roy. 'Lovely hat,' she said.

'It would look nicer on you.'

Someone banged on the pub door, and Betty sighed. Ten minutes before opening time.

'We're closed,' shouted Roy. 'Come back at twelve.'

'Open up.'

'It's Taffy.' Roy unlocked the door and militiamen filed in.

'I know you won't welcome this, but we're requisitioning the pub,' said Taffy. 'Won't be for long.'

'Where's Miss Small?' said Roy.

'We've had a falling out,' said a militiaman. 'We're here to make a point.'

They all made themselves at home, half filling the pub. 'Beers please,' said Taffy.

Roy joined Betty behind the bar and Taffy addressed a regular who'd appeared in the doorway. 'Don't mind us.'

But old Mr Clarke didn't venture in, walked off.

'What's happened?' asked Roy. 'We've always argued the toss. What's different now?'

'Saint Joan wrote to the town mayor and his reply got her all riled up,' said Taffy. 'She wants to teach him a lesson.' He took a swig of beer. 'I told her, shell the town hall at night as we agreed. They'll still surrender.' He stared into his drink. 'But she says he's insulted her and the whole Irish nation.'

'Doesn't sound like Saint Joan,' said Roy.

Betty gave out the last beer. No, that didn't sound like her.

'She says shelling a deserted building isn't enough,' said Taffy. 'Wants to show him she means business. And if folk die, so be it.'

Betty sat down on a spare chair. Dear heaven.

'I've family in the town,' said Taffy.

'So have I,' said another man.

'What does Mr Morley think?' said Betty.

'He agrees with Saint Joan,' said Taffy. 'Recruitment's down, so the sooner the town surrenders, the better.'

'Why not shell the empty town hall and see what happens?' said Roy. 'A few days won't make any difference.'

'I told her that,' said Taffy, 'but she won't budge.'

CHAPTER 36

In the inn, still wired from battling the militia, Hugo, Freddy, and Rupert attacked their breakfasts. Sophie fed the dogs sausages and mashed up a boiled egg for Bella.

'The Volunteers are collecting bodies for burial,' said Hugo. 'I'll ask them to collect Hayden and the other man.'

'Let's talk about something else, something inconsequential.' Ethel shot a sidelong glance at Rupert.

'You can't play the ladylike card anymore,' said Rupert, a glint in his eye. 'Not after that terrifying demonstration of your talents.'

'Indulge me,' said Ethel.

'The petty cash should come through soon,' said Rupert. 'What about a new hat?'

Ethel looked shocked. 'You can't buy it for me. That would be … unseemly.'

Rupert laughed, so loudly that Mrs Gregory almost dropped her crockery tray.

Sophie hadn't seen Rupert laughing since his mother's death. The atmosphere lightened.

After breakfast, they all ventured out onto the high street. A beer van was parked up by the inn, a young lad rolling a barrel towards the basement steps, and Bella twisted in her sling towards the noise.

Sophie checked up and down the street. Delivery vans were on the road, the shops were open, and people were out shopping. Seemed normal, except that along the pavement was a body covered with a white sheet. 'You'd think everybody would stay at home.'

'We're not hiding away in the inn, are we?' said Rupert.

'And the militia's gone, at least for now,' said Sophie, patting Charlotte.

Hugo fastened the top button of his brown coat. 'And people need to work.' He kissed Sophie on the mouth, a lingering, tender kiss, then headed off to his Volunteer-shift. The urge to call him back, to keep him safe, was intense, but she held her tongue.

Rupert and Freddy strode into the bank, and Sophie walked on with the other women. The post office queue was longer today, the end of the line lost to sight. An enterprising café owner was selling the men hot drinks.

Freddy and Rupert caught them up as they reached the bakery.

Lizzie hurried them inside. 'The militia attack sounded horrific. Is everyone all right?'

'Unscathed,' said Rupert, hanging up his coat and sitting at the table. He waved an official-looking flyer. 'The mayor's holding a public meeting.'

'What about?' asked Sophie.

'Doesn't say,' said Rupert. 'Just an *Important Announcement*.'

Rose was racing tiny cars around the rug, and Sophie put her daughter beside her, opened the toy box, and found more cars.

Bella assessed her collection, then swiped all of Rose's cars onto her own pile. When Rose tried to rescue them, Bella pushed her over. Lizzie's daughter fell in a heap, too surprised to cry out.

Sophie rushed to sit Rose up again and wagged her finger at Bella. 'No.' Sophie returned Rose's cars to her and, slowly, so Bella got the point, allotted one of Bella's cars to Rose. 'Every time you steal her toys, you'll lose one of yours.'

Bella made a face, reminding Sophie of Freddy, and Sophie made a face too. Rug World was small, but it mattered. And in Rug World, Mummy's rules prevailed.

'Our tax is paid, but there'll be another bill to pay next year.' Freddy glanced at Rupert, then down at the table.

Right. Rupert had paid the Laceys' tax bill.

'With the Manor in ruins, despite the risk of mines, we must emigrate,' said Freddy.

'I fear so,' Anne said.

Sophie stood up from the toy cars, her mind filled with Hugo. If it was hard for him to reach the lift now, it would be close to impossible from the US. He'd need to cross the Atlantic by ship, would have to travel to Shorten on the train. But by then, the militia might control the railway. Would he emigrate, or stay here, near the lift?

The back door banged open, and Harry Richards came in, wearing a formal coat and a cloth cap. He removed the cap and smoothed his red hair. 'Good morning.'

Alice rushed up to him and cried into his chest, and Harry embraced her, embarrassed. Alice wiped her eyes.

'I knew the militia were attacking last night,' said Harry, 'but I couldn't find a way to warn you. Then another baby arrived, a breech.' He frowned. 'Where's Hugo?'

'He's okay,' said Sophie. 'Doing a Volunteer-shift.'

Lizzie took Harry's coat and cap.

'The town's hardly any distance by car but it's a hearty

walk on foot. I'm quite done in.' Harry sat in the armchair. 'I heard on the broadcast that you're all living in an inn. I should secure lodging there.'

'The Old Bell's full,' said Rupert.

'We have to share a room.' Freddy gave Rupert a pained look.

'You must stay here,' said Lizzie. 'We have a spare room upstairs.'

Harry smiled at her and accepted a cup of tea. 'It's perfectly horrid at the Manor. Miss Small and Miss James are parading around the hospital wing as if they own the place.'

Freddy's lips tightened.

'I'll return to the Manor if I'm needed but meanwhile, I intend to make myself useful at the town hospital,' said Harry. 'Miss Small has obtained more shells. If the mayor here doesn't surrender, she'll target the town.'

Rupert picked up the flyer from the table. 'That's what the public meeting's about.'

The town hall was Victorian and Empire-huge, but by six that evening, the assembly room was packed. Scruffy errand boys and tired shopkeepers rubbed shoulders with prosperous housewives and neatly turned-out maids.

Unable to get further in, Rupert and Freddy stood just inside the main door, and made space for Sophie, the Armstrong sisters, Lizzie, and Miss Kemble. Hugo was still on his Volunteer-shift, and Anne and Clarissa had stayed in the inn to mind the babies and dogs. Harry had gone to the hospital.

At the far end of the assembly room, seated on an elevated stage, stern men in loose grey suits surveyed the townsfolk. One stood up and cleared his throat. He had grey, whiskery hair and sunken blue eyes, and his creased three-piece suit stretched across his stomach. 'Good evening.' The mayor's raised voice silenced the restless crowd. 'I've called this meeting because I have received letters from Miss Small at the Manor.' He said, 'Miss Small' with a contemptuous hiss. 'In her first letter, she threatened to shell the town.'

An alarmed babble rose up.

'Do not concern yourselves,' said the mayor. 'Miss Small will have received my reply this morning. I informed her that as a woman, even an *Irish* woman, she won't use her artillery to shell the town. And I also told her, in no uncertain terms, that we will not surrender.'

'You should have called the meeting before,' shouted a man near the front. 'That decision's ours to make, not yours.'

More angry shouting came from the crowd.

'I used my executive powers,' said the mayor, cutting through the hubbub. 'When Miss Small replies, I will display her letter here.'

Freddy paled. 'The lady's reply won't be a letter.'

'Dear God,' said Rupert. 'What a stupid man.'

Sophie's stomach dropped. How many shells did Miss Small have? Could she flatten the town?

'Please remain calm,' said the mayor. 'It's a ruse on Miss Small's part, to avoid fighting for every street. You can rest assured that our Volunteers remain vigilant.'

'Does the bakery have a basement?' Rupert asked Lizzie.

'No.'

'Join us at the inn,' said Rupert.

'What about the first bake tomorrow?' said Miss Kemble.

'It'll have to be later,' said Lizzie. 'I'll put a note on the door.'

The crowd's heckling was now drowning out the mayor.

'We should go,' said Sophie.

'Miss Small won't shell the inn or the bakery,' said Ethel, as they hurried outside. 'They're not military targets.'

'She authorised the mine in the lane,' said Freddy, 'knew it could kill Bella.'

Sophie glanced back at the town hall. 'If the mayor's final letter was as crass as his speech, Miss Small might target him.'

~

That night, after everyone else had retired to the basement, Sophie waited up for Hugo to return from his shift. When he finally came into the inn, it was well past eleven.

'The next guy was late,' he said, closing and locking the door behind him. 'Nothing's happening.' He shrugged off his brown coat.

Sophie told him about the meeting and the mayor.

'What an idiot. How did he get elected?'

'According to Lizzie, the all-male voters liked his rousing speeches,' said Sophie. 'We're all sleeping in the basement.'

'I was so looking forward to snuggling with you.'

'Hopefully, it'll only be a couple of nights.' Sophie kissed him. 'Harry's here.'

'Alice must be glad.'

'Now most of the house is gone, Anne and Freddy are set on emigrating.'

Hugo's mouth twisted. 'Right.'

'There might be a way you can come with me to America and, if you still want to, directly call the lift to go home.' She drew a calming breath.

'I'm listening.'

'We know the lift lands in different geographical locations here.' For centuries, the landing spot had been in the cellar of The Crooked Gate, not the lane. 'If somewhere in

Virginia, there's a weak spot or tear in this universe, I can call the lift from there.'

'You're clutching at straws. Weak spots or tears are rare. And even if there was a landing spot in Virginia, or somewhere else in the States, how would you find it?' He turned away from her and strode off to the basement.

CHAPTER 37

At dawn the next morning, Sophie's first waking thought was of Hugo striding towards the basement without her. The hollow, lonely sensation from last night was stronger. She waited for it to fade. But it didn't.

She'd slept beside him, but he'd given no sign he'd noticed. He was disconnecting from her, and there was nothing she could do.

Leaving Hugo and the others sleeping on blankets and pillows on the floor, she made her way with Clarissa out of the inn. Despite sleeping in her day clothes and stinking of beer from barrels stored in the basement, Clarissa looked neat and elegant in her formal coat. Sophie, in her ski gear, felt like a smelly scruffbag.

'I suppose we haven't time to bathe and change?' said Clarissa.

Sophie yawned. 'The first batch will be late as it is.'

They scurried along the cold deserted high street and were glad to reach the bakery.

'Hopefully, the beer smell won't taint the flavour of the bread,' said Sophie, as she unlocked the door.

Clarissa measured out ingredients into mixing bowls. 'If my parents don't reply to my letters by tomorrow, I'll go into the bank and use their telephone.'

'Would the bank manager let you?'

'He allowed Rupert that courtesy.' Clarissa filled more bowls. 'I would like your advice.'

What advice could Clarissa possibly need from her?

'A delicate, private matter.'

Sophie frowned as she made her first dough. She was hardly an expert in Shorten etiquette.

'It concerns Freddy, and you know him well,' said Clarissa.

Sophie nodded, still stirring.

'I wrote to Papa to ask if he could purchase a property in America, for Freddy.'

Sophie stopped stirring.

'In New York.'

Lord Maine had deep pockets. 'Freddy must be over the moon.'

'I haven't told him.'

'Okay…'

'Freddy talks about making his fortune in America,' said Clarissa, 'but they're silly, harebrained schemes.'

'It would be good if your father can help him.'

Clarissa bit her lip. 'I need to be sure he's marrying me because he loves me. *Not* because Papa could assist us.'

'But hasn't Freddy already proposed?' Sophie assumed he had, or at least spelled out that he would soon.

'No.'

'He's proud,' said Sophie. 'And with the Manor in ruins, he can't offer you a secure home — or anything.'

Clarissa doubled down on the stirring.

'Hey, go slower, or you'll have to start again.'

Clarissa stepped away from the bowl.

'Tell Freddy, you don't care about him making money in America, that you just want to be with him. And if he doesn't get the hint, *you* should propose.'

Clarissa looked horrified. 'I couldn't possibly!'

'Be bold. You'll know in an instant from his reaction that he wants to marry you.'

'Too humiliating…'

'Only if he says no.' Sophie finished her mixing. 'Yes, he'll be surprised, but not as much as you might think. He was impressed with your gun skills.'

Clarissa smiled weakly. 'You seem very certain. Has he confided in you? Said how he feels about me?'

'Before we left the Manor, he told me flat out he was serious.'

Clarissa's face cleared.

'New York's an exciting, vibrant place.' Sophie pictured a town house and elegant soirees. 'Faint heart never won fair Freddy—'

Boom.

Clarissa glanced at Sophie in alarm and Sophie's heart lurched.

'Should we stay put?' said Clarissa.

Another boom, even louder.

Sophie dashed down the corridor. Please let it not be the inn. She opened the front door.

A few delivery vans were on the road and the shops were still closed, as you'd expect. But in the distance, low in the sky, was a fiery, red glow.

Clarissa stood beside her. 'That's the edge of town, towards Derby.'

'Sounded way closer.' Sophie shuddered. Back in the kitchen, she switched on the wireless. Static.

'We should finish the baking,' said Clarissa.

~

Long before eleven o'clock, the opening time Lizzie had pinned on the door, a restless queue formed outside the bakery.

'Thank goodness we're ready.' Clarissa slipped on her coat and went to the front door.

Sophie put on her jacket, heaved the last box of loaves along the passage, and sat beside Clarissa.

The first customer thrust a shilling into Clarissa's hand, grabbed the bread from Sophie, and hurried away.

The red glow in the sky was still there, and across the street, people were hurrying towards it, some carrying gardening shovels, others pushing wheelbarrows.

'What's going on?' asked Sophie, as she handed over another loaf.

'The militia's blown up the filling factory.' The customer scurried off.

What was a filling factory?

'There's hundreds that work there,' said a skinny woman, taking her bread. 'I can't bear to think about it.'

A young boy dropped his shilling in the box. 'It'll be us next.'

'If the mayor doesn't resign, he'll be lynched,' said a woman behind him.

At home, photos of a destroyed factory would have been on Sophie's phone in minutes. Here, she could only imagine it. Difficult to know which was worse.

After the last loaf was sold, and the door closed, Sophie said to Clarissa, 'What's a filling factory?'

'Makes munitions for the government, for the army.' Clarissa walked with her to the kitchen. 'Cartridges, screening smokes…'

'Screening smokes?'

'A device so soldiers can move across open ground without being seen.'

'You're well up on this stuff.'

'Everyone is,' said Clarissa. 'Believe me, I'd much rather concern myself with fashion and parties.' She wiped down the table and Sophie turned on the wireless.

Crackle. '*Ninety-two women are missing, ten confirmed dead...*' Hiss.

Sophie's stomach dropped and she switched it off. 'All the workers in the factory are women?'

'Women make the tools of war. Men use them.'

'Government slogan?'

'It's what Papa says.'

Lord Maine had a way with words. 'We should call by the inn,' said Sophie, 'then go to the factory to help.'

They grabbed their coats and hurried to the inn.

Everyone was in the dining room, but no one was talking. The only noise came from a crackling fire in the grate and Bella, sitting by Freddy on the floor, hitting her picture book with her fist.

Hugo stood up, and Charlotte leaned into Sophie's legs.

'We've saved you some breakfast,' said Freddy. 'Mrs Gregory's gone to the factory.'

'Will you go?' asked Alice.

'Yes.' Clarissa sat down beside her.

'We're committed to the next baking batch,' said Ethel, glancing at Alice.

'And I start my Volunteer-shift in ten minutes,' said Rupert.

Anne addressed Sophie. 'I'll mind Bella and the dogs.'

'Thank you, but I'll take Charlotte to sniff out survivors.'

Charlotte blinked her agreement. Good. Less noticeable than her nod.

Sophie ate a slice of cold toast, a hard-boiled egg, and downed a cup of tepid tea.

'Mrs Gregory's sister works at the filling factory.' Anne seemed composed, but her inscrutable expression made it hard to tell.

Sophie hugged her and kissed Bella on the brow. 'I'm glad you're too young to understand,' she said to Bella, then stroked Charlotte, wishing Charlotte didn't understand either. She'd lost some of her determined optimism. Enhanced DNA had a downside.

Hugo, Freddy, Sophie, and Clarissa joined the sea of people heading towards the red glow, but now some were returning. Many were in tears, others stony faced.

'It's no use,' shouted an older woman as she stumbled past them.

What did she mean?

Before they reached the factory, a wave of heat hit them, warming their faces, and when they saw what the glow was, they paused in shock.

Charlotte couldn't sniff for survivors or even bodies. What had been a building the size of a football field was ablaze. Two fire engines were pouring out water, but the fire was too big. Would burn for days.

Skeletal stumps of trees that had been caught in the destruction looked like something out of World War One. Smaller blasts were still erupting across the site, and black smoke was billowing into the sky, reeking of rotten eggs.

A woman was on her knees in front of them. Mrs Gregory. Sophie knelt too and put her arms around her.

'Jane's in there,' sobbed Mrs Gregory.

Hugo helped the inn owner to her feet. 'Come away.'

As they guided Mrs Gregory to the inn, Sophie could still feel the searing heat from the factory on her face.

Anne was sitting in the inn foyer, Bella on her lap.

'Let's go to your room,' said Clarissa, leading Mrs Gregory upstairs.

Sophie shook her head at Anne and walked Bella through to the dining room. Freddy disappeared off to the basement and returned with a bottle of brandy. He took a clean water glass from a table and set off upstairs.

Sophie left Bella with Anne and went with Hugo into the kitchen. The breakfast dishes had been cleaned and were drying on racks.

She put the kettle on the stove. Anne must have washed up. Likely she hadn't done that since she came through the lift.

Hugo opened a cupboard.

'That egg smell at the factory was bad.'

'Stuff that goes into shells.' He set out crockery on a tray and sighed. 'I wish we hadn't come back.'

Regret swept over her, and she hugged him. 'All we can do is keep going.'

They returned to the dining room and poured tea. Clarissa stoked the fire. Jack was dozing by the grate and Charlotte was lying near him, wide awake.

Freddy added a drop of brandy to the tea.

'There's a photograph of Mrs Gregory and her sister in the small parlour off the kitchen.' Anne was near to tears.

'Miss Small must have known the factory workers were women,' said Sophie.

'Of course she did.' Anne frowned into her cup. 'Targeted to provoke maximum outrage, discredit the mayor, and force the town to surrender.'

Betty Hill was alone with her son in The Crooked Gate. After the broadcast about the filling factory, Roy had gone there. So had Taffy and the rest. She added coal to the fire and picked up a crayon Frank had dropped. She normally relished the quiet, but this morning's silence was suffocating.

She'd lasted a day in the filling factory in Derby. For twelve hours, she'd worn gloves and a mask and poured toxic liquid into shells half as tall as her. The eggy smell had made her clothes stink and no amount of washing could shift it.

Just one of those shells exploding would have been a death sentence.

The inn door opened and Roy marched in. 'Only two survivors so far, and they're in a bad way.' He hung his coat and hat on the rack. 'Taffy's joined the Volunteers, so have his mates.'

'They've changed sides because of the factory?'

'And what's happened in London.' He snatched her *Vogue* magazine from the armchair and turned to the front cover. 'The Duchess of York is dead. Shot through the head.'

'*No.*'

'Happened yesterday. This picture's all over the papers.'

'Who shot her? I mean, why?'

'The London militia. They didn't mean to kill her.'

'Oh, it was an accident?'

'No,' said Roy, grimacing. 'They meant to shoot the king.'

The morning after the factory was shelled, Roy went to the town and didn't return to the pub till the afternoon.

'I was starting to worry,' said Betty.

'The post office queue was very long.' Roy handed her four black armbands. 'You should sew these onto our coat sleeves.'

'For the duchess?'

He looked solemn. 'And the factory girls.'

'Where's your shotgun?'

'I gave it in.'

Betty stared at him. 'Why on earth did you do that?'

Roy pulled a flyer from his trouser pocket. 'These are everywhere.'

She took it. A stern soldier was pointing out with his finger. *Your country needs YOU.*

Betty scanned the lines of smaller text. *Leave the militia by the last day of January and claim a double unemployment payment! Secure immunity from prosecution: hand in your weapons and sign the Declaration. Don't delay!*

Roy sat down wearily by the fire.

'You signed this … Declaration?' Betty sat opposite him, the leaflet still in her hand.

'We need the money.'

'You should have waited. We should have talked about it.'

'Volunteers marched me to the post office. I put the gun

in a box and that was that,' said Roy. 'Anyway, we've got yours.'

'And I'm keeping it,' said Betty.

'If I handed it in, there'd be more cash.'

'They wouldn't give you the money again.'

'You're probably right.' Roy sighed. 'Pity you can't sign the Declaration.'

'Why can't I?'

'Only men can sign.'

'Where does it say that?' Betty peered at the leaflet.

'Just how it is.' Roy shrugged. 'I'll go back next week for the normal payment.'

'You shouldn't.' He was fully employed, working in the pub. 'They'll start checking.'

'Get a brew on.'

Betty made tea, then sat beside the fire. Frank lay on the floor beside them with his book, though he'd coloured in all the scenes.

'I reckon half the Manor militia have signed the Declaration.' Roy bent down and ruffled Frank's hair.

Would her brother have taken to Roy, or resented him? Roy's relaxed approach to life was so different from Will's. Her brother had been a worrier. Like her.

Roy gave her an affectionate smile. 'Cheer up, Mrs Hill. You'll be Mrs Ducker soon.'

A week after Roy signed the Declaration, a sharp morning breeze blew into the pub as the front door opened and shut.

'Mr Morley,' said Betty. 'This is a nice surprise.'

He doffed his cap. 'Good day to you, Mrs Hill. Mr Ducker.'

Roy stood up. 'Would you like a cup of tea?'

'Thank you, but I mustn't tarry.' Mr Morley looked serious. 'We fought valiantly, sacrificed many worthy souls, but change is in the air.' He paused. 'I just popped by to tell you I've left the militia. And contrary to superstition, this Friday 13th might be auspicious.'

'If you say so,' said Betty.

'Is it true Saint Joan's done a runner?' Roy asked him.

'Discretion was the better part of valour,' said Mr Morley. 'Irish citizens aren't covered by the amnesty.'

'What will you do now?' said Betty.

'From each according to his ability, to each according to his needs.'

Betty frowned. She'd heard the slogan. Forgotten what it meant.

'Writing is a higher calling. I'll contribute regular articles to *Workers Weekly* and I have plans for a novel.' He put on his cap. 'Let us beat our swords into ploughshares.' He left, closing the door behind him.

'He's changed his tune.' Roy sat down and read his newspaper. On the *Daily Herald*'s front page was a photograph of the duchess's funeral in London. Roy did a low whistle. 'A million people turned out. A million.'

'You were right about the glue,' said Betty.

'Glue?'

'The royal family uniting the country.'

'The militias are finished, men leaving in droves.' Roy read the next page of the paper. 'The post office is taking on more staff.'

The pub door creaked open and old Mr Clarke walked in.

'We're thinking of doing lunches. Fish and chips.' Betty smiled at him.

'What a lovely idea.' Mr Clarke smiled back, his grey moustache twitching. 'When are you starting?'

CHAPTER 39

The same morning that Mr Morley cut his ties with the militia, Freddy was reluctantly accompanying Clarissa on a walk.

'It's too cold for walking,' said Freddy, missing his fur hat. He had no credit to buy another.

'Only as far as the road.' The path behind the bakery wound through tired-looking scrubland.

'These two weeks have been so difficult,' said Freddy, 'I haven't had to think about it. But now I can't stop.'

'Thinking about what?'

'Returning to the Manor before we emigrate. In her letter, Mrs Rawlings said the surviving wing is habitable, but it sounds ghastly.'

'Freddy?'

'Yes.' He turned towards her.

'Will you marry me?'

Freddy blinked. Had he misheard?

'I'm proposing to you,' said Clarissa. 'If you don't wish to marry me, please say so and I'll depart for London forthwith. By all accounts, London's safer.' Her bottom lip trembled.

'Um.' She'd floored him… 'Of course, I'd love to marry you.' Freddy kissed her, a slow, lingering kiss. 'But we can't become engaged…' The ring Sophie had returned to him was somewhere in the ruins of the Manor. 'I'll purchase an engagement ring in America.'

'The ring can wait,' said Clarissa, 'but I'd like you to announce our engagement.'

Freddy kissed her again. 'I will announce it. This very day.' He squared his shoulders. 'And I'll turn my mind to the United States. Rupert has suggested I carry out speaking tours. Apparently, they're all the rage.'

'What's a speaking tour?'

'Americans pay to hear someone speaking, telling them about … something.'

Clarissa looked sceptical.

'Let's announce our engagement.' Freddy turned on his heel.

But Clarissa held his arm. 'Before we do, stop thinking about America.'

'I must.'

'We don't need to emigrate. I spoke to my father on the bank's telephone yesterday, and he had a much better idea.'

'What sort of idea?'

'He'll pay your ruinous taxes as long as necessary.'

Freddy's stomach dropped. 'I won't be in debt to Lord Maine. I'm already in hock to Rupert.'

'You won't be in debt to Lord Maine,' said Clarissa. 'It will be your father-in-law assisting us to set up our home. It's entirely different.'

Freddy sighed. 'Can I have time to consider?'

'If this is your pride … no.' She put her arm through his. 'And he wants to fund the rebuilding of the Manor.'

Freddy gasped. 'All of it?'

'Yes.'

'Goodness.' That would cost a fortune.

'Two years ago, when I expected to marry Hugo, Papa bought me a house in Eaton Square. We can live in London on and off until the Manor's finished.'

'I give in,' said Freddy. And it felt glorious. No need to tell anyone about the unusual manner of the proposal.

They walked to the bakery, arm-in-arm.

Sophie was at the back door, and she was grinning.

'You knew,' said Freddy.

Sophie's grin widened. 'Might have done!'

In the kitchen, Freddy grinned too. Miss Kemble and Lizzie were out but everyone else was there. 'I have news.'

CHAPTER 40

The following morning, four of the Laceys' patrol vehicles rattled along the road towards the Shorten estate. Sophie, Bella, and Hugo were in the back of the second car.

Hugo pulled up his jacket collar against the wind. 'I've been thinking about the Duchess of York.'

'It's good that such a horrible crime cost the militia the war,' said Sophie.

'I think it may lose Britain another war.'

She squinted at him. 'You've lost me.'

'Elizabeth Bowes-Lyon in our universe became queen when her husband became King George VI.'

Sophie knew this. 'And when he died, their daughter Elizabeth was crowned.' The future Elizabeth II here wasn't much older than Bella.

'At home, she played a small but positive role in World War Two.'

'Did she?' Sophie's history lessons at school had focused on the Nazis. Elizabeth Bowes-Lyon hadn't featured.

'She refused to flee to America during the Blitz, and when

the Luftwaffe targeted Buckingham Palace, she famously said, 'I'm glad we've been bombed. Now we can look the East End in the eye.'

Sophie nodded. The East End of London, the docklands, where military supplies came through, had suffered the worst in the Blitz. The district was also the poorest part of the city.

Hugo adjusted his ski hat over his ears. 'The queen's resolve bucked up the king, and their decision to stay contributed hugely to morale.'

Sophie held onto the half-height door as the vehicle swerved around a bend. 'So, without her, the royal family here might bail?'

'And if they do, that could have a tiny ripple effect that could grow, as in Chaos Theory.'

Sophie searched her memory. 'The effects of a butterfly beating its wings on one continent expand out, causing a massive storm on another.' She tightened her grip on the car door. 'Britain here could lose the war.'

'In infinite universes, the Nazis must win in some. Perhaps in many.'

Disturbing idea. 'But without World War One here, a second war might not happen.'

'Let's hope not.' Hugo looked straight ahead, a muscle tensing in his jaw. 'If Miss Small has abided by the agreement, before she left, she'll have handed over a map showing where the mines are. As soon as the lane's safe, I'll cross universes.'

His sense of urgency rang an alarm bell. 'Have you found out something new about the lift?'

Hugo shrugged. 'No.'

The convoy drove through the Manor's open metal gates and stopped on the drive. Beyond the moat, the blackened ruin of the house was stark and jagged against the pale winter sky. Sophie and Hugo climbed out of the car and stood in silence, lost for words.

Charlotte jumped from the first car and stared at the house. Freddy and Anne coaxed Jack out, and they all walked slowly forward, taking in the damage.

Freddy and Anne led the way across a makeshift wooden bridge that spanned the moat. The historic drawbridge hadn't survived.

What was left of the Manor was generically dark and scarred, but some shapes were identifiable: a coffee table, a floor lamp.

Jack pulled backwards on his lead and Freddy gently moved him forward. Charlotte was keeping close to Sophie, subdued, and Sophie fixed her gaze on the remaining gable, remembering the Manor as it was.

The butler and housekeeper were waiting outside the undamaged wing. Freddy shook hands with them.

'Mr Brown and Mr Gambon departed yesterday.' Mr Crawford's face was as hard to read as ever.

'That's a relief,' muttered Anne.

'Why didn't they leave earlier and claim amnesty?' asked Freddy.

'They were stubborn individuals,' said Mr Crawford. 'When they left, Mr Brown said he'd been worn down by surly, resentful servants. I'm unsure what he meant.'

'The militia were billeted upstairs,' said Mrs Rawlings, briskly, 'but the bedrooms are just about habitable.'

Everyone followed Mr Crawford and Mrs Rawlings into the surviving wing. A stable door had been hung up to protect the exposed corridor from the elements.

Sophie paused by the unflattering portrait of Elizabeth I. Uncannily unscathed. The monarch's staring eyes seemed to follow Sophie as she walked on. Maybe here, that woman would be the *only* Queen Elizabeth.

In the hospital bay, all the beds were stacked against a wall. The royal blue carpet was back on the floor, the fire was lit, and on the wide mantelpiece above the fireplace was a small wireless. Upright chairs had been arranged around a scarred, rectangular table. The room's antiseptic smell was gone, replaced by the faint whiff of furniture polish.

Anne sat at the table and glanced up at the butler and housekeeper. 'Thank you for this.'

Everybody joined Anne at the table, the scraping of chair legs muffled by the carpet. Bella looked about, curious. She hadn't been in here before.

Maids were in the kitchen area of the bay, making tea. As crockery was laid out, Mr Crawford handed Freddy a large brown envelope. 'From Miss Small.'

Inside were two Ordnance Survey maps. The first was of Shorten town and the surrounding area and was littered with dots drawn in black ink. The other map was of the Manor and the estate. Freddy tapped a black dot that marked the mine in the lane. 'This map stops a mile further on.'

'Indeed,' said Mr Crawford. 'No mines beyond that.'

Sophie's heart sank, Hugo's desire to leave flooding her mind. *This version of me has only one life and I'd like to seize it. Have a regular life at home, a career.* She resisted the urge to catch his eye. How long would he stay? A few days? A week?

'With the kitchens gone,' said Mrs Rawlings, 'meals have to be cooked in the servants' hall.'

'Please sit with us and take tea,' said Anne.

After a moment's hesitation, the senior servants joined them.

'Life is gradually returning to normal.' Freddy gave Clarissa a happy glance.

'We were very pleased to hear of your engagement,' said Mrs Rawlings.

Clarissa cleared her throat. 'My father was distressed

about the fire and will assist with rebuilding the Manor.' This, more sensitive, revelation hadn't been included in letters.

Mr Crawford and Mrs Rawlings competed with looks of polite surprise.

'Mama would like us to return to Armstrong Hall,' said Alice, 'but there's no rush.' She smiled at Harry.

Ethel nodded, her eyes on Rupert.

Charlotte, by Sophie's chair, had adopted her careful, 'I'm just a dog' expression.

'Can you show us where my father is buried?' said Freddy to the butler.

'I'm happy for everyone to accompany us,' said Anne, standing up.

It was a ten-minute walk to the graveyard inside the moat.

Richard's grave was next to Lady Georgina's. Nearby, another cross with A.P. on it, marked a new grave. Alan Parkes.

CHAPTER 41

$\mathcal{A}$ part of Sophie hadn't accepted Richard was dead, but seeing his grave made it real.

Charlotte bowed her head, and Jack stayed near Freddy, uncharacteristically still. Yes, he knew his old master was gone.

But Bella wriggled in her sling, restless. Soon, she'd start pointing at the graves and gurgling. Sophie slipped away.

As soon as they were out of sight of the graveyard, Bella settled, so instead of returning to the Manor, Sophie headed to the families' building.

Since the fire, she and Lucy had exchanged innocuous letters, Lucy summarising Tiana's gardening efforts, Sophie describing the town shops.

Tiana opened Lucy's door and clumsily hugged Sophie, careful not to squish Bella.

Lucy jumped up from the armchair. 'You're a sight for sore eyes.'

'Yay, no cast!'

'It's healed, but one leg's a bit shorter than the other,' said Lucy. 'I can live with a limp.'

Sophie kissed her on both cheeks. 'How are you feeling? You know, with…'

'Okay.' Lucy sat down and patted her flat stomach. 'Early days.'

Sophie took off the sling, put Bella on the floor, and straightened. 'The man who attacked you is dead.'

'Oh.' Lucy swallowed.

'He broke into the inn in the town,' said Sophie. 'Ethel shot him.'

Lucy exhaled. 'It's done with, then.'

'You don't seem surprised about Ethel,' said Sophie. 'I was gobsmacked.'

'I trained the Armstrong sisters and Clarissa a while ago. Discreetly.'

Tiana sat on the wooden chair. 'We're delaying telling Anne about the pregnancy. She must be in a terrible state.'

'She might welcome something else to think about,' said Sophie. 'Come on, Lucy, get practising. Talk to Bella.'

Lucy peered at the baby like she was an alien. 'Hello.'

Bella screwed up her face. 'Bah!'

'You need more practice,' said Sophie, her tone light-hearted. She sat on the floor beside her daughter. 'The lane's safe. You could go home to have the baby.'

'Sooner rather than later,' said Tiana. She shot Lucy an excited smile. 'My flat on campus is big enough for two, plus a baby.'

'It'll be a big change,' said Lucy. 'But we can always come back, once the baby's old enough?'

Tiana did her half-shrug. 'We'll work it out.'

'Life here's going to get easier.' Sophie told them about Lord Maine rebuilding the Manor.

'That's wonderful,' said Tiana.

Lucy knelt beside Bella and cautiously held her hand. 'Something else to look forward to.'

~

Later that morning, in the surviving wing of the Manor, Sophie and Hugo followed Mrs Rawlings up narrow stairs to the next floor.

Their bedroom was Shorten-huge, but there was no fireplace, the medieval window leaked, and there were six single beds arranged in regimented rows.

Sitting on the nearest bed, Sophie wrestled Bella into the fleecy Babygro, then settled her on the floor.

Hugo sat on another bed and the springs complained. 'This is better than camping but without the perks of glamping.'

Sophie fastened up her ski jacket, picturing Hugo in a posh tent with mod cons. 'Have you ever glamped?'

'No.'

Maud came in and Sophie beamed at her.

'How was it, with the militia?' Hugo asked Maud.

'Suffice to say, I'm very glad the Laceys are back.' Maud looked around, frowning. 'I'll bring more blankets.'

'What was here before the militia moved in?' Sophie asked her.

'Stored furniture when the summer ball was on. Sofas, armchairs.' Maud frowned again. 'All lost in the fire.' She glanced down at Bella. 'I'll mind her while you have dinner, Miss.'

Hugo examined a stain on the floorboards. 'This looks like blood.'

'The militia brought beer, had fights up here.' Maud smoothed a crease on a pillow. 'You'll never guess about Mrs Rawlings.'

'You're right,' said Sophie. 'I won't.'

'She and Mr Crawford are getting married.' Maud said 'married' as if was unthinkable — or unfeasible.

'That's good news,' said Hugo.

'It is,' said Sophie. 'I wonder why they waited so long?'

'It's not the done thing,' said Maud, 'for housekeepers and butlers.'

'Lady Lacey wouldn't have stopped them,' said Sophie.

'Mr Crawford's a stickler for propriety,' said Maud. 'But perhaps he thought after all the trouble, nobody would mind.'

'I presume Mrs Rawlings lost her husband many years ago?' said Sophie.

Maud seemed confused. 'She's not a widow. All house-keepers are called Mrs.'

Hugo was nodding but Sophie shook her head. Even now, Shorten's barmy rules could surprise her.

The hospital bay had reverted to its previous name: the large drawing room. And that evening, they ate dinner there.

The dress code, by necessity, was the clothes they'd been wearing when they'd escaped the Manor fire. Suits for the men, day dresses for the women, except for Sophie, who was conspicuously casual in ski clothes. The meal was yummy, if not piping hot, and there was wine and French brandy from the town.

Freddy tucked into his roast beef. 'Lord Maine believes the house can be rebuilt within two years. He's already commissioned an architect.'

'Will you rebuild it in the same style?' Sophie fed Jack and Charlotte slices of beef. 'Or something art deco and modern?'

Freddy smiled at his mother. 'I'm under strict instructions to build it just as it was, but with central heating.'

'So long, Frank Lloyd Wright.' The 1970s song played in Sophie's head.

'Absolutely,' said Anne, and across the table, Hugo grinned.

After dinner, they drank brandy, and Freddy switched on the small wireless.

'This is the British People's Alliance, now partnered with the British Broadcasting Company. A general election is to be held on 23rd February. Ramsay MacDonald, the leader of the Labour party, welcomed the news…'

'Good,' said Alice, turning it off. 'Nothing that affects us.'

'It certainly does affect us,' said Freddy. 'If Mr MacDonald forms the next government, taxes will go up even more. Another officious tax letter was delivered this afternoon.'

'Once the Manor's rebuilt, you should open it to the public,' said Sophie. 'People will pay to go on tours.'

Freddy looked horrified.

'Not around the bit you live in,' added Sophie.

'The bit we live in,' echoed Freddy. 'We'll live in all of it.'

'The Manor needs to pay its way,' said Anne. 'I visited National Trust houses at home. I know roughly how it'll work.'

'I'd appreciate your advice about Radden Hall.' Rupert swirled his brandy. 'The militia have gone but apparently left quite a mess. I must return tomorrow to supervise the clean-up.'

Beside him, Ethel was stony-faced.

After Ethel trooped upstairs to retire with the other women, Sophie took Rupert aside.

She lowered her voice. 'Are you dumping Ethel?'

'Dumping?'

'Casting her off.'

'Oh, I see,' said Rupert. 'Absolutely not. I've assured her we'll marry once my house is in a fit state.' He paused. 'If

Ethel were to accompany me before we marry, it would fuel gossip.'

'Since when have you cared about gossip?'

Rupert shot her his knee-trembler smile. 'Since Ethel.'

Five minutes later, Sophie went up with the dogs to the makeshift bedroom.

Bella was asleep on the floor, wrapped up in a blanket, and Maud was sitting on a bed in her coat, re-reading her favourite Penny Dreadful. The cover of *Varney the Vampire* featured a coffin and a skeleton menacing a sleeping girl. Not steamy, or gory. Silly horror.

Maud closed the book and stood up. 'Jack feels the cold, Miss, so I've knitted him a new jacket.' She was whispering, not wanting to wake Bella. 'And a coat for Charlotte.' She picked up two garments from the bed.

Sophie held the soft black wool against her cheek. 'Thank you.'

'Mr Crawford and Mrs Rawlings have been planning their wedding in secret for months,' said Maud. 'Everybody's invited.'

'When is it?'

'Next Saturday.'

In a week's time. Hey ho. This wedding guest would be turning up in ski trousers and a top.

Maud left, and Sophie secured the woollen jacket on Jack and, after some resistance, on Charlotte. 'It may be undignified but keeping warm is more important.'

Charlotte looked pained but resigned.

Hugo came in.

'What happened to talking politics after dinner and drinking more brandy?' whispered Sophie, one eye on Bella.

'It felt weird. Everything's different now.'

Unlikely the custom would make a comeback. Sophie felt a perverse pang of nostalgia.

Hugo pulled a bed close to another, the legs screeching like an outraged owl, and sat on it.

'Shush.' Bella stirred but didn't wake.

He unlaced his boots. 'Rupert's forked out for a catered marquee in the village for the new Mr and Mrs Crawford. Should be a good bash.'

Sophie undressed fast, put on the nightdress she'd bought in the town, and slipped into the bed beside Hugo's. She snuggled down under the blankets. 'So many weddings. Rupert and Ethel, Alice and Harry, Reynolds and Miss Parry. And Lizzie will marry her fit firefighter.' Lizzie knew how he took his tea. A sure sign.

Hugo changed into his pyjamas just as fast and got into his bed. 'Was the firefighter fit?'

'All firefighters are,' said Sophie. 'Well, the guys. Condition of employment.'

'If you say so.' Hugo lay flat and pulled the covers up to his shoulders. 'Lucy and Tiana are going home after the wedding. I'll go with them.'

Her heart felt heavier, and she winced. 'Please don't do this. Don't make me choose between you and Bella.'

He reached over and squeezed her hand. 'You already have.'

CHAPTER 42

Rupert insisted on funding a general shopping expedition to the town, and a few days later, arm in arm with Hugo, Sophie was in Little Shorten, tottering up the church path, her feet squeezed into court shoes.

Women's fashions in this alternate 1920s hadn't quite caught up with the 1920s at home, but Sophie's pink dress was more flapper than Edwardian fussiness, and her matching beret featured a single cream feather. Her pink coat was also simple, barely reaching her ankles.

The men wore the same morning suits worn at posh weddings at home, with top hats.

'Perfect weather, cold but clear,' said Sophie. Weddings were like buses. None for ages, then they all turned up close together.

Hugo seemed distracted, probably thinking about going to the lift tomorrow.

Sophie stopped walking. Watching a happy wedding, all the while knowing Hugo was leaving her, was unbearable.

Hugo paused too. 'What is it?'

'Two more weeks. Please.' She cast around for why two

weeks. 'That would give the lift time to drop off Lucy and Tiana and be ready for you.'

He looked conflicted but kissed her on the forehead. 'Okay.'

Too short a reprieve. Should have asked for longer.

In the church, there was a buzz of happy chatter. The convention of the bride's family and friends sitting on one side of the aisle, with the groom's relatives on the other, didn't work for this occasion. The Laceys and their guests had been seated at the front, while servants and their families were randomly spread out on other pews. Tiana and Lucy waved, and Sophie grinned back. She nodded at Maud. Freddy had engaged a temporary nanny to watch Bella and the dogs.

As Sophie sat down on the front pew, Anne said, 'The first of a joyful flurry of weddings.' Anne didn't sound joyful, was thinking of Richard. Sophie gripped her hand.

A few moments later, Wagner's *Bridal Chorus* from *Lohengrin* started up on the church organ, and Mrs Rawlings walked down the aisle in a plain, ankle-length white dress. Sophie had only ever seen her in black. She looked younger. The housekeeper smiled politely at the guests on either side, but you could tell that inside she was beaming.

The butler was standing straight as a soldier waiting for her and didn't glance round. Mr Dignity, even today.

As the couple made their vows, Hugo put his hand over Sophie's, remembering their wedding, as she was.

Every wedding was different, and so was every marriage. 'Lucy and Tiana are getting married at home,' Sophie whispered.

'Despite the … circumstances,' said Hugo, 'it's worked out fine. They'll be a lovely family.'

The strains of *Be Thou My Vision* began and the congregation got to their feet to sing. The hymn was the same here, and Sophie knew the beautiful words by heart from childhood. But as she sang, her mind was with Tiana and Lucy. Tiana didn't want to return to Shorten once Lucy's baby was born. Hopefully, one of them would compromise.

After the service, to cheers from onlookers, Reynolds slowly drove Mr and Mrs Crawford in the least battered car through the village.

Betty Hill stood at the edge of the green with her little boy, staring at the wedding car. She continued staring until after it disappeared down the road, before hurrying to the impressive marquee. Her cheap mac provided little protection from the cold.

Sophie's pink coat was stylish but summer-thin, and she was glad to get inside the heated pavilion. Belling heaters, much bigger than Lucy's, were powered by electric cables connected to the pub.

Hugo headed to their allocated table and Sophie sat next to him. Rupert hadn't skimped on the place settings. The mats were royal blue, like the Manor's had been, and the cutlery shone in the electric lights suspended from the marquee's ceiling.

Sophie downed her first glass of champagne and accepted a second.

'Slow down,' said Hugo.

She wanted to get smashed, blot out that he'd soon be leaving, but she set aside the glass.

Rupert and Ethel joined them, with Clarissa and Freddy.

'I *love* weddings,' said Clarissa. 'Hugo, I wish you could stay until ours.'

'And ours,' said Rupert.

'It's a shame,' said Hugo.

Freddy glanced at him. 'And a difficult decision.' He sipped his champagne. 'But it'll be fascinating to see what pictures are on the doors.'

'It's not a fun day out,' said Hugo. 'We must never be complacent.'

Sophie frowned. 'You do know something.'

'About what?' said Hugo.

Sophie studied him over her water glass. 'About Janus.'

'Only what you know.'

There'd been no room in the holdall for her lift-puzzle notebook, and Sophie hadn't missed it.

'I shouldn't have made light of crossing in Janus' ship,' said Freddy. 'I'm just tipsy and happy.'

Sophie smiled and pushed her full champagne glass towards him.

CHAPTER 43

The morning after the wedding, Lucy and Tiana were driven down the lane by Reynolds, and Hugo and Freddy came too. Sophie had cried off.

In a second car, driven by another chauffeur, was a kitbag with Lucy's possessions and two other large bags, crammed with water flasks and canned food. The basics, if Janus dumped them in a hostile universe.

Hugo gripped the vehicle door as they clattered along, the icy wind stinging his face. *You do know something.* Sophie's suspicion at the wedding had spooked him. His notebook was well-hidden in a drawer in their Manor bedroom, and she had no reason to rummage in there, but he imagined his sketch of the walking staff from *Classical Myths and Legends* glowing like a neon sign. If she found it, she'd remember it could reset the lift — and Janus.

He moved his hat to better protect his ears. It would always hurt that Sophie had chosen Bella over him. Rationally, of course he accepted that her baby's needs should trump his… That didn't help.

'I'm not sure Sophie's right, that the lift requires time to cross to your universe and then return to pick up more travellers,' said Freddy. 'Time may behave differently within a black hole.'

Tiana was nodding.

'I've honestly no idea.' Hugo reminded himself for the nth time that lacking the gene, Janus couldn't read his mind, but his heart was still racing. He forced himself to take measured breaths.

Reynolds manoeuvred around the large hole left by the exploded mine and Seddon, the chauffeur driving the luggage car, did the same. 'We must repair that,' said Freddy. 'It could blow a tyre if hit at speed.'

'Sounds as if a lot has changed at home,' said Lucy.

'Technology moves on, but most things are the same,' said Tiana. 'Though I might have lost the visiting scholar tenure by now. If my "burn-out" story doesn't fly, we can go to the States.'

'California…' said Lucy. 'What about hospital costs?'

Tiana did her one shoulder shrug. 'I did well out of the divorce.'

'Organising my passport will be a challenge,' said Lucy. 'I'll have been presumed dead for decades.'

'We'll sort it,' said Tiana.

After twenty minutes of sedate-Seddon-Reynolds driving, they reached the Janus stone and they all got out except the chauffeurs.

'I'm glad you put this stone here,' said Tiana. 'You could install a lamp post for people who arrive in the dark, like in Narnia.'

'Too far out for an electric lamp post.' Lucy shot her an indulgent smile.

Hugo scanned the lane. The verge and the hedge looked the same. Unremarkable. But the unease in his guts was a physical ache. Lucy and Tiana needed to give precise destination instructions to Janus.

Janus…

Primeval fear flooded him, and he fought an irrational urge to run. Get a grip. Janus was trapped in his ship. Outside of it, he was powerless.

The chauffeurs turned the vehicles around, ready to return to the Manor.

'I won't call the lift,' said Freddy. 'Janus will know I don't want to travel.'

Hugo consciously controlled his breathing. In, out. In, out.

'I *really* want to travel,' said Tiana. 'Janus.'

'Janus,' said Lucy, sounding less certain.

Lucy and Tiana gasped.

'I can't see it,' said Hugo through gritted teeth. With all his soul, he didn't want to.

'Sorry,' said Tiana. 'Hugo Harrington. And we shouldn't leave out the chauffeurs. Reynolds. Seddon.'

In front of the tall hedge, the gold lift shimmered and became solid. Hugo swallowed. If Janus had been unaware of him before Tiana said his name, had that changed? He fancied he could feel the malevolent presence. Shut it out.

'There's one picture on the doors,' said Freddy. 'A narrow, angular tower.'

Tiana nodded. 'The university accommodation block, in all its brutalist glory.'

Lucy was watching the lift, mesmerised.

The arrival bell rang out and the doors shuddered open. In the already chilly lane, the temperature plummeted.

Hugo exhaled. Calmer now, and he felt no presence. The universe destination number, assigned eons ago by the lift's builders, was memorable, but Tiana and Lucy were stressed, might forget. '666.'

'I know what to say,' said Tiana.

'So do I.' Lucy squared her shoulders.

'Keep safe.' Hugo hugged them in turn. 'I'll phone as soon as I arrive back.' They'd exchanged mobile numbers.

Freddy shook their hands. 'Bon voyage.'

Tiana and Lucy hurried into the lift, dragging their kitbags, and the doors closed. Seconds later, the lift faded and was gone.

'The plan to have corrective surgery on Miss Hemming's leg is sound, but she seemed apprehensive,' said Freddy. 'Is she worried about the operation? I hope she wants to travel enough to facilitate a smooth crossing.'

'She wants to travel,' said Hugo. Lucy's pregnancy wasn't his story to tell.

'Goodness, goodness,' said Reynolds. The chauffeurs had left the cars and were staring at the empty verge.

'The poor fellows are in shock. We should drive,' said Freddy. 'I've missed it.'

'Are you sure?' asked Hugo.

'Absolutely.' The mine hadn't dulled Freddy's love of cars.

'Are you alright to drive, Hugo? You look done in.'

'Just cold.'

CHAPTER 44

Two weeks after Lucy and Tiana left in the lift, Hugo returned after breakfast to his cold Manor bedroom. He took the lift-puzzle notebook from his sock drawer and flicked the pages until he found the sketch of the walking staff. Such an innocuous-looking object and yet it could kill a god…

If he took the notebook with him and the lift's software scanned it, Janus might be unconcerned, assume this 'lesser being' thought it just a walking stick. On the other hand, presented with a reminder of a device that could end him, who knew what capricious, sadistic Janus would do? Would his most important algorithm — not harming travellers — hold? If it didn't, Janus would swat him like a fly.

The sketch was committed to memory. He should tear out the page and burn it. No. Janus would realise a page was missing. He should burn the whole notebook. Sophie's lift-puzzle notes were safe in 21st century London. Apart from this sketch, it had the same info.

Hugo collected Sophie's jacket and his own and picked up

the dog coats. Charlotte had indicated by nodding that she wanted to see the lift again, and as she and Jack were inseparable, Jack was coming too.

Downstairs, in the large drawing room, Sophie and Clarissa were kneeling on a blanket. Clarissa was making a toy sheep kiss a pig and run away, producing happy gurgles from Bella.

Sophie was clutching Bella's keys-rattle, just watching them. She'd been fighting tears since the moment she woke up. This was always going to be horrible.

Jack was dozing by the fire, but Charlotte was lying on her front, holding open *Peter Pan* with one of her paws. Despite how he was feeling, the sepia illustration of a baby flying around a room made Hugo smile.

Clarissa was unfazed by the labradoodle reading a book. Freddy had shared everything with her, including Charlotte's new abilities.

Hugo strode over to the fireplace, selected a log from the basket, and dropped it in the grate. Then he threw in the notebook. For good measure, with a poker, he pushed it further under the burning wood. The cardboard cover curled inwards, and it was gone.

As he turned from the fireplace, a weight lifted from his shoulders. 'It's time.'

Sophie kissed Bella on her brow. 'Be good till I get back.'

'She's always good,' said Clarissa with an indulgent smile.

Hugo knelt on the floor and cuddled Bella, breathing in her milky baby smell, then got to his feet. He fastened the dog coats on Jack and Charlotte. He pocketed Charlotte's lead but clipped the other lead to Jack's collar. The cloudy film covered both his eyes, making him entirely blind.

Clarissa stood up. 'Safe journey.' She shook hands with Hugo.

The survival kitbag was by the door. He hauled it onto his shoulders, took Jack's lead, and Sophie and Charlotte followed him outside.

The rubble from the old house was being cleared and men with large drawings under their arms were measuring the ground with yellow tape.

'Won't be too long before the house is resurrected,' said Hugo. '*Grand Designs* for real.'

Sophie didn't reply, was welling up.

As soon as he'd trawled the internet for walking staff info and formed a plan, he'd return. Lucy would call the lift for him. He kissed Sophie tenderly, her tears tasting salty on his lips. 'This isn't forever.'

On the drive, everyone had gathered to say their good byes in the winter sunshine. Anne hugged him, and he embraced the Armstrong sisters in turn, before shaking hands with Rupert and Harry.

The car engine was already running, and Freddy climbed into the driver's seat. The dogs bounded into the back and Sophie got in beside them, her face shiny with tears. She didn't wipe them away. More were coming. Charlotte nuzzled up close, trying to comfort her.

Inside Hugo, apprehension about crossing in the lift was dwarfed by dread that he'd soon be so far away from Sophie. Logically, researching the walking staff could secure all their futures but part of his brain was screaming at him not to get in the car.

He made himself secure his bag in the boot and took the shotgun seat in the front — with an actual shotgun. Not required, but having a lethal firearm to hand was a hard habit to break. Like the vehicle's wartime medical kit.

Freddy drove cautiously down the drive and they passed through the open gates. The metal sheeting and barbed wire had been removed and a gamekeeper was repainting the metal latticework.

Out of habit, Hugo checked the shotgun, but the lane was tranquil and deserted, and Freddy kept a steady speed.

When they rounded the final bend and saw the Janus stone, Freddy sped up.

Pop.

A bullet? A tyre blowing?

The car lurched, veering from side to side, and Freddy fought to control the steering. Sophie screamed and Hugo gripped his door. No seat belt. No airbag. Going to die.

The vehicle careered off the road, thumped violently in and out of a ditch, and slammed into a tree.

The impact threw Hugo across the lane. He tried to roll but thumped into another tree. Pain reverberated down his spine, and he cried out.

He lay there in shock, winded, and everything hurt... Okay, probably a good sign. Sit up. A shuddering breath but he managed that. Now stand up.

There. He leaned against the tree trunk. His back was agony, his right shoulder ached, and his vision was blurred. But he could walk.

The dogs were struggling to stand on the road, whining. Sophie was on her knees, clutching her arm. But Freddy was lying near the Janus stone, entirely still, a gash across his brow.

Grab the medical kit.

The front of the car was crushed in, grey steam billowing from the bonnet. Hugo wrenched open the door, stretched into the seat well, and the world spun. He straightened. Take deep breaths.

He bent down again — slowly — and picked up bandages and an antiseptic tin.

Blood from Freddy's cut was pooling on the grass. 'He's

breathing,' said Sophie. Charlotte was licking Freddy's face, but he wasn't responding.

Hugo smeared dark crumbs from the tin over the cut and tied a bandage tight around Freddy's head, fixing it with a safety pin.

'Where's Reynolds?' said a woman's voice.

Betty Hill was standing in the road with a shotgun. In her coat and small hat, she resembled a 1920s gangster. She'd shot out their tyre—

'Is he badly hurt?' Betty looked horrified but didn't lower the gun.

'Yes,' said Hugo.

'Where's Reynolds?' Betty repeated, her voice insistent.

'At the Manor,' said Sophie.

'The broadcast said Reynolds was driving.' Betty scowled at the wrecked car.

'Mr Lacey decided to drive.' Hugo tied another bandage over the first, already soaked through. 'What do you want with Reynolds?'

Betty pointed with her shotgun to where the verge met tarmac. 'That's where he was. Where he died. His head bashed in.'

'Your brother,' said Sophie.

'Attacked and left to die.' Betty levelled up the gun.

'It wasn't like that,' said Sophie.

'What *was* it like, then?' Betty's lips thinned.

'After we called the lift, your brother attacked Reynolds.' Sophie spoke in a rush. 'Reynolds was messing with something under the car bonnet and had a spanner... It was self-defence.'

'Whatever Parkes told your brother, it was invented to frighten him,' said Hugo. 'Parkes didn't want the lift opened because in our universe, he was wanted by the police.'

Betty bit her lip. 'He said if you meddled with the lift, it would ruin us, kill us all.'

'You know that's not true,' said Hugo. 'We called the lift before and nothing happened to us, or you.'

'Something sent him insane.' Betty's mouth twisted.

'That wasn't the lift,' said Hugo, sitting Freddy up against the stone.

Betty lowered the shotgun, seemed to wilt. 'I don't know what to believe.'

'Janus,' said Sophie, loudly. 'Hugo.'

The lift duly appeared, shining gold. Did it appear faster the more times you summoned it? The pain in Hugo's spine spiked, and he gasped.

'Just one picture,' said Sophie. 'A tall tower.'

'University tower block.' That should mean he'd get home.

With a familiar rattle, the doors shuddered open, and the high clang sounded. Charlotte went into the lift, Jack limping beside her.

Freddy's best chance. 'We carry him together,' said Hugo, grabbing Freddy's shoulders.

Sophie bent to pick up his feet but yelped and lost her grip. 'My arm. I think it's broken.'

'I'll drag him,' said Hugo. 'Can you carry my survival bag?'

Sophie nodded. 'One good arm.' She darted to the car.

'What are you doing?' Betty followed him across the verge.

'The lift heals injuries,' said Hugo, panting with the effort of dragging Freddy. He stumbled over the threshold and laid Freddy down.

'Janus, put Freddy in stasis to stop him losing blood,' said Hugo.

Silence.

'Obey Hugo as you would me.' Sophie dropped the holdall and knelt next to Freddy.

'Sophie Arundel-Harrington,' said Janus, 'you must step away from Freddy Lacey.'

She stood back. A soft azure barrier appeared around Freddy, outlining the shape of him, sprawled on the floor. The robot arm slammed out of the wall, the steel hand equipped with an array of razor-sharp tools. Hugo had seen it before, but Sophie hadn't. She paled.

'Precision surgery,' said Hugo.

Outside the lift, Betty was shaking her head, bewildered. She couldn't see the lift, or them.

'Seeing the lift might give Betty closure,' said Hugo.

'Betty Hill,' said Sophie.

Betty's mouth fell open.

'Right.' Sophie drew a deep breath, seemed to be struggling to focus. 'Janus, take Hugo Harrington to universe 666 so he arrives and thrives there safe and well.'

They'd spent a while perfecting the wording.

'Janus, heal Freddy Lacey, then return him here, to universe 422,' said Sophie. 'Ensure that he arrives safe and well in universe 422 and thrives here.'

'Your arm requires attention,' boomed Janus.

'Don't worry, I'll get it sorted in Shorten.' She was slurring her words.

'Healing such a complex fracture is beyond the capabilities of creatures in 422.' Janus' baritone echoed in the lift.

'Oh, you're right,' slurred Sophie. She shuffled past Freddy to the rear of the lift, crumpled, then curled into a foetal position.

What had happened to her? Hugo hurried over and grabbed her shoulder. She was deeply asleep. 'Sophie, wake up! You're staying with Bella.' Sophie didn't stir. He dragged her towards the threshold.

Rattling. The doors were closing. Hugo lurched forward with Sophie, but the doors shut in front of him.

'All travellers will be healed,' said Janus. 'Sleep.'

Hugo's lids fluttered shut and coherent thought faded, lost in the resonance of Janus' voice. He lay down, welcoming the touch of the cool floor.

CHAPTER 45

$\mathcal{H}$ugo was woken by the loud arrival clang. He blinked and looked around the lift.

'Universe 666,' thundered Janus like a supernatural bus conductor.

Freddy was on his feet, fastening up his ski jacket over his suit. The horrific wound on his brow was gone, though his clothes were still bloodstained.

Sophie was standing beside Freddy, examining his face. 'Miraculous.' She spoke slowly, as if words were difficult, unfamiliar. 'Not even a scar.'

'How are you feeling?' Hugo asked Freddy.

'Odd. Not all there.' He was slurring his words.

Understandable, given his head injury. The memory of the car crash was vivid in Hugo's mind but everything after he'd got into the lift was fuzzy, an uneasy, living dream. He frowned, confused. Why was Sophie here? Where was Bella?

'Janus, how did you seal the wound?' slurred Sophie.

'Glue.' Janus' tone was smug.

'I'm glad my arm's sorted,' slurred Sophie. 'Good as new.'

Was she drunk? There was something important … but Hugo couldn't remember what.

The doors opened, revealing an almost deserted students' union, but just beyond the lift threshold, oblivious to the lift, and them, was a skinny girl peering at her phone.

Charlotte was by Freddy's legs, tilting her muzzle, staring at the girl. Jack copied her. The next instant, Jack darted towards Sophie, his tail wagging, and Charlotte danced around the lift, literally bouncing for joy.

Hugo gulped. 'Jack's eyes.' The cloudiness over his pupils wasn't there. He could see again!

'Thank you for removing Jack's cataracts, Janus,' slurred Sophie. 'You're wonderful.'

'My pleasure,' the deep voice purred.

'What a lovely surprise.' Freddy put Jack's jacket on him and clipped on his lead. 'The students' union's not very crowded. Interesting.' He smiled inanely.

Nothing Freddy hadn't seen before.

Charlotte stopped bouncing and Hugo secured the dog coat on her. She didn't notice, staring at nothing.

'Hugo, could I stay at your house?' asked Freddy. 'I've an uncommon desire for a fast-food burger.'

They were both drunk. Hugo slipped his holdall onto his back. 'No problem.' He took Jack's lead and stepped with Freddy into the students' union, willing his own foggy brain to clear.

Sophie and Charlotte barged into the skinny student and the girl scowled before sauntering off.

The lift doors rattled shut.

'Take heed, travellers,' boomed Janus from inside the lift. 'Now and forever, we part ways. Others have more need.'

Hugo froze. What was happening?

Jack sat down beside Charlotte who was shaking her head.

Freddy and Sophie's attention was on a lunch notice, pinned to a board. Had they not heard what Janus had said?

Hugo was still struggling to think straight. Janus had to appear when summoned. One of his core algorithms—

'All creatures evolve. So does Janus.' The lift's gold faded to grey and disappeared.

The instant the lift had gone, Hugo's brain fog cleared, and he remembered. Janus had put Sophie into a coma, preventing her from leaving the lift and returning to Bella.

Sophie and Freddy were now scanning the hall, as if noticing the students' union for the first time.

'What's going on with you?' Worry sharpened Hugo's tone. He pulled off his heavy holdall and dropped it on the floor.

Panic flashed in Sophie's eyes. 'Why am I here?'

'The car swerved,' said Freddy. 'I don't understand.'

But in that moment, Hugo understood, and he swayed with the horror of it. 'I'm so sorry.'

They looked at him. Not drunk. Confused.

'Janus suppressed your thoughts and inserted his own,' said Hugo. 'Freddy, he made you believe you wanted a burger more than you wanted to return to Bella.'

Freddy was trembling. 'No.'

'Sophie, he put you into a coma to keep you in the lift.'

'I'm going back,' Sophie shouted, her voice cracking. 'Janus.'

Freddy yelled 'Janus!' with authority.

The lift didn't appear.

'He's got around the summoning algorithm,' said Hugo. 'He's cut us off.'

Anguish twisted Sophie's face. 'No, no, *no.*'

Hugo gathered her into his arms, and she collapsed against him, crying into his chest. Freddy sank to his knees and put his head in his hands.

Hugo stroked Sophie's hair, despair turning his stomach. How could he have been so stupid? Of course, Janus had known about the sketch. He saw the past, the present, and the future, in every parallel universe. He knew if any walking staffs survived. And he also knew if — or how — a staff would end him.

But the most important algorithm of all had held. Janus hadn't *ended* them.

Deep, desperate sobs were wracking Sophie's whole body. 'How? Why?'

Bella's trusting face filled Hugo's mind and his eyes prickled with tears, but he pushed Sophie gently away from him. He had to stay strong. 'We should go to London. Recover ourselves. Wait here while I collect our stuff from Elliot and Lorna.'

Freddy and Sophie didn't respond but Charlotte nodded.

Hugo hurried off across the hall and slipped through the security door after someone else.

Elliot was in. 'Good to see you.' He smiled as he led the way into the small sitting room. 'You know, Lorna would love to go with you on your next adventure. I would too.'

'I'm afraid you can't. No one can. The lift's cut us off.'

Elliot raised his eyebrows.

'No more travelling between universes,' said Hugo. The words seemed to echo round the flat.

'You sound relieved.'

Was he? He supposed he was. But relief was edged with a bitter guilt that soured his throat. He drove his hand through his hair. 'What date is it?'

'You always ask that.' Elliot looked at his phone. '28th August.' He strode over to a kitchen cupboard and took out a plastic bag. 'Here's your phones and car keys. Where's Sophie and Bella?'

Hugo accepted the bag. 'Bella's in Shorten.'

'But if the lift's cut you off…'

'We'll never see her again.'

Elliot gasped. 'That's … terrible.'

'I know this is rude, but I have to get back to Sophie and Freddy.'

'Freddy's here? I thought he was staying in Shorten.'

'He meant to,' said Hugo. 'Honestly, it's a mess.'

Hugo returned to Sophie and Freddy, who were standing silently with the dogs where he'd left them.

'Come on.' Hugo picked up his holdall and they followed him towards the exit.

Outside, it was hot and still. A glorious summer's day. Hugo removed the dogs' coats, removed his own jacket, and walked towards the road, the clothes draped over his arm. Sophie, Freddy, and the dogs trailed behind.

They soon reached the car in a side street. Hugo dropped the holdall in the boot and found Charlotte's travel harness. He picked up George's. Should fit Jack.

Once the dogs were belted up in the back of the car, Sophie flopped in beside them.

Freddy took the front passenger seat and Hugo slid behind the wheel, plugging in his phone to charge. As soon as it registered, Hugo messaged his mother with their cover story. *Left the travellers. Coming home.* He'd filled up with petrol before they'd parked. No need to stop on the way.

He fastened his seat belt, drove onto the main road, and glanced in the rear-view mirror. Jack was huddled close to Charlotte who was half lying on Sophie's lap. Sophie's head was bowed like a defeated soldier.

When they joined the motorway, Sophie and Freddy appeared to be asleep. He hoped they were. He set cruise control, welcoming the chance to think. Janus had incidentally given Hugo Harrington everything he wanted. He was home and safe with Sophie. He should be *more* relieved. But how could he be? Losing Bella would haunt them for the rest of their lives.

The moment that book had fallen from the bookcase in Shorten, revealing *Myths and Legends*, Janus cutting them off had been inevitable. Not sharing what he'd discovered, even burning the notebook, had made no difference. Other versions of him must have found the sketch, or not, understood its significance, or not. And Janus had always known.

The walking staff danced in his mind, mocking him. *Reset Janus*. How had he thought he could hoodwink a god? An entertaining joke for Janus. But Hugo didn't have to play along. Safely crossing between universes was a stupid pipe dream and telling Sophie and Freddy now would only give them false hope, prolong their grief. He'd have to take this secret to the grave.

He indicated and moved into the slow lane. His grandmother had kept an incredible secret for that long. She'd worked with Alan Turing in World War Two in Bletchley Park, helped crack the Nazi codes. After her death, when that work had been declassified, Hugo's father had been staggered to see her name, displayed under 'Naval Personnel' on the Roll of Honour.

But his grandmother's secret hadn't been tested day after day, her loved ones' suffering bound up with it... His promise to Sophie after their wedding repeated in his head. *No more secrets, forever.*

If there was even the slightest chance the walking staff could give them a way back to Bella, wasn't he duty-bound to tell them?

CHAPTER 46

In Sophie's dream, Bella was determinedly practising walking in the small drawing room. She reached the armchair and looked up at her mother. 'Bah.'

Sophie woke with a start and blinked in the dark. The duvet she was lying on was soft, modern. She was in Hugo's bedroom in 21st century London.

And Bella was gone.

Despair ran through her like poison. She'd hadn't said goodbye and could never explain. She rubbed her temples, a memory surfacing. When Bella had been so sick, she'd pleaded with the universe. *Save her. I'll do anything.* Was this the bargain? Saving Bella's life in exchange for losing her forever?

Hugo was sound asleep, his arm around her.

Sophie screwed up her eyes. Don't cry. Hugo needed to sleep.

The night before, Sophie had managed to call her aunt, and she'd lied, reassuring her that all was well. Hugo's mother was abroad, their family dog in kennels, and Hugo's father was working late. So Hugo had ordered takeaway. The food had been tasty, but she and Freddy hadn't eaten much or drunk any wine. Hugo, though, had finished his own portion, half of hers, and polished off a bottle of Shiraz by himself.

Misery had different layers. Her own layer wasn't helped by … anything. Maybe her body and her brain were shutting down?

She gently moved Hugo's arm and climbed off the bed. The room was stiflingly hot. She'd slept on top of the duvet in just her knickers. In the dark, Sophie stepped on her clothes, left in a heap where she'd dropped them, and felt something hard under her toes.

She slipped her hand into the pocket of her trousers and froze. Must have pocketed this before she left the Manor. Her fingers closed around Bella's keys-rattle until the metal dug into her palm. Slowly, she gave in to silent tears.

When she eventually stood up, she checked her watch. Four in the morning. She'd never get back to sleep now.

She put on her summer dressing gown and slid her feet into flip flops. Watching TV in the basement wouldn't stop her thinking about Bella, but she'd go anyway.

The dogs hadn't stirred on the floor, stretched out on their fronts. Echoing Hugo's sleepy embrace, Charlotte's front leg was resting over Jack's.

Sophie crept downstairs, tying the dressing gown as she went.

Freddy was in the basement, dressed in knee-length shorts and a T-shirt. He was standing up, wearing the VR headset. She touched his arm and he jumped.

He removed the headset. 'You can't sleep either.'

Sophie gave him the rattle and he took it. She hugged him and they sobbed together.

Long minutes later, Sophie said, 'Does the game help? Take your mind off it?'

'Not really.' Freddy put on the headset.

Sophie retraced her steps up one flight of stairs to the kitchen. She made tea and returned. Freddy accepted his tea, and Sophie sat in the squishy chair and drank hers. Talking wouldn't help, might make this terrible ache worse. She flicked through channels on the TV. Nothing held her attention. She turned it off, curled up and dozed.

She was woken by natural light streaming through the high-up windows from the sunken corridor outside. From the floor above came the sound of the front door shutting. Hugo's father leaving for work.

Freddy pulled off the VR headset. 'I could sleep now.'

He went off to the Stables, a separate, self-contained flat, and Sophie returned to Hugo's room.

Hugo was in the shower, and the dogs were awake. Sophie sat on the bed with them, burying her face in their fur.

When Hugo emerged from the bathroom, a towel wrapped around his middle, he sat beside Sophie and kissed her on the forehead. 'Keep strong,' he said quietly.

'If you're broken, how can you be strong?' She wiped her eyes. 'Janus cured Jack, an act of kindness. Then he did the cruellest thing he could. For *no* reason. I can't bear to be awake. Every morning, Bella will be the first thing I think of, and every night, she'll be the last. Always.'

An hour later, Hugo fried sausages for the dogs and cooked a full English breakfast for three.

He pressed a screen icon on the red coffee machine, and it loudly ground its beans. A fresh, deep-coffee scent joined a sultry breeze whispering through the open French windows.

Sophie stared at her plate. Fried eggs, a huge pile of sautéed mushrooms, and two hash browns.

'Please eat,' said Hugo, 'or you'll waste away.'

'I want to,' said Freddy, looking at his breakfast. 'I want to waste away.'

This felt surreal, sitting in Hugo's kitchen in a T-shirt and shorts. If only she could shut her eyes and then be in Shorten…

Hugo sat down with his coffee and attacked his breakfast. Jack's restored sight seemed to have turbo-charged his appetite, and his eyes were on Sophie's meal. But Charlotte's attention was fixed on her mistress, and she gave Sophie a meaningful look. Eat.

Hugo finished his breakfast, then tapped on his phone. 'Missed calls from Tiana.'

'Likely, I will have too.' Sophie's mobile was in Hugo's bedroom, still in the carrier bag. Phoning her aunt had been upsetting enough. She hadn't wanted to talk with anyone else, even Isha, her closest friend.

Tiana answered on the second ring and Hugo put the phone on speaker.

'Is that you?' Tiana's Californian twang sounded loud and sharp.

'Definitely me,' said Hugo. 'Is all well with you and Lucy?'

'Fine.' But Tiana sounded anxious.

'I'm here,' said Sophie.

'As am I,' said Freddy.

'I thought you guys were staying in Shorten,' said Tiana.

Lucy came on the call. 'Where have you been?'

'Sorry, I should have called yesterday,' said Hugo. 'We're in London.'

'From where?' said Tiana.

'From the lift,' said Hugo. 'Obviously.'

'When did you leave Shorten?' asked Lucy.

'A fortnight after you,' said Hugo.

Silence. 'Okay,' said Tiana. 'We've been here almost six months.'

Hugo paled.

'Oh.' Sophie tried to take that in.

'We're a bit tired,' said Hugo, 'but we'd like to properly catch up soon.'

'I'll send my new number.' Lucy ended the call.

'What's the date today?' said Freddy.

Hugo glanced at his phone. '29th August.'

'Ninety-two years and two months difference between the universes. It should be March, not August.' Freddy frowned. 'The students' union wasn't crowded because it's high summer, the holidays. I should have realised.'

'You were in no state to realise anything.' Sophie felt sick. All those weeks in stasis, in Janus' power. The crossing times varied, but six months... 'Why did he keep us asleep for so long?'

'Janus can keep travellers in stasis until the end of the last universe,' said Freddy.

'The more pertinent question is,' said Hugo, almost to himself, 'why did he release us yesterday?'

The question hung in the air.

'There could be automatic safety mechanisms,' said Sophie, 'including a time limit, if travellers are uninjured or their injuries have healed.' She shuddered. 'But while we were unconscious, he discovered how to circumvent being summoned.'

'Did you hear what Janus said, when we were out of the lift?' asked Hugo.

Sophie and Freddy shook their heads. So did Charlotte.

'*Now and forever, we part ways,*' quoted Hugo. '*Others have more need.*'

Freddy sighed. 'Are there any other travellers? I suppose we can't know.'

'We've never seen anyone else in the lift,' said Sophie, 'but we've no idea what the ship really looks like. It might have different rooms, different floors.' She exhaled. Thinking this through was creepy, but for a few seconds, she hadn't thought inconsolably about Bella.

'*All creatures evolve. So does Janus.* His last words before the lift disappeared.' Hugo took a long sip of coffee, seemed to be steeling himself. 'This is my fault.'

'How can this possibly be your fault?' said Sophie.

'Janus keeping us unconscious, then cutting us off. It's all linked to a sketch I stumbled across in Shorten.'

'I don't follow,' said Freddy.

'There's a very small chance we could turn the lift into a safe ship,' said Hugo. 'Free of Janus.'

Freddy jerked upright. 'Why on earth didn't you mention this before?'

'I knew you'd found out something.' Sophie's stomach twisted. 'You lied to my face. What happened to *No more secrets. Forever?*'

'I didn't share because once you knew and called the lift, Janus would have known, and figured out how to hurt us — or worse.'

'Okay…' said Sophie. Not getting them killed trumped sharing, though her heart wasn't buying the logic. Anger vied with hurt. But mixed in with both was a flicker of hope.

Hugo fished a notebook from his trouser pocket. The blue plastic cover was scuffed, the pencil still attached.

'My lift-puzzle book.' Sophie kept it in her bedside drawer here. 'Where's yours?'

'I burned it in Shorten,' said Hugo. 'I worried Janus would see the drawing while we were in the lift.' He thumbed through her notebook and opened it, setting it on the table.

The pencil sketch she'd drawn in medieval Georgia. 'Janus' staff.'

'The other drawing was of the same walking staff,' said Hugo. 'But it was in colour, with perspective and in 3D. It showed the thickness of the main stick and the complete shape of the head.' He pointed at the drawing. 'The sketch I found was a clue that directly threatened Janus.'

Curiosity about a clue was lost under anger and resentment. 'You knew Janus would cut us off.' Sophie seethed. 'You kept it secret because you wanted me to leave Bella, come back with you.'

Hugo flinched. 'I swear, that's not how it was.'

Sophie briefly closed her eyes. 'I'm sorry. I know you wouldn't have done that.'

'You should have told us.' Freddy glared.

'With hindsight, yes I should,' said Hugo. 'But I wanted to go home to research the walking staff, and I believed because Janus couldn't read my mind, he wouldn't know.' Hugo sighed. 'But he did.'

Freddy's brow creased. 'Your drawing, Janus leaving us in stasis, then cutting us off, could be coincidence.'

'If it is, this is a pointless rabbit hole,' said Hugo.

'How does your sketch threaten Janus?' said Sophie.

'It'll take a while to explain.'

Of course it would. Sophie grabbed her notebook and retreated to the loo off the hall. She locked the door and sat on the closed toilet lid.

Residual resentment that Hugo hadn't shared was slowing down her brain. She looked again at the sketch. She'd copied this from a much older picture: the heart-shaped top with the hollowed-out centre and inside it, the letter T. At the time, it had been mildly interesting. A curiosity.

She took a deep breath. If Hugo had found a way back to

Bella, she needed to focus, make it work. She stood up, stepped into the hall, and hurried to the kitchen.

CHAPTER 47

When Sophie returned to the kitchen with the lift-puzzle notebook, Charlotte was sitting on a chair between Hugo and Freddy, resting her front paws on the table. She was concentrating, staring at Hugo's phone.

Hugo was reading aloud, his finger on the screen. '*Janus' walking staff indicates his knowledge, guiding the way.*' Charlotte's brow furrowed. She could easily read the words, was likely thinking through underlying meanings.

Sophie sat opposite them, pushed her breakfast plate aside and set down the notebook, open at the sketch page. 'Where did you find your drawing?'

Hugo set aside his phone. 'In a Victorian book in the Manor library. *Classical Myths and Legends: A Convenient Guide* by George Herbert.'

'Oh,' said Sophie. 'George Herbert. H. G. Wells' first names reversed.' Two years ago, after she'd read *The Time Machine* in the Manor Library, she'd realised that Wells had travelled in the lift.

'A pen name,' said Freddy.

'How did I miss that?' Hugo hit his brow with his hand.

'But why not use his regular, well-known name? Couldn't have helped sales.'

'How does this threaten Janus? Help us get to Bella?' Sophie couldn't hide her impatience.

'Whoever drew the sketch in the Manor's book in the 19th century signed it with their initials.' Hugo wrote 'I. M.' on the sketch. 'They copied it from an actual walking stick.'

'Janus'?' said Freddy.

'How it survived all that time, I don't know,' said Hugo.

Sophie's brain whirred. 'Maybe it didn't.'

Hugo frowned.

'We know Wells crossed universes, saw alternate futures, because of his sci-fi books,' said Sophie. 'But what if he visited ancient Rome? Maybe he brought the walking staff home as a souvenir?'

'More likely than it surviving without a scratch for two millennia,' said Freddy.

'I googled *Classical Myths and Legends* this morning,' said Hugo. 'The British Library has a copy. And if that book has the same drawing, that means the walking staff existed here in the 19th century — and may have survived into the 21st.'

Where was Hugo going with this? Sophie's brain seemed to be working, but she was none the wiser.

Freddy steepled his fingers together. 'In Georgia, Naga said the walking stick only looked like a walking stick to people without the gene, and the device could summon Janus out of the lift so he could walk around.' He hesitated. 'Do you think Janus really has two heads?'

Sophie sighed. 'Hugo, I still don't see how this helps.'

'Naga mentioned, almost as an aside, that walking staffs were also used to reset the ship's software.'

Sophie's heart missed a beat. 'Reset ... back to factory settings? Janus would no longer be sentient?'

'Exactly,' said Hugo. 'He'd be what he was before. Advanced technology, but only that.'

'Goodness,' said Freddy.

Charlotte fixed her large eyes on Hugo.

'I get it now,' said Sophie. 'Wow.' No wonder Hugo was stressed. Resetting Janus meant killing him.

Freddy drummed his fingers on the table. 'Janus would only have cut us off if resetting him is a real possibility. Perhaps in some universes, different versions of us do just that?'

'This is too complicated.' Charlotte nuzzled into Sophie's arm, worrying.

'Only individuals who share the builders' DNA can summon Janus,' said Freddy. 'And before he cut us off, we had to be physically near the lift to call him. Logically, the same would apply to using the walking staff.'

Sophie grimaced at the sketch. 'So, even if we find the staff, we can't get close enough to reset Janus because we can't summon him.'

Freddy's shoulders slumped. 'And the lift is the only way to Bella.'

'It isn't,' said Hugo. 'Sophie, don't you remember what Naga said? There's another ship. Juno.'

'Less advanced … but wasn't there something wrong with it?'

'I have no idea what you're talking about,' said Freddy.

'You weren't there when Naga mentioned Juno,' said Sophie, 'and I remember now. A crossing in the other ship took longer than usual and the passengers ran out of food and water. They all died.'

'So, Juno has no way to protect travellers from the passage of time,' said Freddy.

'That happened after a lot of crossings,' said Sophie.

'The risk would be the same, regardless of how many

previous crossings,' said Freddy, patiently. 'Whenever you toss a coin, the odds don't change.'

Charlotte looked at him, alarm in her furry face, and Sophie's throat dried. 'Russian roulette.'

Hugo addressed Freddy. 'If you could summon Juno, be with Bella, would you risk a second trip back here?'

'No,' said Freddy, his tone vehement.

Sophie glanced at Hugo. 'And you wouldn't come with me to Shorten?' she said. 'Forever.'

'You know that's a big ask.'

Sophie's shoulders slumped.

But Freddy sat up straighter. 'In theory, I could call Juno to reach Bella. And Clarissa.' He got to his feet, carried his breakfast plate and his coffee over to the microwave to reheat them. 'I should take the risk. Just once. Juno should land in the same spot Janus does, in the students' union.'

Hugo drove his hand through his hair.

'You wish you hadn't told us.' Sophie stared at her cold breakfast. 'I half-wish you hadn't.'

'You'd have remembered about Juno,' said Hugo. 'Sooner or later.'

Freddy sat down with overcooked fried eggs and scalding hot coffee. 'Do you know anything else about the ship? Other risks?'

'I don't,' said Hugo.

Sophie tried to think it through. 'Say we find this walking staff. What if we use Juno once, *not* to cross to Shorten, but to arrive in a place and a date when we're sure someone summoned Janus. Then reset him.'

'Yes,' said Freddy. 'When Mummy called the lift, or Miss Hemmings did, or Alan Parkes.'

'Or when Tiana called it,' said Sophie. 'There might be a parallel universe where time travels at a slower rate than here but not as slow as in Shorten, so we could go to the

1980s or to 2003, or a few weeks ago. Wait for the right moment.'

'The multi-verse theory has many versions,' said Freddy. 'It's possible there are billions of such universes, all different in tiny or large ways.'

'So, the lift is summoned in some, but not in others.' Sophie tapped the sketch.

'How would we ever locate the right universe?' said Hugo. 'We'd be looking for a needle in a haystack.'

'A needle in an infinite number of haystacks,' said Freddy.

Sophie dragged her eyes from the sketch. 'We don't need to call Juno or go anywhere. Lucy and Tiana are here. They can summon Janus.'

'I'd be surprised if they could,' said Hugo. 'Janus will have grounded everyone we know with the gene.' He grimaced. 'Janus is the master of time. We can't outwit a god.'

'We shouldn't get ahead of ourselves,' said Freddy.

Sophie thought back to her pre-course university reading, before this mad adventure started. 'In *Sir Gawain and the Green Knight*, the true nature of the quest doesn't become clear until the end, and Gawain's willingness to pursue it, to sacrifice himself, subverts the inevitable outcome.'

Hugo winced. 'Not liking the "sacrifice" bit of that.'

'The best quests are straightforward,' said Freddy, 'with knights and dragons, and a happy ending.'

'Trouble is,' said Sophie, 'I always root for the dragon.'

Freddy managed a smile and he tucked into his breakfast.

'The pictures on the lift doors are destinations, real or symbolic.' Sophie flipped through her notebook and stopped when she came to the sketch of the cottage on fire.

Freddy narrowed his eyes. 'I hate fire.'

'I saw this image on the doors when I first went into the lift,' said Sophie, 'but not since. All the other pictures, the Manor, me with the sword, the baby, have happened, so surely that means I'll see the cottage picture again, either on Juno's doors or Janus'? And whatever it represents will come true.'

'Which means?' Hugo asked her.

'I'm not done crossing universes.'

'Each traveller's destinations change on each crossing,' said Freddy. 'Probability comes into it. Some may be fleeting.'

'Or,' said Hugo, 'they're fixed, fated.'

The notebook pages fluttered in a sudden gust of wind from the open French windows and the pages settled on the sketch of Janus' staff. Freddy traced the drawing with his forefinger, lingering on the heart-shaped top.

'Let's go to the garden.' Sophie stood up. 'Get some fresh air.'

Outside, Sophie took calming breaths. 21st century London air wasn't the best, but in this quiet part of Wimbledon, there was no traffic noise, only birdsong, and the garden was a delight, the apple tree by the terrace resplendent with fruit.

Bella loved this tree. She'd lain in her pram for ages, looking up at it, fascinated by the leaves quivering on the branches...

Time seemed to slow.

'Despite the unfavourable odds, we should search the British Library,' said Freddy. 'See if that *Classical Myths* book has the sketch. Today.'

'You can't just walk in,' said Hugo.

'Why ever not?' said Freddy. 'It's a library.'

'Anyone can wander round the public rooms,' said Hugo. 'But to request a particular book, you have to apply in person for a Reader Pass and show a valid passport and driving licence.'

Freddy frowned. 'I won't be allowed in.'

'I've got ID,' said Hugo.

Freddy patted Jack. 'Why is everything so difficult here?'

The August sun was hot on Sophie's arms and legs, and she moved into the shade of the apple tree.

Hugo joined her and searched her face. 'Checking inside the book is one thing. What about the endgame?'

Killing Janus. Fear slid down her spine, but she reached for a stronger force. A mother's love for her child. And Freddy's reasoning was sound. *Janus would only have cut us off if resetting him is a real possibility. Perhaps in some universes, different versions of us do just that?* They could do this. Give it a try, at least. Their only hope.

Sophie ruffled Charlotte's head, then reached for Hugo's hand. Freddy held Sophie's other hand.

'First, the British Library,' said Sophie. 'One step at a time.'

Hugo and Freddy's hands tightened over hers, their skin comforting and smooth, and slowly, like blossom budding on a tree, resolve took hold. Yes, they could do this.

And the step after that?

Kill a god.

≈

≈

≈

I hope you enjoyed *Defiance*.

If you did, let people know.

Reviews are the most effective way of building awareness of a book you've enjoyed. While I love telling people about the *Shorten Chronicles,* honest reviews bring books to the attention of other readers.

If you didn't buy *Defiance* direct from my Fantasy Bookshop, I'd really appreciate it if you'd leave a review (short as you like) where you bought it.

Thank you!

HUNTED

Sophie's adventures continue in the fifth book of the **Shorten Chronicles.**

Check release dates, special offers, discounts, and more: *www.rosalindtate.com*

Buy direct and support the author: *https://bookshop.rosalindtate.com*

About the Author

Rosalind Tate lives in Gloucestershire, England, and holidays on the Cornish coast. She served in the British military, then worked as a journalist and a lawyer.

Rosalind's enjoys speaking at authors' and readers' conferences, talking about publishing and encouraging new authors. When she's not behind her computer, you can find Rosalind reading her favourite books, walking her dogs, swimming, or watching sci-fi and fantasy shows.

Rosalind has three grown up children, a tolerant husband, and two utterly gorgeous dogs.